NOTHING'S EVER LOST

Emma G. Rose

Imperative Press

Hampden, Maine

Imperative Press
Hampden, ME
www.emmagauthor.com

Publisher's Note: This is a work of fiction. Names, characters, places, and incidents are a product of the author's imagination. Locales and public names are sometimes used for atmospheric purposes. Any resemblance to actual people, living or dead, or to businesses, companies, events, institutions, or locales is completely coincidental.

Book Layout © 2017 BookDesignTemplates.com
Cover Art by Kelsie Witt
Cover Design by Ashley Hinson Dhakal Designs

Nothing's Ever Lost/ Emma G Rose -- 1st ed.
ISBN 978-1-7339079-0-3
LCCN 2019905476

To my cousin Nick, who died by suicide.
&
To my Jack, who made this book possible
just by existing in the world with me.

"no one's ever lost forever
when they die they go away
but they will visit
you occasionally
do not be afraid."

— "LOST" AMANDA PALMER

CONTENTS

Chapter One

Anna couldn't find her phone. It wasn't in her room anywhere, which meant it had to be downstairs. The question was, where? And, more importantly, could she find it before Jack got there to pick her up? She did not want to be the one who delayed their first beach trip of the summer.

She rushed down the stairs so fast she almost tripped halfway down, but she managed to catch the banister just in time. At the bottom, she slid to a stop in front of her mom's office door. It was open, which meant it was safe to interrupt her. Well, safe-ish.

"Mom, have you seen my cell phone?"

"I have not," her mother said in a clipped voice, not looking up from her work. "Do you need me to call it?"

"No, I can handle it myself, thanks."

Anna started to leave.

"Tell your brother TV time is over."

"He's going to whine about it."

Anna's mother waved her hand, as if to say, *Thank you for pointing out the obvious, run along now.*

Anna ran along. On the walk to the living room, she tried to remember where she had last seen her phone. It wasn't in her room, she was certain of that. It wasn't in the bathroom, she knew because she had checked. It had to be in the living room somewhere. She'd been texting last-minute plans with Jack before bed last night.

In the living room, she found her brother sitting on the floor about five feet from the television, a juice box on his knee. Cartoon colors danced across his face.

"Nathan, Mom says no more TV."

"Five more minutes." As predicted he was whining.

"It's a commercial. By the end of the five minutes you'll be watching another show and won't want to shut it off."

Anna grabbed the remote and clicked the TV off. Nathan heaved the world's biggest, most pathetic sigh. He dragged himself upright and stormed off in the direction of the kitchen.

Anna rolled her eyes at his back and began searching for her phone. It wasn't on the side table next to Dad's chair. It wasn't on the coffee table. It wasn't on the charger. There was only one place left to look: the couch.

She held her breath and stuck her fingers between the couch cushions. You never knew what you might find in the space between. It was where gross thing went to die. Once, Nathan had dropped a grape down there and it had turned into a little puff of mold that squished between Anna's fingers. She'd squealed, and Nathan had practically fallen on the floor laughing while their older brother, Michael, sighed and told her not to be so dramatic.

Today she was lucky. She found seventy-five cents in change, which probably belonged to Michael. On the rare occasions when he wasn't at work or driving around in his very own car, which he had paid for himself and refused to let anyone else drive, he was always sitting with his ankle propped on his knee, making all the change in his pockets slide out and fall between the cushions. Oh well, finders keepers. She stuffed the coins into her pocket.

Between the next set of cushions she found her phone. It was pretty much dead. She stuck it on the charger and went into the kitchen to make the sandwiches. Jack was already three minutes late, which meant she had only about twelve minutes to make their lunch before he showed up.

She got the bacon going and then pulled out the other ingredients. It took almost no time to slap some peanut butter on some bread. She just had to wait for the bacon to cook. While she was working, Nathan wandered in and sat down on a stool on the other side of the kitchen.

Anna prodded the bacon with her spatula, and a drop of hot oil leapt from the pan to her wrist. She hissed through her teeth and jerked her arm away from the stove. That had hurt—a lot—but she didn't have time to whimper about it. Jack would be there any minute.

Nathan rocked the stool from side to side, making a thumping noise each time a pair of legs hit the floor. It was annoying.

"Stop it," Anna shouted, not turning around.

"I want to come too." Thump-pause-thump.

"You're going to break that stool."

"Mom said I could rock as long as I promised to buy her a new one if it breaks."

Anna scooped the bacon from the pan and dumped it onto a paper-towel-lined plate.

"Fine, but who's going to buy you a new skull?"

Nathan ignored this.

"Besides," Anna continued, "you're ten. How exactly would you pay for it?"

Nathan snorted. "I get an allowance," he said with all the haughtiness of the know-it-all teenager he would someday be. Then he ruined it by whining, "Why can't I come?"

Anna flapped her hand at the bacon to make it cool faster. "This is a trip for grown-ups."

"You are not a grown-up."

"Okay, it's a trip for teenagers then." She poked at the bacon. It was cool enough to pick up, but only just.

"I'll be good," Nathan whined.

Anna snatched pieces of bacon from the plate and dropped them onto slices of peanut-butter-covered bread. "Why can't you go bother Michael?"

"He's working."

"Of course. Well, go play Mario then."

Nathan slumped across the breakfast bar. "Can't. Dad took it away. He said I wasn't allowed to waste another beautiful summer day staring at a tiny screen."

Anna felt a breath of sympathy. She'd heard that line from Dad before, usually in relation to her phone. Nathan must have sensed his advantage, because he started begging again.

"Please?"

"No."

"Please?"

"No."

"Pleeeeze?"

Their mother appeared in the doorway, a handful of papers in one hand. Their argument had apparently been loud enough to reach her office.

"Nathan, you're too young to go to the ocean without an adult," she said.

Then she turned on Anna. "And how many scholarship forms did you fill out this week?"

"Anna's an adult," Nathan said.

"Mom, it's summer," Anna said.

"No she isn't, but when she is, she'll have a mound of debt because she didn't want to put in a little effort." Their mother shook the handful of papers as though they were past-due notices on Anna's future bills. Anna knew Mom was right in theory. But when she had a job, a real job as an architect at some big firm in Austin or Chicago, she'd make plenty of money to pay back student loans. The odds of actually winning a scholarship seemed too small to waste her summer on.

Sunlight glanced through the room, reflecting off the windshield of a car pulling into the driveway. Anna stuffed the sandwiches into a zip-top bag and dumped them into her lunchbox.

"Jack's here. I've got to go." She kissed her mother on the cheek. "I'll do it tomorrow, I promise."

"That's what you said yesterday."

"No matter what. I promise."

Her mother looked skeptical—her signature look. "Be careful."

That sounded like permission to leave. Anna ran for the door. "I'm always careful," she said. She grabbed her backpack on the way out, and nearly crashed into Jack, who was halfway across the mudroom. Anna pushed him back toward the front door.

"Let's get out of here before my mom thinks up something else for me to do. I brought peanut butter and bacon."

"You're awesome."

"I know. You have the sour gummy worms?"

He raised two cellophane packages for her inspection.

"Sweet." Anna thrust the lunchbox at him and swiped the candy out of his hands.

Anna's mother called her name from somewhere on the other side of the house. "Quick, out, out." She practically shoved Jack through the door.

When they were safely in the car, Anna said, "I am going to be so dead later."

"As long as it's after we get back from the beach." Jack backed the car out of the driveway. "What did you do?"

"I don't know, but I don't want to stick around and find out." Anna ripped open the first bag of gummy worms.

"Well, sorry I'm late," Jack said. "I spent at least twenty minutes convincing Ella that she couldn't come with me."

He dropped one hand off the wheel to dig through the cargo pocket on his shorts. He came up with a small red toy, which he stuck on the dash. Anna squinted at it. It was a plastic octopus, about the size of a golf ball. The expression on its face suggested that there should be little cartoon birds flapping circles around its head.

"What is that?" Anna asked.

"Ella gave it to me. She said that if she couldn't come with me, I had to take Octavius so he could tell her all about it later."

"Couldn't you tell her about it later?"

"She says he's better at telling stories than I am, because I always make things up."

Anna didn't know what to make of him. Half the time, Jack acted like his sister was the most annoying child on the planet, and the other half he might as well be six years old too. Anna couldn't tell which half this was, so she said, "All right, let's get this octopus to the ocean."

Jack flipped on his blinker and turned left onto the main road. It would take them through the center of town, with its single stoplight, and onto the highway.

As they drove past the coffee shop, Jack said, "Do you want to stop and say hi to Michael?"

"No, he'll just say he's too busy to talk."

"He takes his work really seriously for a guy who smells like burned coffee fifty percent of the time."

"Yeah, no kidding. You want a gummy worm?"

"Sure."

By the time they'd gotten off the highway and onto Route 1A, Anna had opened the second bag of sour gummy worms. She lounged in the passenger seat of Jack's car with the bag in her hand and her feet on the dashboard.

Jack glanced at her. "What are you grinning about?" He almost had to shout to be heard over the wind and the radio.

"I'm just happy, that's all."

Anna selected a red-and-yellow gummy worm from the bag and bit it neatly in half. She looked at the yellow half worm between her fingers. Somewhere she had heard, or maybe read, that an earthworm could survive if you cut it in half. They had two hearts or something, so if one died, the other could go on beating. It didn't seem likely. No matter how many hearts you had, being cut in half seemed like a ticket to a cozy bed six feet under, which probably wouldn't be so bad if you were a worm.

She was about to ask Jack if he had heard the heart thing too, when the first words of "Mexican Wine" came through the speakers. She hadn't heard that song in ages. Anna handed Jack the yellow half of the worm and leaned forward to turn up the radio.

He glanced at the half worm in his hand, then shrugged and popped it into his mouth. His foot rested heavier on the gas pedal. The speedometer needle slipped past ninety.

They were flying around one of the sharper curves when Anna offered him the blue half of a blue-and-orange gummy worm. He lifted one hand off the wheel to take it from her.

Anna saw it first, the eighteen-wheeler overturned across both lanes of the road. She screamed. Jack was swearing, slamming on the brakes. Too late.

The hood snapped when it crumpled against the undercarriage of the eighteen-wheeler. The tires squealed. The brakes locked. The airbag inflated, filling the car with fine powder. It smelled of fireworks and talcum powder.

A metal shaft shattered the windshield and tore through the airbag toward Jack's face. Anna turned her head. Her knees slammed into her chest, emptying her lungs. She watched her leg break. A splinter of bone erupted through the skin. The pain split her world in half.

Chapter Two

There was nothing, nothing in the whole universe, except one thought blazing orange in Anna's mind: get out of the car.

She scrambled over the console between the front seats and lunged for the rear passenger door. Her hands fumbled for the handle. Darkness squeezed her brain. She thought she might pass out again. And then the door opened. Her hands and knees hit the asphalt. It should have hurt, but it didn't.

She rolled over. Shards of glass fell from her knees. They'd stuck there but hadn't left any cuts. A suspicion raised its hand for attention at the back of her brain. She ignored it, inspected her arms and legs and found them undamaged. Weird, she would have sworn . . . but no. She pressed her hand against her shin. There was her leg, safe, without even a bruise.

She'd been terrified. She told herself she'd imagined the bone tearing through . . . The idea she'd been avoiding strained out of its seat, waving its raised hand and making little grunting noises. She turned her back on it. Maybe if she ignored it, it would go away.

"Jack," she said, quietly at first, then more loudly. "Jack!"

"I'm here, I'm fine. Are you okay?"

He came around the car to meet her. He too was unbroken, unbruised. Anna shoved more memories into the darkness. She had always been good at ignoring the things that were too unpleasant to think about.

Jack extended his hands to help her up. As she stood, she caught a glimpse of the front seat of the car. She turned away quickly, but not quickly enough. She felt dizzy and realized it had been a long, long time since she had last taken a breath. It must have shown in her face, because Jack grabbed her elbow. "Whoa, hey, are you okay?"

Slowly, purposefully, Anna turned her back to the car.

"Jack," she said. "Do this."

She pressed her right hand over her heart like a first grader preparing to pledge to the flag. Jack's eyebrows lowered in confusion. He mimicked her. Both stood motionless for a long string of seconds.

The whole world was silent. No birdsong, no far-off traffic. Panic slithered up the base of her spine. She looked away from Jack, at the blue sky, at the long curve of empty Maine highway with trees standing guard on either side.

"Anna, this is real, isn't it?"

"I'm pretty sure it is."

"Only . . ."

Jack had once confided to Anna that he was terrified of turning out like his uncle Steve, who'd had some sort of psychological break and killed himself before Jack was even old enough to remember. Whenever weird things happened, he expected Anna to reassure him. She was like his security human. Of course, that only worked if Anna was the sane one, and at the moment she wasn't certain she was.

"It seems real to me," she said, which was true. It seemed incredibly real, the kind of real you usually get for only a second or two when you see something so beautiful, it jerks you out of everyday life and reminds you that the very beating of your heart is a kind of miracle. Except right now her heart wasn't beating.

"So you're saying we're d—"

But there was another sound.

"Shh."

"You shushed me. We're probably—"

She heard it again. It sounded like a groan.

"There. You heard that?" Anna ran toward the cab of the overturned semi, her sandals making no sound on the scatter of broken glass. She scaled the side of the truck like a jungle gym. At the top, she peered down through the cracked window.

"The driver's alive," she said.

"We should get him out," Jack said. "There's gas all over the place."

"Get up here. I can't lift him on my own."

While Jack climbed up beside her, Anna tried opening the door. She had trouble working the handle. Her fingers were clumsy, like she'd fallen asleep on her arm and woken up with pins and needles. It made grabbing things difficult. But if she concentrated, she could make her hand work the way she wanted it to. The door opened.

Anna dropped down into the cab of the truck.

"Where are you going?" Jack asked.

"You're stronger. I'll boost him as high as I can. You pull him up."

While Anna unbuckled the truck driver's seat belt, she wondered if she would be able to lift him. A full-grown man with a slight beer gut, he must weigh at least two hundred pounds—more, maybe—and she was a teenage girl who ran track.

Jack leaned down into the cab. "Are you okay?"

"Fine," Anna said, as though saying it could make it true. "Are you ready?"

She wrapped both arms around the man and lifted. He felt lighter than he should have, much lighter. She tried to tell herself that it was adrenaline helping her, like those women who lifted cars off their babies, but the image of her leg breaking flashed through her mind again, and she knew she was lying to herself.

Lying on his stomach and reaching into the cab, Jack could just barely grab the fabric of the man's shirt.

"I can't get a good grip. Lift his arms up."

Anna sighed. "Hold on."

She planted one foot against the dash and lifted. Her grip slipped up to the man's armpits, forcing his arms to rise. Now Jack could reach him, but the angle wasn't right.

"I need more leverage."

"Just hold him up. I'll try to lift him higher."

With some bickering, they managed to get him out. Anna clambered up the back of the seat toward the door. She was still waist-deep in the cab when another wave of dizziness hit her. That gave her hope. If what she feared was true, she shouldn't be feeling dizzy, should she?

When they were on the ground again, Jack took her arm. "You sure you're okay?"

"Are you?" Her tone was an accusation. "Let's just get this guy out of here."

Together they dragged him toward the side of the road. The farther they got, the harder it was to hold on to him. As they reached the road's shoulder, Jack dropped the man's feet.

"What the hell?" Anna said.

"My hands just slipped or something," Jack said.

"Don't think about it."

"What?"

"Anything."

Jack lifted the man's feet again. "Should we be doing this? I mean, will we get into trouble for this?" The truck driver's left foot hit the ground.

"I told you not to think about it."

Jack picked up the foot. "But isn't this meddling with fate?"

Anna puffed hair out of her eyes. "A: it was your idea, and two: screw fate. We're dead."

Shock flickered across Jack's face. It was the first time either of them had said it aloud.

"This is probably far enough," Anna said, pretending she hadn't noticed Jack's expression. They laid the truck driver in the grass on the side of the road.

"Is he alive?" Jack asked.

Anna crouched next to the unconscious man. She pressed two fingers against his throat to feel for a pulse, but her hand passed through his skin. She screeched and pulled it away.

"Jack!" she cried.

And he was there, pulling her to her feet. His hands felt solid, real.

The truck driver groaned and turned his head.

"He's alive," Anna said.

Behind them the truck exploded, silently. Jack saw the flash first and pushed Anna back, shielding her with his shoulder. Anna shoved him, more or less gently.

"Your concern is touching, but not particularly useful at this point," she said.

"Well, excuse me for breathing."

"You're not, you know."

He slumped, only a little, but enough that Anna noticed. "Yeah, well, sorry for that too," he said.

Anna patted his arm. "I forgive you."

"Do you think—"

"If you two are quite finished," a voice broke in.

Startled, they swung around. A man had appeared seemingly out of nowhere. He was standing on the shoulder of the road a few feet from them. His head was shaved. His khaki pants were impeccably ironed, and his black polo shirt had a name tag clipped to it. Anna thought he looked like a cell phone salesman.

He read from the clipboard in his hand, "Jack Xavier Pratt, Anna Evelyn Poplin, and Todd Gagnon."

When they stared silently at him, he repeated the three names.

"I'm Jack, and this is Anna. We don't know any Todd."

The man looked past them. "No, perhaps not," he muttered, and wrote something on his clipboard.

Anna and Jack followed his gaze to see what he had seen—the truck driver was sitting up, gaping at the remains of his truck, which was blazing now. A thin trickle of blood slipped down his forehead.

He seemed alive, though Anna wasn't sure she was the best person to judge, at least, not right at the moment.

The man offered his clipboard to Jack. "If you could sign here, please."

The first inkling of fear crept into Jack's voice. "Wait a second. What is this?"

"It is a standard release handing you over to my custody for the next part of your journey to The City."

Anna was only half listening; she'd just figured out what had been bothering her about the man's face. He had no eyebrows, no eyelashes, no hair of any kind. His face was just a skull with skin stretched over it. Although that described pretty much everyone, this particular face gave her a chill in the center of her soul.

"Oh my God. You're Death."

His long, skinny index finger tapped the name tag on his shirt. It said *Death* in bold black letters and underneath, in smaller print, *Afterlife Transportation Specialist*. To the left of the words was a picture of a scythe with a shiny silver blade.

Anna stamped down the shock. She could handle this. "I expected you to be taller and, you know, bonier."

Death seemed taken aback. "Yes, well, times have changed. Sign here, please."

"Where's your scythe?" Jack asked.

"As I said, times have changed. Focus groups have found that the old farm metaphors mean little in the modern world." He sounded like he was reading from a script.

"So you carry a clipboard instead?"

"Yes, but I do not enjoy it. Now, if you could sign here, *please*."

"What happens if we don't sign?" Jack had always been distrustful of authority figures with paperwork.

"Then you are doomed to roam through the rift as lost souls, searching throughout eternity for a portal into death."

For an instant Anna felt like she was looking at an optical illusion. Death was still standing in front of her in khakis and a polo, but at the same time, he also seemed to be seven feet tall and wearing a coarse, black robe. The clipboard was both a clipboard and a six-foot scythe. It made Anna's brain hurt. She blinked and the image disappeared.

"Got a pen?" she said.

A plastic ballpoint appeared in Death's hand. He watched them sign.

"And here, and initial here, and here, and here . . ."

~

Joe Gunderson had been a pastor for so long that even alone in his own car, in the privacy of his own head, he thought of himself as Pastor Joe. He knew it was strange. That didn't stop him from doing it.

He was driving up Route 1 toward Ellsworth when he saw black smoke pouring into the clear blue sky ahead. He slowed the car. As he inched around the curve, he saw an eighteen-wheeler spilled sideways across the road. It was on fire.

"Oh my God," he said, and meant it.

He pulled into the breakdown lane and turned on the emergency flashers. He hoped that if the sight of the smoke didn't slow oncoming vehicles, the flashing lights would warn them that something was ahead. But he was too late, he realized as he drew closer. There was already a car buried front-doors-deep under the tractor trailer.

He pulled out his cell phone and dialed 911.

The woman who answered asked him the nature of his emergency. As he told her, he noticed a man slumped on the side of the road.

"There's a man here. His head is bleeding," Pastor Joe told the operator.

He drew closer, saying, "Sir? Sir, an ambulance is on the way. Are you all right?"

"The angels saved me," the man said.

"He's okay, a little banged up," Pastor Joe told the operator. He got down on one knee and touched the man's arm. His eyes were vacant. "He might be concussed." Then he said to the man, "You should lie down until the ambulance gets here."

The man's gaze slid away. "They picked me up and carried me. I should be dead."

"What about the occupants of the other car?" the operator asked.

Pastor Joe looked at the mangled vehicle. He knew the scenes of death. In more than twenty years of serving the community, he had prayed with families while their houses burned. He had answered phone calls that led him out into the night to stand at deathbeds. He had presided at funerals. He didn't have to go and look into the depths of the wreck to know that anybody in the front seat had to be dead.

He could just wait for the ambulance to come. They would be here soon. Besides, this injured man needed him. But what if he was wrong? What if someone was still alive? What if, because of his inaction, someone was allowed to slip away, frightened and in pain and all alone? Could he live with that?

"I'll look," he told the operator. He climbed to his feet.

The man on the ground mumbled, "They said I was forgiven."

Focused on the car, Pastor Joe barely heard him. "Stay here, please."

He said a prayer for strength and approached the crumpled vehicle. The heat of the nearby fire coaxed sweat to stand out on his forehead. His eyes watered from the smoke. Pastor Joe bent to look through the rear passenger window.

"No one in the back," he reported.

He took a deep breath, clutched the phone, and glanced as quickly as he could through a gap in the twisted metal.

"In the front, two dead. Teenagers. A boy and a girl."

In the brief instant before he looked away, his eyes took in details he would later wish he hadn't seen. The boy—his face a pulpy mess skewered by a metal shaft, his hands tangled in the punctured air bag. The girl—curled with her knees to her chest, bone sticking out of her left leg, her head lolling toward him. Something electric blue was tangled in her hair. It suddenly seemed vital that he find out what it was. He looked again. A gummy worm. It was half of a blue gummy worm. He felt acid rising in his throat.

"Sir, are you still there?" the operator said in his ear.

Pastor Joe had to swallow before he could answer. "Yes. I . . . Wait."

He thought he had seen. Yes.

"She's breathing," he shouted. "Praise God, she's breathing."

Chapter Three

Anna thought she had blinked. Suddenly they were somewhere else. Death was gone. The road was gone. She and Jack were standing in some sort of waiting room, in front of a reception window. "Anna Poplin and Jack Pratt," the receptionist was saying. "Please take a seat. The doctor will be with you shortly."

"What's going on?" Anna whispered.

Jack shrugged. "Isn't it obvious? It's Death's waiting room."

"But we already saw Death."

Another shrug.

They slumped into a pair of bile-green chairs. The walls were sickly mint, decorated—and that was a charitable word—with pastel drawings of flowers and fruit in cheap pasteboard frames. There weren't any windows to the outside.

Only two other people were waiting. One was a red-haired man, the other a middle-aged woman in the kind of hat women wore on Easter Sunday. None of this made sense. If they were in Death's waiting room, shouldn't it be crowded? Thousands of people died every day. Where was everyone? It wasn't like Death had local offices. Did he? Maybe they were in the waiting room for people who died in Maine, or even just in the greater Bangor area. At this point, anything seemed possible.

Nobody moved. Nobody spoke. Seconds ticked by in silence. Anna stared at the black-and-white plastic clock on the wall. It had no numbers, and both hands seemed to be pointing to just shy of twelve o'clock.

Anna nudged Jack. "There's something weird about this place."

"Gee, I can't imagine why Death's waiting room would be weird. I feel right at home."

"Sarcasm is unattractive," Anna said. "Except when it's me using it."

Jack shook his head. He seemed sort of dazed. Anna didn't blame him. She wasn't feeling all that chipper herself. She stared at the clock. It hadn't moved. Watching it carefully she began to count. When she got to sixty, she was sure. At 120 she was certain.

"Jack, that clock isn't moving."

"Don't worry. We haven't been here that long."

"No, I've been watching. It hasn't moved at all. It's always eleven fifty-nine. Maybe it will always be eleven fifty-nine. Maybe this is it, purgatory or—hell, or whatever." She suddenly felt dizzy again.

"Anna, calm down. Maybe the battery's dead."

Anna jumped up, startling the red-haired man and drawing a "harumph" from the hat lady. Up close, she could see that the clock had only one hand. What good was a clock with one hand?

She climbed onto a chair and tried to take the clock off the wall. It was stuck. She set her fingernails in the seam between the wall and the clock and pulled. It didn't move. Anna pulled harder, lost her footing, and slipped backward off the chair.

Someone caught her. It was the red-haired man. He set her on her feet quickly and backed away like she might be contagious.

"Thanks," Anna said. "Hey, you have a watch on. Can you tell me what time it is?"

The red-haired man sat down again. He scowled at his wrist. "It's dead. Just like me. Just like you." He leaned forward and covered his face with his hands.

Anna hurried back to her chair.

"You okay?" Jack asked.

"Oh yeah, fine. I think Red over there might be a bit . . ." She made a whirling motion beside her ear.

"Nice of him to catch you, though."

Anna opened her mouth to say something, realized she didn't know what, and sighed. She leaned her head back against the chair.

The door next to the reception window opened. A woman in white scrubs called out a name. The red-haired man climbed to his feet. He didn't look at them as he passed. The door clicked shut behind him. Silence fell.

"What do you think happens in there?" Anna asked.

Jack drummed his fingers against the arm of his chair. "It's a doctor's office, right? So I guess we're going to be examined."

"For what? We're dead. That's like taking a test after graduation."

"I don't know, for lividity, maybe?"

Anna cocked her head. "I don't think that word means what you think it means."

"Of course it does. It means, like, aliveness, as in, the doctor checked the body for lividity."

"Yeah, no," Anna said. "I think it means, like, red and splotchy. Or angry. It might mean angry."

"Red and splotchy because you're angry."

"You would be angry too if you were red and splotchy."

The hat lady gave them an exasperated look. They were apparently disturbing her prayers. Anna and Jack fell silent.

Anna slumped back against her chair and examined her ponytail for split ends. Jack was bouncing his leg, shaking both of their chairs. She put her hand on his kneecap and pushed down. He stopped. She pulled her hand away.

Anna studied the so-called wall art, trying to identify all the flowers. She used to know lots of flowers, from when her grandfather ran a nursery. Most of these were unidentifiable. They seemed to have been drawn by a first grader with a palette of puce, gamboge, and cerulean. She wasn't sure if those were actually the right names for these colors, but they were the only ones that sounded ugly enough.

"I'm so bored." Anna sighed and crossed her legs. "It's like a morgue in here."

Jack snorted. Anna squinted at him. She played the sentence back in her head and giggled. "I can't believe I said that."

"A fatal slip of the tongue," Jack said.

"I could just die of embarrassment," Anna added.

Jack bit his lip, trying to hold back a smile. "How mortifying."

Now they were both giggling.

"Young man, young lady," the hat lady interrupted her prayers. "Don't you know where you are?"

They stopped laughing abruptly. Anna was careful not to look at Jack as she nodded.

"You should behave more decently," the woman continued. "Your soul is about to be judged by God. You must prepare yourselves."

Anna tried to look penitent, but Jack said, "We should be more respectful. This is a grave situation."

Anna laughed so hard, she almost fell out of her chair. It wasn't that funny. She knew it wasn't that funny. But she couldn't seem to stop.

The hat lady snorted regally, stood up, and moved to the other side of the room. She settled in her seat like a hen in an egg box, closed her eyes, and resumed her prayers.

Eventually the door opened again. A name was called. The hat lady waddled away, with one last disapproving glare. Jack and Anna were alone.

They weren't laughing anymore. Anna watched Jack and wondered what he was thinking. He was staring into space, as though his mind was far away.

"What's up?" Anna asked.

"I was thinking . . . If I hadn't stopped for gummy worms, we could have left earlier. We might have gotten there before the truck crashed. We could be at the beach by now."

"Jack, you can't . . ."

The door opened. "Anna Poplin?"

Jack followed Anna to the door. "Can't I go with her?" he asked the nurse.

The nurse shook her head and favored him with a small smile. "Don't worry, you're next."

Anna turned to Jack. "See you on the other side?"

"Of course."

She followed the nurse through the door and down a narrow corridor. Like the shoes of all nurses in the history of health care, this nurse's shoes squeaked with every step. She opened a seemingly random door and shepherded Anna into a small examination room.

"The doctor will be right with you. No need to undress."

The door clicked shut behind her. Anna was alone. In an effort to distract herself from the weirdness of what was going on, she looked around the examination room. It was exactly like every other one she'd ever been in, except there were no posters on the wall. The closest thing to decoration was a rack of pamphlets on a counter across from the exam table.

The plastic rack had six slots, but they were all filled with copies of the same pamphlet. The cover said "Dealing with Death." Anna grabbed one before sitting down. She glanced at the picture of a rust-colored desert with a narrow road running through it. The subtitle underneath said, "Knowing the Facts About Your Afterlife." Anna opened the pamphlet and read:

> *What is death? Death is a condition caused by a breakdown of vital processes in the physical body. This can occur due to old age, traumatic injury, or illness. This should not be confused with the entity known as Death who guided you from your life to your afterlife.*
>
> *Common Symptoms and Signs: Cessation of heartbeat, reduced need to breathe, lack of appetite, inability to interact with living creatures, feelings of depression or hopelessness, increased laughter, desire to reach The City, heightened spirituality or religious sentiment.*

The Three "R's" for Dealing with Death: Although there is no cure for death, there are things you can do to mitigate your symptoms.

1. Remember: Death happens to everyone, but no two afterlives are exactly alike. Your afterlife has been tailored to meet your individual needs.

2. Relax: You may feel some strong or conflicting emotions as you begin your afterlife. Remember to relax and keep things in perspective.

3. Request: Afterlife service professionals are here to assist you, but they cannot read your mind. If you want to know something, ask.

Anna closed the pamphlet. The back page had two lines of large text. They read, "It's your afterlife. Make the most of it." Anna rolled her eyes and turned her attention to the door. She could hear shoes squeaking toward her.

Someone rapped on the door of the examination room but didn't wait for Anna's answer before opening it. The doctor who entered was a pleasant-looking woman with her hair done up in thousands of tiny braids. She wore a pair of black slacks and a magenta-colored button-down shirt under her white lab coat. A couple of pens protruded from the breast pocket. Like everyone Anna had seen in the afterlife thus far, she carried a clipboard.

"Hello"—she glanced at the clipboard—"Anna. My name is Dr. Stevens. How are we doing today?"

Suddenly it all seemed so normal. Anna felt off balance, like she didn't know what was real. Had she died? Or was she at a regular checkup? She had memories of a car accident and a broken leg and . . . other things she didn't want to think about, but here she was. Nothing broken. Fine.

Anna stared at the doctor. "Am I hallucinating?"

Dr. Stevens didn't answer right away. First, she sat down on a stool across from the examination table. Then she balanced the clipboard on her knee and leaned her arms on it. Finally, her gaze found Anna's. "Are you?" she asked.

"I thought . . . there was an accident, and we—Jack and I, I mean—we hit one of those big eighteen-wheeler trucks, you know, and I thought . . . well, it seemed like . . . we died."

The doctor's posture relaxed. "Oh, probably. Give me your arm."

Probably? Dazed by the flippant reaction, Anna extended her right arm. Dr. Stevens took out of the pocket of her lab coat something that looked like a miniature blood pressure cuff. She wrapped it around Anna's arm.

"But, I'm seventeen."

Dr. Stevens paused midway through pumping up the cuff. "I don't see how that's relevant."

Anna blinked a few times. What was wrong with this woman? Couldn't she see the issue here?

Anna tried to explain. "People aren't supposed to die at seventeen. I'm supposed to graduate from college, get a job, get married. Maybe have some kids or travel to Australia or something." She was beginning to sound hysterical now, she knew, but she couldn't help it. "I'm supposed to die in my sleep when I'm like a hundred and four."

Dr. Stevens smiled. Her voice was gentle even though her words weren't. "And who told you that."

"Nobody. It's just . . . I thought . . ." It was real. Oh God, it was real. Anna wanted to cry, but she had forgotten how. It wasn't the kind of thing you usually had to remember. Usually, your body just did it. She bit the inside of her cheek. It didn't hurt.

"You see, Anna, everyone has a set amount of time. Look here."

Dr. Stevens pulled a plastic model out of a drawer. It was one of those props in the shape of an organ, without which no examination room seems complete. This one looked like a Gobstopper that had been cut in half to reveal the layers of color. A clock with the hour hand missing was embedded in the center.

"During the course of your life you can spend your time, or borrow it, buy it, waste it, or wish it away." As she talked, she rotated the clock hand to match her words. "But when it's gone"—here she pushed the hand all the way around to twelve o'clock—"that's it."

She laid the model down gently. Anna's eyes lingered on the minute hand pointing to the end of her life.

"Why doesn't anyone tell us this? If I had known I only had seventeen years, I would have—"

"What? Lived better? Appreciated things more? No, you wouldn't have." Her voice was firm. "Every person in the world knows that he or she could die at any moment. Disease, accidents, heart failure, even the air you breathe can kill you. You worry that Death will come someday, yes, but you never really believe it until he calls your name."

Dr. Stevens seemed to realize she was ranting, and stopped herself. She returned her attention to the blood pressure cuff.

Anna watched it hiss down. Why was the doctor bothering? Her blood pressure couldn't possibly matter now.

"Hmm," the doctor said.

"Hmm, what?"

The doctor tapped the gauge with one perfectly manicured pink nail. "Have you ever heard of the concept of a near-death experience?" she asked.

Hope bloomed in Anna's heart. "Yes," she said.

"If you were actually dead, I would be getting a zero reading. But if you look here . . ." She tapped the gauge again. The thin red needle was quivering at the tick mark above the zero.

"So I'm not dead?"

"Not yet."

"Then why am I here?"

The doctor avoided Anna's eyes as she removed the cuff. "Trust me, Anna, this is best. Your body is not a comfortable place to be right now."

"What do you mean?"

"People have near-death experiences when conditions in their body are too extreme for consciousness to exist. It saves you from fully experiencing the pain of your injuries."

"But I'm going to wake up, right?"

Dr. Stevens sighed. "Maybe. It depends on what's wrong with you, and how quickly you get to a hospital, and how badly your body has been damaged."

"What about Jack? Is he having a near-death experience too?"

"I can't tell you that."

"Why not?"

"Well, first of all, he isn't my patient, so I don't know, but even if he was, I would have to honor doctor-patient confidentiality."

"In the afterlife?"

"Of course. I'm still a doctor, wherever I am." She wrote something on the clipboard. "You'll have to ask him."

"Okay, fine, so how will I know if I've died or not?"

"If you die, you'll almost certainly feel it. If you don't, you should wake up in a hospital bed sometime in the near future, but then it won't matter, because you probably won't remember this conversation."

"Why not?"

The doctor tilted her head. "I don't know. But have you ever heard a story about a near-death experience that included a calm discussion with a doctor?"

"No."

"Neither have I." The doctor stood up. "It's probably best to get on with your afterlife. None of us can know what will happen tomorrow." She tucked the clipboard under her arm. "Do you have any other questions for me?"

Anna drew herself up tall and took a deep breath. "I'd like to know, please, which way I'm going. It'd be nice to know now, just in case I still have the opportunity to do something about it . . ."

The doctor smiled again. It was a nice smile. "It doesn't actually work that way."

Anna deflated. "You mean you can't tell me?"

"I mean it's not that simple. There's no eternal punishment, and no bonus prize for being good."

"But I thought . . ." Anna stopped. She didn't really know what she thought, or if she'd ever thought about what would happen when she died.

"Think about it," the doctor said. "When you were little and you did something wrong, your parents punished you. Why?"

"I guess so I wouldn't do it again."

"Exactly. Then what would be the point of eternal punishment? You can't do it again."

"Then what does happen next?"

"Only one way to find out." Dr. Stevens held the door open and gestured for Anna to walk through. "Oh," she added, "have a lollipop. You're not too old for lollipops, are you?"

Anna plucked the lollipop from her outstretched hand. "You are never too old for lollipops."

As Anna walked through the door, she squinted at the lollipop wrapper. It was clear cellophane, but there were words printed along the bottom in white: *It's your afterlife. Please keep it clean.*

Anna turned to make a sarcastic remark about this to Dr. Stevens, but the door was already closed. Anna stared at it. A feeling of spaciousness told her she was outside, but that didn't make sense, did it? She let her eyes pull her head to the right.

Rust-colored sand lay in all directions as far as she could see. It was broken only by a narrow, unmarked road of slightly darker sand, reaching out of sight in both directions. The scene seemed familiar. It took Anna a moment to place it. It looked like the picture on the dealing-with-death pamphlet.

But the light was strange, like twilight on a lake during that few moments before moonrise when the water was somehow brighter than the sky. And the sky here was empty—no stars, no clouds, no color— just nothing, forever.

Chapter Four

There was nothing where the sky should be. It made Anna dizzy, and she had to close her eyes. In the silence of the dark, she realized she wasn't breathing. She took a deep breath, held it, and felt no need to either release it or take another one. She felt again that crushing sense of reality. She was dead and this was the afterlife and she was all alone.

A voice cut through the roaring in her ears. "Anna?"

"Jack!"

He was standing a few steps behind her with a lollipop in his hand and a bewildered expression on his face. Anna threw her arms around him.

"Hi," he said. He didn't give her his usual bear hug. Instead he patted her back in a distracted way.

He had clearly noticed the sudden change of scenery.

"You got one too," she said.

"What?"

Anna rolled her eyes at him and presented her candy for inspection. "A lollipop. What color is it?"

"Oh, right. Purple." He wasn't really paying attention. He was looking over her shoulder at the nonexistent sky.

"No fair, I got green. Want to switch?" she said, trying to keep her tone light.

She waited for him to answer. "Jack!"

"Huh?" His eyes snapped to her face.

"I said, want to switch?"

They traded. Anna immediately tore off the wrapper and popped the lollipop into her mouth.

"Holy grape-ape, Batman," she said, candy clicking against her teeth. "This is quite possibly the best thing I've ever tasted."

"It's like the first bite of a cold Granny Smith apple," Jack said. "When you've been at the beach all day and you're hot and tired and you stop at the convenience store and they have this one little display of fruit and you buy one, because the idea of sugar makes you queasy. And when you bite into it, you immediately start to salivate because it's just a little bit tart."

Anna stared. "Yup," she said.

Jack looked thoughtful for a moment with the lollipop stick protruding from his mouth like a slender cigarette. "So, what do we do now?"

"We're standing on a path. I guess we're supposed to follow it," Anna said.

"Or we could go back inside?"

The door had no handle on the outside. Jack pounded his fist against it. Nobody answered. He let his arm drop and just stood, staring at the door. He was clearly thinking something through.

Anna left him to it and walked around the outside of the building. It was no bigger than a garden shed. When she came back around, Jack hadn't moved.

"The building's too small," she said.

"Shouldn't there be a hallway here?" Jack said. "I swear my exam room only had one door."

"Yes."

She noticed a black mesh trash can next to the door and realized she was still holding her lollipop wrapper. She threw it into the bin.

"So if I went from the hallway into the room, then I should've come out of the room into the hallway. This is impossible."

"Yes," Anna said again. *Impossible* was the only word, really, for any of this. "Not to add to the weirdness, but my lollipop wrapper disappeared."

Jack looked into the can. "Maybe it blew away?" he said.

"There isn't any wind," Anna said. "Actually, I'm not sure there's any air. Where did it go?"

"Here, let me try." He pulled his wrapper from his pocket, held it out over the mouth of the trash can, and opened his hand. The wrapper wafted down, like a leaf drifting toward a lawn, and disappeared.

"You saw that," Anna said.

"I saw it. Maybe they do it with mirrors?"

Jack started to reach into the can. Anna grabbed his elbow.

"What if your hand pops out of existence?"

"That couldn't happen."

Anna stared at him. He drew his arm back slowly. "So this path . . ."

"Right," she said. "Which way?"

Without hesitation Jack extended an arm. "That way."

Anna started to ask, "Are you sure?" and stopped. He seemed so certain. Did that mean he was dead? Was an afterlife compass something you got when you died? She could ask him right now, just ask him flat-out what the doctor had said. But no, that was silly. Jack was fine. They were both fine. Again, she pushed away the memory of the inside of the car, holding to the hope that maybe they could both come out of this okay.

"You're right," she said. "Let's go."

For a while there was only the sound of their footsteps whispering in the sand. Normally they wouldn't have paid any attention to the noise—they would barely have heard it—but there was nothing else to hear.

Anna looked sidelong at Jack. He was thinking something sad. She could see it in the clenching of his eyebrows. Eventually, he said, "I wonder what they'll tell Ella."

"There's something over there." Anna pointed farther down the path.

"What is it?"

"Can't tell. Come on."

She grabbed hold of Jack's hand and ran, giving him the choice to follow or be dragged. Normally, Anna liked to run. She was a sprinter, and enjoyed the quick bursts of motion that made her muscles strain and her lungs burn. She didn't enjoy this. She might have been sitting still for all the exertion she felt. It was awful.

The thing, when they reached it, turned out to be a metal box on a post. Small round holes were punched into the side, forming the outline of a phone handset. Inside the open front of the box they could see a black pay phone with a silver cord and shiny square buttons.

"Are there no cell phones in the afterlife?" Jack asked.

"The sign says dial zero for assistance," Anna said.

Jack nudged her aside. "Forget that. I'm calling my mom."

"That's sort of creepy. What are you going to say?" Anna realized she'd almost asked the question she didn't want to ask, and talked faster. "I mean. It seems like you shouldn't freak her out unless you have a good reason. Besides, it probably wouldn't even work. What's the area code for the real world? There's probably some special code to call the real world."

"Okay, fine. Let's dial zero then."

Anna picked up the phone. The familiar sound of a dial tone buzzed in her ear. She pressed zero. The tone cut off.

"It's ringing." Jack leaned closer. Anna tilted the handset so he could hear too.

A voice said, "Hello, you have reached the afterlife assistance service. To hear this menu in English, press one. *Para continuar en espanol, prensa dos. Pour continuer en française, presse...*" Anna pressed one.

"If you know your party's extension, you may dial it at any time. Otherwise, please listen carefully, as our menu options have changed. If you are wondering where Jesus is, press one. If you are looking for your seventy-two virgins, press two." Anna slapped Jack's hand away from the phone. "If you are waiting for your next life assignment, press three. All other questions, press four."

Anna pressed four. Another recording started. "If you feel your death has been in error, press one. If you need directions to The City, press two. For our business hours—" Anna pressed two.

"You should have pressed one," Jack whispered.

Anna shook her head. If afterlife phone menus were anything like during-life phone menus, attempting to file a complaint would only result in more phone menus.

"Thank you for calling the afterlife assistance service. All of our associates are currently helping other travelers. We look forward to assisting you with all of your afterlife needs. Please hold for the next available associate." The voice clicked off, and a tinny jazz recording filled the earpiece.

Anna slammed the phone down.

"What did you do that for?"

"I am not waiting on hold in the afterlife. Let's just keep walking."

They walked. The landscape never seemed to change. One long, low dune of rust-colored sand looked exactly like the next. Anna kept her eyes on the path to avoid looking at the empty sky. Though the candy was long gone, she still chewed on the end of her lollipop stick. It was something to do. Jack had stuck his behind his ear like a pencil.

After a while Anna felt like she should be tired. Her feet didn't hurt, she wasn't thirsty or hungry, but she was bored.

"I feel like I'm trapped in one of those old cartoons where they reuse the same background over and over during the chase scene," she said.

"How far do you think we have to walk?" Jack asked.

"Honestly, I have no idea," Anna said. "Maybe we should go back."

"Back where?"

"To the pay phone."

"You said you didn't want to be on hold."

"I don't, but"—she swept her arm out to encompass the landscape—"there's nothing out here. At least we know where the pay phone is."

Jack pivoted on his heel in midstride, ending up facing the way they had come. "I didn't think of it before," he said, "but maybe there's a shuttle bus."

"You mean like the ones that take you from the airport to the hotel?"

"Sure." He started to walk back up the road.

"That's ridiculous," Anna said.

"No more ridiculous than a trash can that disappears trash or a pay phone in the middle of a— Wow."

"What?" Anna stepped toward him.

Jack thrust one arm out toward her. "No, stay there."

She froze. "What's wrong?"

"This isn't the right way. Can't you feel it?"

Anna didn't answer. Had she felt something? She'd taken only one step and hadn't really been paying attention. It was hard to be sure.

Jack took another step. His legs seemed to be resisting him, so he looked like he was trying to walk through knee-deep snow.

He said, "Do you remember when we did the ropes course in gym class, and there was that one challenge where you had to climb to the top of a telephone pole and then jump to a trapeze bar, and even though you had a harness and a whole team of people on the ground minding the ropes, when you were standing there, your whole body was screaming at you not to jump?"

"Yeah."

"This is like that, but worse," Jack said.

"Come back then, genius."

Jack turned around and came toward her without any sign of effort.

Anna looked at the emptiness all around them, then down at her feet. Her father was always telling her to be patient, to think things through. "Impatience will bite you in the butt," he'd say. *Daddy, you should see me now.*

"It might not even be there anymore." Jack said.

Anna shook away her memories. "What?"

"The pay phone, it might not even be there. A whole doctor's office disappeared. Why couldn't a pay phone?"

"Either way, it looks like we're playing a side scroller."

Jack raised his eyebrows at her.

"You know," Anna said, wiggling her thumbs to mime playing a video game, "like Mario. You go right or not at all."

"Oh good, then we know where we're going."

"We do?"

"Yup," Jack said. "Look for a castle with a ginormous flagpole."

"Thanks. That's really helpful."

Anna chewed on the lollipop stick. "Where do you think we are going though?"

"The doctor said something about a city."

Anna knew she probably wasn't going to get a better opening than this. She could ask him now, ask him and know and deal with the knowing. She opened her mouth, but the words wouldn't come.

She remembered something else her dad used to tell her: "Don't ask questions you don't want answers to."

~

Ella had spent at least sixteen of the last twenty-four hours trying to convince Jack, Mom, Dad, and, when no one else would listen, the cat, that she should be allowed to go to the beach, too. By the time Jack left that morning, Mittens was all for it, but everybody else had said no. So Ella decided she would go to the beach with *her* friends.

She pilfered a towel from the hall closet and went into her bedroom to gather up her best friends: Mr. Stuffy, Barbie, Legs the

Frog-man, Sarah, and Optimus Prime, who had belonged to Jack until he decided he was too old to play with toys. Ella had tried to point out that he still had a bunch of toys on the shelf in his room, but Jack said they didn't count because they were collectibles and were in mint condition and would be worth money someday, and if she touched them, he would shave her head while she slept.

Ella didn't actually believe he would do it, and she had no idea what mints had to do with anything, but she left his stupid toys alone anyway.

She talked to her dolls as she loaded them into her red plastic cart. "Sit down, Mr. Stuffy. Legs, stop pulling Barbie's hair. Now, does anyone have to go to the bathroom? Are you sure? I'm not stopping once we leave. I mean it."

She threw the towel over her shoulder and pulled the cart down the hall. On the stairs, the front wheels spun in the air as the back wheels thump, thump, thumped from step to step.

"Ella!" Mom had probably been calling her for a while. She sounded about one second away from adding middle names.

Ella looked up. Mom was standing at the bottom of the stairs, her hands on her hips. With Ella three steps from the bottom, they were nearly eye to eye. "What are you doing?"

"Taking my friends to the beach."

The cart thumped down two more steps. "Fine, why not? But no one goes swimming," Mom said. "I do not want to fish Barbies out of the pond again."

Ella planted her hand on her hip. "They couldn't help it. They were shipwrecked."

"And no boating either."

"Okay, okay." Thump, thump, thump.

Mom stepped back to let Ella and her cart pass, then followed her up the hall.

"Do we have any sunscreen?" Ella asked as Mom turned and went into the living room where she had been folding clothes. *The Price Is Right* was on.

"You don't need it. I put some on you an hour ago." Mom sat down on the couch and picked up a pair of Dad's shorts.

"Not for me. For Sarah."

Mom sighed as she folded the shorts in half. "Can't you pretend?"

"Mom, Sarah is a baby and she has very sensitive skin. If she doesn't have sunscreen, her skin will turn all red and peel off, and then when she's old, she'll have wrinkles, and nobody wants that."

This argument seemed to win Mom over. At least she was smiling by the time Ella finished. "Okay, okay." She set down the folded shorts and got up. "Is the spray-on kind all right?"

"Sarah likes that kind best."

"Of course she does," Mom said.

Ella had only managed to buckle one of her sandals by the time Mom came back with a spray bottle that looked a lot like the water-filled one she used for ironing.

"That's the wrong foot, you know."

Ella levered the sandal off with the toes of her other foot. "It's not my fault. I'm dyslexic."

"You're not dyslexic."

"I could be."

"You read me almost all of Frog and Toad last night."

Ella kicked the sandal under the shoe rack. "I don't need shoes anyway."

"What if you step on a bee?"

"I'll squish him."

"Good plan. No swimming, right?"

"Right."

Mom held the screen door while Ella maneuvered her cart outside. Ella bumped the cart down the porch steps. The door thunked shut behind her. She crossed the grass to the pond, stopping briefly beside the playhouse Jack and Daddy were building for her. It pretty much only needed a roof now.

"We'll have a housewarming party. Won't that be fun?" she said to the dolls. "It'll be a real grown-up party. We can get Mom to make us petits fours, and everyone can sit around drinking fancy juice."

When they reached the pond, Ella laid out the towel and began to unload her friends. She picked up Sarah first, since she was in greatest danger of burns and wrinkles. Ella sprayed the sunscreen. "Stop squirming. I'm almost done, and then you can go and play."

Next, she picked up Barbie. "Remember, no swimming. You practically just ate breakfast, and if you go swimming now, you'll probably get cramps and drown and then I'll have to jump in after you and Mom will yell."

She listened to the doll for a moment. "Yes, I guess it's okay if you just put your feet in. But just your feet." She found a handy rock and propped Barbie against it, with her stiff plastic feet touching the water. "Happy now? Good."

She picked up each toy in turn, talking to them and pausing now and then to listen to their responses. "No, Uncle Jack isn't coming. He's at a different beach with Anna. I know you're disappointed, but Uncle Jack promised he would play with us tomorrow. We have a tea party scheduled at three o'clock. I know you don't like tea. Don't worry. I'll put grape juice in your cup."

Finally she reached for Optimus Prime. As her fingers brushed the plastic, a sharp pain stabbed her forehead. She fell on the ground, both hands on her head.

The pain disappeared. But it had been there, and it had been scary. She scrambled to her feet and sprinted for the house. "Mommy!"

She reached the screen door, sobbing and gasping for breath, just as her mother opened it.

Mom knelt and grasped Ella's shoulders. "Honey, honey, what's wrong?"

Ella tried to speak, but tears choked her.

Mom hugged her. "Honey, I can't understand you. Take a deep breath. Tell me what happened."

Ella tried, but her words were still garbled.

"Your head? Did you hit your head?"

Anxious fingers ran through Ella's hair, searching for bumps and cuts.

"No, my head hurt."

"You have a headache?"

"*No.* My head hurt."

"Okay, okay. It's okay now." Mom picked her up and carried her to the couch, now cleared of all but a single stack of Jack's white undershirts. She laid Ella down, took one of the folded shirts, and set it over Ella's eyes, blocking out the bright morning sun.

"You lie here. I'm going to go get you some cold water."

Ella mumbled. She heard Mom leave the room. The fan was spinning above her head. She could feel the breeze on her hair. A cupboard shut. Water ran.

Ella startled awake when the phone rang. The shirt slid to the floor. Mom came in and reached over Ella's head to pluck her cell phone off of the side table.

"Hello . . . Yes, speaking."

Ella tried to track only one blade of the fan as it spun. It was hard to do. Her eyes kept wanting to lose focus.

"Is he . . . Is he okay?"

Mom's voice had gone shaky. She was clutching the phone so hard, her fingertips had turned white. "Where?" she said.

Ella sat up. "Mom?"

Mom didn't answer. She was nodding, nodding. "Okay. Yes. Thank you." For a moment after she ended the call, she stood there, staring at the wall behind the couch. Nervous, Ella made a small noise in the back of her throat. Mom looked down at her. Her eyes focused.

"Get your shoes. We're going."

Ella sat up. "Going where?"

Mom stabbed a button on her phone, speed-dialing, and pressed it to her ear. "Just going."

"Is it a surprise?"

"Shoes. Now."

Ella jumped up and ran for the stairs. They were going to the beach! It had all been a big joke they were playing on her, so that she would be surprised. Jack would be there, and Anna, and maybe even Daddy. That's who Mom had to be calling. Maybe he secretly had the day off from work.

Ella rushed frantically around her room until Mom called her name. She barreled down the stairs and skidded to a stop in the front hall. She had shorts on over her bathing suit, floaties on her arms, and her goggles perched on her head.

Mom took one look at her and laughed until she cried.

Chapter Five

Anna spotted something blue in the distance. That was a relief. The emptiness, the sameness, the complete and utter nothing had started to get to her. A few minutes more of that and she'd probably start screaming. Once she started, she wasn't sure she'd know how to stop.

The blue whatever-it-was hugged the ground and stretched as far as she could see to the left and right, which was more or less forever. It moved like water, but there was something off about it.

"What is it? A river?" Anna asked.

Jack squinted at it. He shook his head. "It's too blue."

"What do you mean it's too blue?" Anna said. "Water is blue."

"Not like that. That's, like, swimming pool blue."

As they got closer, Anna realized he was right. The thing was clearly man-made. It was, in fact, nothing more than a thin layer of water flowing over a strip of blue plastic. It looked like an endless slip-and-slide, if such a thing could be twice as wide as a freeway. Far out across the blue, Anna thought she saw a rowboat floating impossibly high on the water.

"I don't get it," Jack said. "What's it supposed to be?"

"Look at this." Anna pointed to a sign by the side of the road. It stood at about knee height and was angled to allow them to read it without bending. The top line read, *Styx*, and under that, *This installation made possible by the Afterlife Beautification Commission and the Hereafter Historical Society.*

"So it's what, public art?" Jack asked.

"Looks like it."

"Wonderful."

A squeaking pulled their attention back to the river. The boat was moving slowly toward them. It was on a sort of low trestle with four small castor wheels. A man in a gray hooded cloak stood in the back of the boat, forcing it forward using a long guide pole. The thing swayed from side to side with each thrust of the pole. The wheels squeaked mercilessly.

The whole situation was funny, if you ignored the imposing cloaked figure whose face they had not yet seen. Anna wondered if he would be a skeleton. But that wouldn't be right, would it? Judging from everything that had happened up to now, there was probably a heavily tattooed pirate with an eye patch hidden under that robe.

When the boat-cart thing got closer, Anna realized it was actually moving backward with the butt end facing them. Soon, she was able to make out the words *Argo Across II* written in peeling paint.

Jack groaned.

"What?" Anna asked.

"Argo Across? That's really, really dumb."

"Boat names are supposed to be dumb. What does *Argo* mean?"

"It's the name of Jason's ship. You know, Jason and the Argonauts, who found the Golden Fleece."

"Ah."

Jack nodded, still staring at the thing coming toward them. "And if we're sticking with the Greek mythology theme, that means the ferry captain is Charon."

"Sharon? Isn't that a girl's name?"

"Sharon with a *C-h*," Jack said.

When the rowboat finally reached the bank, the wheels pressed the plastic into the red dust. Two tiny plumes of black drifted out of the indentation, like drops of food coloring in a tub of water. The sight made Anna uneasy, but she wasn't sure why.

Charon, if that's who he was, bent to throw a coil of rope toward the shore. As he stood, his hood fell back, revealing dark brown curls framing a face half hidden by a beard.

"Not the guy I would have chosen to represent Charon," Jack muttered.

The rope landed in front of Anna. She grabbed it and wrapped it once around her hand. It seemed like the right thing to do, although she didn't know why. The bottom of the boat didn't even touch the water. It wasn't as if it was in danger of floating away, and if it somehow did, you could just walk across the plastic and get it back.

"Hello," Jack said.

Charon looked at them without speaking. He seemed to be waiting for something. A little nervously, Anna began to coil the rope.

Jack tried again, "I'm Jack and this is Anna."

Still nothing. The man's eyes were a brown so light, they were almost gold. He stared through Jack and Anna. It was hard to tell if he was actually seeing them. Did he even speak English? Jack raised his eyebrows at Anna.

"Um, permission to come aboard?" Anna said.

Finally, the ferryman spoke. "Come aboard."

His voice surprised her. It was warm and deep. She had been expecting thin, desiccated.

Jack climbed onto the boat, which rocked alarmingly under his weight and squeaked like a mouse with its tail in a trap. Anna followed him, bringing the rope along. The boat kept rocking long after they both sat down. Charon seemed unconcerned. He stood in the stern, guide pole in hand, and let the boat rock under him.

"You may drop the rope," he said to Anna.

She sat down next to Jack and placed the coiled rope gently in a pile by her feet. Charon nodded once, as if confirming a job well done.

With a lot of levering and a deafening noise, he forced the boat out toward the center of the river. Anna leaned over the side to watch the blue plastic pucker under the wheels. Sure enough, puffs of black rose from the plastic each time the wheels slowed. She leaned closer to get a better view.

Jack grabbed her arm. "You'll fall," he said.

She pulled it away. "I won't, and if I did, I could walk to the other side. What are you worried about?" She knew what he was worried about. That black stuff gave her the same feeling as a cockroach running across your toe. Anna looked over the side again. It was only plastic with a puddle on it. Why did it worry her so much?

She leaned toward Jack and whispered in his ear, "Are you seeing a giant slip-and-slide?"

"Yes, but . . . just don't lean over."

"Why?"

"It just seems like a bad idea, okay?"

Anna narrowed her eyes at him, but sat back in her seat. "Okay."

Charon blinked and said nothing. Near the middle of the river he stopped propelling the boat. It squeaked forward on its own for a moment and then ground to a stop. The wheels went silent. Anna was happy about that at least.

Charon laid the pole across his knees and leaned forward. Anna noticed that he was wearing jeans under the robe. His feet were bare. She could even see the dark hairs curling on his toes.

"Now then," Charon said, drumming the fingers of his free hand on his knee. "We must discuss payment."

"We don't have any money," Jack said.

"We no longer take payment in money. A foolish thing to do, really. What use is gold to us here? We amassed piles of gold and silver. Mountains of it." He gestured as he talked, making the boat sway and creak. "And then times changed, and the coins were no longer even made out of precious metals but bits of copper and lead and nickel, worthless even if we could spend them." Charon dismissed the money with a wave of his hand. "Of course, even the most precious coins weren't really coins at all, but the memory of coins."

"What do you mean?" Anna asked.

He turned his dark eyes on Anna. "This is the underworld, child. Everything that comes to us here is nothing more than a memory, an imprint of something that exists or did exist in the living world. So what were we to do with the memory of billions of coins?"

He stared at the opposite shore, as though seeing his mountains of gold piled there. "They were worthless." He shook his head.

"Then we met a man on the riverbank who offered to tell us a story as payment for his passage. We thought, *Why not? A story has to be worth at least as much as the memory of a coin.* As he talked, we saw the story in here." He placed one finger against his temple.

"In your imagination?" Anna said.

"Yes!" he nearly shouted, and then he lowered his voice, speaking urgently, leaning forward. "But until then, we did not know we possessed one. You humans cannot understand. You have lives that begin and end and are full of thoughts and memories and experiences. For the first time in our existence we had a memory that was not the river, an experience that was not the river, a thought of something that was not the river. From that moment we resolved to ask for payment not in worthless coins but in stories." His large hands clutched his knees. "Give me a tiny piece of your life. You've had so much, you'll hardly notice that it's gone."

"But, aren't you basically an actor?" Anna said. "I mean, this is like Shakespeare in the Park, not the actual River Styx. It's not even really a river. How can you have no memory of anything else?"

"What is an actor?"

Anna looked to Jack for help.

"It's a person," Jack said, "who pretends to be someone else for money."

"Oh, a con man."

Jack paused. Finally he said, "Kind of like that, but not quite. He does it to entertain people."

"And they give him money in exchange?"

"Well, even actors have to eat."

Charon nodded. "We know about eating. That's when you bite and swallow things. Humans need to do this when they are alive."

"Right," Anna said. "Wait. So you're saying you're not human?"

"We don't think so."

"What are you then?"

"We are Charon, ferry captain on the River Styx. We transport souls from the empty desert into the afterlife."

"But this is an art installation." Anna enunciated the words carefully. "It isn't real."

Charon's face crumpled at the edges. "We are real."

"Well, yes. Obviously. But the river isn't."

"We are the ferry captain on the River Styx. We are real; therefore the river is also real. This is called logic."

"You can't just say 'therefore' and call it logic," Jack said.

"This is our river, and we say it is real." Charon's voice boomed in the emptiness.

Anna bit her lip. Jack gave her a look that said, *You started this and you had better figure out how to finish it before he throws us overboard.*

Anna tried reason. "A real river has more water in it."

"The Styx has water."

"But a real river has more. You can swim in it. I could have walked across this and barely gotten my feet wet."

"Don't be foolish, child. A human cannot walk on water."

"I'll show you. Look."

Anna stood, making the boat rock wildly, and clambered over the side.

"No!" Charon and Jack both grabbed for her as she slipped over the edge. Her feet broke through the plastic and into something icy and viscous below. She tried to kick, but the cold almost instantly numbed her legs. She could hardly feel them.

Inky blackness billowed all around her, staining the bright blue plastic like a bruise. She wanted to scream but was terrified of that water filling her lungs. Dark water closed over her head. Sudden and complete darkness. Something, many somethings, brushed against her arms, her legs, her torso. She lashed out against them.

A hand grabbed her by the hair and heaved. Charon pulled her straight up and onto the deck with merely a grunt.

Dripping but safe, Anna clung to him. He patted her back like a man who thought "there, there" was the ultimate in comforting tactics. Anna forced herself to let go of Charon's robe.

Jack reached out to support her as she shifted carefully toward her seat. She brushed his hand away and sat down. She didn't want to infect him with the darkness, which she was sure still clung to her.

"Are you okay? What happened? Where did you go?"

Anna couldn't answer him. She looked down at her hands, her shorts, her legs. They weren't stained as she had expected. The water that dripped from her hair was as clear as a spring. Still, she felt unclean.

"If he says it's a river, it's a river," Anna said. Her fingers clutched the solid wood plank that served as a seat.

Charon shook his head at her. "That was a foolish act."

"Are you okay?" Jack asked again.

Anna looked down the river, where the darkness was dissipating in the current. "Tell the man a story so we can get off this thing."

"But—"

"Please, Jack." She heard the whine in her voice and tried to say it more firmly. "Please."

Even after she turned her head away, she could feel Jack's eyes on her. He seemed to be waiting for her to say something else. She kept silent and closed her eyes so she wouldn't have to look at that damn sky anymore.

She felt Jack fidget. Then he spoke.

"We were at a birthday party. Everyone in our eighth-grade class had been invited."

Anna opened her eyes. She couldn't believe he had picked this story. He could have told the one about the time he caught the lawn on fire, or the time they barricaded the road to stop the ice cream truck, or even the one about the snowmen, but no, he was actually going to tell this one. Right now. With her sitting right beside him.

"Anna and I were dating at the time."

Anna closed her eyes again.

"It had been a few weeks, but I still couldn't believe my luck. I had wanted to date her since the day we met. I'd asked her out once before this, but she . . ." He faltered. Paused. Rallied. "She turned me down. But now we were dating, and I didn't think things could get any better.

"We had gone bowling earlier at a local bowling alley where we ate cake and ice cream and the birthday girl opened her presents. Then we went back to Kristi's house to wait for our parents to pick us up.

"It was nighttime and dark, but the lights of the gas station across the street made enough light that we could barely see each other. We were in the front yard, under a huge tree.

"I was sort of standing around, trying to ignore the girls whispering to Anna. Whatever they said seemed to annoy her. She shushed them.

"When my dad's truck stopped in the street in front of the house, I said goodbye to everyone and headed for the truck. Anna called after me to wait. She said, 'I want to ask you something.' I waved to my dad and went back to her.

"'What?' I asked.

"She said, 'I don't want to ask you in front of everyone. Come over here.'

"A couple of the girls were giggling. She glared at them to stop. Anna has a good glare when she wants to."

Anna tried it on Jack now, but he seemed to be ignoring her.

"They stopped. She took me by the wrist and led me around behind the shed. Nobody could see us. She turned to me and smiled.

"'What did you want to ask me?' I said.

"She said, 'Nothing. Mostly I wanted to do this.'

"And she kissed me. I didn't know what to do. It was my first kiss. I stood there, shocked. I felt like the rest of the world had stopped and she and I were the only living, breathing things left. Finally, I kissed her back.

"She pulled away. I didn't trust myself to say anything. She was smiling, not really at me, more smiling to herself. I turned around and walked away.

"A couple of the other kids tried to say something to me, but I ignored them. I didn't want them spoiling this. I wandered over to my dad's truck and climbed in."

Jack stopped talking. Anna kept her eyes on the distant shore. She hadn't thought it had meant so much to him, that kiss. Had she even known at the time that it was his first? She wasn't sure.

"Thank you, child. That is a fine payment." Charon was smiling.

Jack nodded. He didn't even have the grace to look embarrassed. Anna said nothing.

They sat side by side, listening to the squeak of the wheels. Anna watched the opposite shore. It didn't look any different from the one they had just left. It was narrow road and empty desert as far as the eye could see. She wondered why the Afterlife Beautification Commission had chosen this particular spot for its art installation. She wondered if the road continued unbroken under the blue plastic. She wondered what the hell had happened back there.

The boat squeaked to a stop. "Thank you for your story," Charon said. "I will remember it fondly."

Jack seemed dazed. He obviously wasn't going to answer. Anna had no idea what was up with him. "You're welcome," she said. "And thank you for bringing us across the river."

"It is what we do," Charon said. He continued in a softer voice. "It is all we do." He bent to pick up the coil of rope and cast it ashore. It seemed to be part of the ritual. But the rope had caught itself on something, the head of a nail protruding from the place where the seat joined the side of the boat.

Charon straightened and held the guide pole out toward them. "Could one of you hold this a moment, please?"

"Sure . . ." Anna began, reaching to take it from him.

"No," Jack said. He caught Anna's forearm and pulled. "No."

"Jack—"

"We have to go. Thank you for taking us across."

Anna wanted to pull away from Jack, but suddenly she felt shaky. Her adventure over the side must be catching up with her. She let Jack drag her past Charon and out of the boat. When she looked back, Charon was standing in the bow, pole in one hand, rope, freed now, in the other. His eyes were sad. He turned away from her quickly.

"What is wrong with you?" Anna hissed.

"Don't you know that story?"

"What story?"

"It was a fairy tale. One of the Grimm ones, I think. There's this boy who's fated to marry a princess. But the king finds out and doesn't want it to happen, so he throws the boy into the river. These two old people find him and raise him, and eventually the king finds him again and tries to have him killed, but it doesn't work, so . . ."

"Reader's Digest version, please."

"Okay, eventually he meets a ferryman who is cursed to never leave his boat. The boy gets the devil's grandmother to ask the devil how the man can be freed, and it turns out all he has to do is trick someone else into taking the oars from him. Then that person would be trapped and he would be free."

"Charon wouldn't do that. He saved me. He just needed help with the ropes."

Jack didn't argue with her. He went quiet for a few minutes, but he was clearly thinking. When he spoke again, he asked, "What did he mean when he said thank you for your story?"

"What do you mean, what did he mean?"

"I mean, what story was he talking about?"

"Cute, Jack."

"What?"

"You were the one who chose the story. Don't blame me if you feel weird about it now."

"Anna, what story? I don't remember anyone telling a story on that boat." His tone got through to her. He wasn't joking. Anna felt like she was falling all over again. She paused in the middle of the path.

"Jack, you just told Charon the story about Kristi's birthday party four years ago."

"How would I do that? I don't even remember Kristi's birthday party. I'm pretty sure I went." His eyebrows furrowed. "You were there too, right?"

Anna covered her mouth with her hand. "Oh my God."

"What? Anna, what the hell is going on?"

Anna moved her hand just enough to let the words out. "You gave him a piece of your life. He asked you to. He said you wouldn't even miss it."

"Holy shit," Jack said. "I don't remember that party at all. I don't remember going. I don't remember talking about it. Tell me this isn't real."

Anna couldn't.

~

Mom always let Ella pick out her own clothes, but not today. Today Mom said, "I want you to wear these."

Ella didn't even complain, because of Mom's face. It was all shadows and lines, and it made Ella sad to look at it. She knew Mom was sad because Jack was dead and he wasn't coming home ever again. That made Ella sad too. Jack had promised to finish her playhouse. How could he do that if he didn't come home? And he'd taken Octavius with him. Was Octavius dead too? She would have to ask Mom.

Ella put on the white dress with the gray flowers and the black sweater her mom had picked out for her. She even put on the shiny black shoes that pinched her feet. Then she picked up Sarah. Mom had said Ella could bring only one friend and the rest would have to get babysat by Barbie. She'd picked Sarah, because Sarah was the littlest and didn't like being away from Ella for long.

"You behave now. And mind Ms. Barbie," she told the dolls. "And no sugar." She turned to Barbie. "If they get all hyped up on sugar, they'll never sleep tonight."

Mom's voice came up the stairs. "Ella, it's time to go."

They were going to something called a wake. Jack would be there. Ella was excited to see him. Maybe if she asked him very nicely, he would come home with them and he wouldn't have to be dead anymore. Or maybe it could be like how Skylar at school stayed at her mom's house during the week and her dad's house on weekends. Maybe Jack would give them joint custody and then he could still play with her some days after school.

Ella took Sarah and started down the stairs. The steps were big, and she had to hold on to Sarah and the railing at the same time. Going down the stairs took a long time. She could hear the grown-ups talking to each other in their don't-let-the-kids-hear-us voices.

". . . not sure we should take her," Ella's daddy was saying.

"We can't shelter her from this, Jim." Mom's voice was doing that shaky thing like she was going to cry. "We can't just tell her he went to live on a farm or something."

"Who went to live on a farm?" Ella asked. "Do they have chickens and pigs and bunnies?"

"Nobody, sweetie. We're just doing grown-up talk."

Lately everyone was always doing grown-up talk. Grandma and Uncle Scott and Aunt Lily and basically the entire family had all come to visit, but everyone was sad and acted like boring grown-ups, even Ella's older cousins. It seemed like there was no little-kid talk left in the whole world.

"Someday I'll be a grown-up," Ella said.

Mom scooped her up off the second-to-last step and hugged her so tight that Ella went "Oof."

"Of course you will, baby," Mom said, and she was crying again. That made Ella want to cry too.

"Rachel, stop. You're scaring her."

Daddy reached out his arms and Ella went into them. Her mom let her go, and then turned away. She was trying not to let Ella see her cry. She knew it made Ella sad. Ella wanted to explain that it made her sad only because she didn't want Mom to be sad, and hiding it just made her sadder, but adults never understood things like that when you tried to explain. She wondered if she'd be so difficult to explain things to when she was an adult.

"Let's get you all settled in the car, okay, Ella Bella?" Daddy said.

He carried her through the house toward the front door. Ella clutched Sarah tightly. She was still excited to see Jack, but she was nervous too. Why was everyone so sad?

"It's just grown-up things," she told Sarah. "You'll understand when you're older." Sarah didn't like that answer much. She knew as well as Ella did that it was the kind of thing adults said when they thought you were too little to know what was going on.

Daddy buckled her into her booster seat and got into the car. He was all dressed up, in a black suit and a gray tie with a white shirt underneath. Daddy never dressed up. A wake must be a very special kind of party. Ella started to get a little bit excited again.

She straightened Sarah's little shoes and rubbed the top of Sarah's bald head. Then Mom came outside and got in the car.

They drove just like they were going to McDonald's. Ella knew the way by heart. She wondered if maybe the wake would be at McDonald's. That seemed like a pretty good place for a party since they had the PlayPlace and all the best French fries. But they turned a new way at the stoplight.

"Sarah is hungry for French fries," Ella said.

"No French fries, sweetie. You ate an hour ago, and I don't want you to get your dress greasy. You know what a messy eater Sarah is."

Ella was both disappointed and delighted by this answer. Sometimes Mom pretended that Sarah wasn't a real baby, and that annoyed Ella. She liked it much better when Mom was nice to Sarah. She kicked her heels against the seat and looked out the window to see where they were going.

Dad stopped the car in front of a great big house. It looked like something out of a movie. It had fancy, tall posts in the front holding up the porch. And it had lots of roofs that all sloped in different directions. There were curly bits all around the top. And sparkly windows painted in all different colors.

When Daddy came to get Ella out of her booster seat, she whispered at him, "Is this a castle?"

Dad smiled, but he didn't look happy. "No, baby. It's a funeral home. We have to be on our best behavior in here. This is a place for grown-ups."

Dad's voice made Ella nervous again. That was his listen-or-else voice, and Ella never liked to find out "or else what." She looked down into Sarah's blue eyes and said, "You be very quiet now, and maybe after, we can get French fries."

"Ella—" Daddy started to say, but Mom interrupted him.

"Let it go, Jim."

Daddy picked Ella right up and carried her on his hip like she was still a little baby girl. That meant she was at eye level with the grumpy-looking man who opened the front door. He opened it before Daddy could even knock, like he'd been watching through the window for them. Ella didn't like that man.

She pressed her face on Daddy's shoulder and smelled his Dad-smell, which was the third-best smell in the world. The first-best smell was Mom-smell, and the second-best smell was cookies just out of the oven.

She felt Dad walking and heard the man talking soft and low, but she didn't listen to him. She was smelling Dad-smell and looking at Sarah's face pressed just underneath her own. She didn't look up again until she heard Mom start to cry. She wished Mom would stop crying.

They were in a new room. It had lots and lots of chairs all set up in rows like when they had gone to see Jack and Anna in the school play. This room wasn't a gym, though. It looked like someone's grandma's house, with carpets on the floors and striped wallpaper. It was also full of flowers. Ella had never seen so many flowers inside before.

Dad put Ella down gently, and she immediately ran over to smell the flowers. They didn't smell like anything, but they were set up in pretty shapes. There was a heart and a ring and big vases with flowers flying out in all directions. In the middle was a shiny wooden box with metal handles. Ella pulled on one of the handles, but the box didn't open.

"Ella!" Dad said. That was his stop-right-there voice. Ella froze.

"Come here."

When Ella got to him, he pointed to a chair in the front row and said, "Sit right there and don't you move until I say so."

Ella sat. She was in trouble for touching the box. That wasn't fair. Nobody had told her not to. How was she supposed to know not to touch something if nobody told her not to? She wished Jack was there. He would tell her why she wasn't allowed to touch the box. Jack loved to explain things to her. He almost wasn't even a real grown-up. Sometimes, he was just a kid like her.

Mom and Dad were talking to the grumpy man. Mom had stopped crying, but the grumpy man gave her a little pillow full of tissues just in case. Then he made them all stand in a line near the front of the room. Ella stood between Mom and Dad with Sarah in her arms. She could see the box she wasn't allowed to touch.

Another man came in carrying a big poster board. It had a picture of Jack on it. He put it on a wooden thing so it would stay up at the front of the room. Mom started to cry again when she saw it. Ella thought she must be really happy that Jack was coming soon. Sometimes people cried when they were happy.

After that, lots of people came. But none of them were Jack. Some of them were people she knew, but lots of them weren't. Most were crying or looked like they were going to cry or like they just had been. All of them wanted to hug Ella. She got tired of it really quickly. She didn't like being hugged by strangers, especially sad ones.

"Where's Jack?" she asked, but she said it too quietly, and nobody heard. She repeated herself more loudly. She was starting to worry that Jack wasn't going to be there at all. Maybe they'd lied to her. Grown-ups did lie sometimes.

Ella's mom knelt down on the floor and hugged Ella tight.

Ella said, "You said he'd be here."

"Honey, Jack is dead."

"I know. He can't play anymore, but you said he'd be here."

Ella's mom started to cry really hard, like she was hurt. Ella couldn't take it anymore. She started to cry too. She cried and she stamped her foot and she wailed as loudly as she could. She knew she was acting like a baby, but she didn't care.

Dad tried to pick her up, but Ella pulled away from him.

"You said he'd be here. You lied!"

All the stupid, sad adults were looking at her, but she didn't care. She ran away, away from Dad and Mom and the grumpy man. She ran right out of the room and down the hall and stopped because she bounced against someone's knees. Ella wanted to keep running, but the person who owned the knees said her name, very softly.

Ella looked up. She knew this person. She'd seen him with Anna before.

He crouched right down next to her but didn't try to hug her. Ella liked that. "My name is Michael," he said. "Do you remember me?"

Ella nodded. "You're Anna's brother."

"That's right." He smiled a very tiny smile.

"Just like Jack is my brother."

"Yes. I'm Anna's big brother."

Ella looked at Michael. He was dressed up too. With a button-up shirt and a tie and his hair all flattened down. But he was down here on the floor with her, not crying or trying to hug her. And he was a big brother too. She could ask him her questions.

"Why isn't Jack here? They said he would be, but he isn't. They said he can't play with me anymore. They said he's dead."

Michael settled down on his knees. He was still a little taller than Ella, but he looked down at her in a way that made her feel better.

"Ella, can I tell you a secret? It's the secret of being a big brother, and I think Jack would want me to tell it to you."

He wasn't answering her question. Still, Ella nodded. She liked secrets. And she'd always known that big kids and grown-ups had them.

Michael leaned close to her. "The secret is that even when he's far away, even when he doesn't talk to you, even when he doesn't have time for games, your big brother loves you."

Michael reached out and touched Ella's shoulder, gently, like she was a ceramic figurine on the mantel that was only for looking at. Ella didn't even mind.

"He loves you so much. And being dead won't change that. Can you remember that secret for me?"

Ella nodded. She stepped closer to Michael and patted Michael on the knee. "You're a good big brother," she said.

"No," Michael said. "I'm really, really not."

Somebody was crying really loudly. Ella looked up and saw that Anna's parents were there, standing way up high, watching Michael talk to her. Both of them were crying, but they weren't making all the noise. Ella turned around. Her parents were there too. Mom had her hand over her mouth, and a noise was coming out that sounded like she was having a nightmare. That scared Ella a little bit. She didn't like to see her mom upset. She looked at Michael.

He hadn't moved. He was just sitting there, his shoulders slumped way down, his hands open in his lap. Ella stepped close to him. She leaned her head on his shoulder and let him hug her.

Chapter Six

Anna was worried about Jack. He hadn't said anything since they'd realized he'd lost his memory. Anna was itching to find out how much he'd really forgotten. Did he actually not remember his own first kiss? But she didn't want to question him when he was in this mood. It would only make things worse. It was Jack who finally broke the silence.

"How do we know that any of this is real?" Jack asked.

"It's real, Jack."

"But how do we know this isn't a dream?"

"I'm pretty sure it's not."

"Maybe I'm lying in a hospital bed somewhere, dreaming all of this," Jack said. "Or maybe, maybe I've finally snapped, like Uncle Steve. Maybe the stress of the accident caused some kind of, I don't know, schizophrenic break or something, and I'm wandering around talking to myself."

"So I'm a figment of your imagination?"

"Possibly."

Anna shook her head. "How can I convince you?"

Jack's face darkened. He blinked, and his eyes remained closed a second too long. For an instant, he looked like the boy she'd first met, seven years earlier, halfway through the fifth grade. He'd been a transfer student from Rhode Island. She'd turned in her seat to see him, standing nervous in the doorway. Then, as now, he had blinked, shutting out the world, and his face was the face of a child waiting for the monster to jump out from under the bed and crunch his bones.

Anna cast around for something, anything to distract him. And to her surprise she found something. Was it a coincidence that something

58

always seemed to appear just when they needed a distraction? Was that how the afterlife worked?

"Do you see that? Like a low cloud in the distance?"

"There aren't any clouds here."

"It's something else then, a mountain, or a town."

As they got closer, they saw that the dark mass in the distance was a pair of buildings connected by a catwalk. The smaller building looked like an office, four stories tall. The larger was maybe six or seven stories, with slotted vents for windows and tall smokestacks on the roof. It looked like a factory. Something about the building bothered Anna, something on the edge of her vision. It wasn't just that it was the only structure for miles. It was wrong somehow, but no matter how hard she stared, she couldn't quite grasp how.

Jack, in a completely useless gesture of habit, shaded his eyes to look up at the building.

"It looks familiar. I swear I've seen this place before," Anna said.

"How could that be?"

"No idea," she said. "But I know I've seen it, maybe in a book or something. I feel like maybe the picture I saw was in black-and-white."

"This is weird. Is it a real place, do you think?"

"Define *real*."

"I'm definitely not the expert on that one," Jack said.

Anna stared at the building and saw what was wrong with it, like a magic picture that suddenly snaps into focus. "No shadow."

"What?"

"It doesn't cast a shadow."

Jack nodded toward the ground. "Neither do we. Strictly speaking there's no sun, so we shouldn't cast a shadow."

"Okay, fine, but where is all the light coming from? I mean, bright as day, not a cloud"—she glanced up at the empty sky and then down again quickly—"not a cloud in the sky. But no sun either, so it should be dark, right?"

"Maybe . . ." Jack paused, clearly at a loss. "Maybe the air glows."

"The air glows. That makes exactly no sense." Anna sighed. "Have I mentioned lately how much this place creeps me out?"

"You're creeped out? I'm lucky I remember my own name."

Anna opened her mouth to reassure him, but was interrupted by a voice. From somewhere over their heads a voice called, "Hey. Hi."

Anna grabbed Jack's arm. "What was that?"

Jack pointed toward the right of the factory. On the roof of the catwalk, a sturdily built man with curly hair was waving at them, sweeping both arms over his head in a broad, here-I-am gesture. His bright-green shirt seemed to punch a hole in the empty sky.

"Who is that?" Jack whispered as they waved back.

"No idea. At least he seems friendly."

"Oh yeah, they all do, right until they eat your memories."

Anna had to ignore that. There was nothing constructive to say. Who knew? He might be right. So far, nothing in the afterlife had been predictable.

"Wait there," the man shouted. "I'll be right down."

As the man moved away from the edge of the roof, Jack wondered out loud, "How do you think he got up there?"

The man jumped off the roof. Anna screamed and jerked her hands up to her eyes. She felt Jack's arm around her, pressing her face into his shoulder. It would have been comforting, except that Anna immediately noticed she couldn't smell him. Normally, this close, Jack smelled like deodorant and sunscreen and, well, Jack. Now all of that was gone. It was as though Anna had the worst cold of her life. A second later she heard a thump, and then, amazingly, laughter.

Anna risked a peek, expecting to see a crater with a corpse in it. The man—no, the boy, actually; he looked to be about their age—was on his feet, dusting sand off the front of his shirt.

"Hey, sorry. Didn't mean to scare you."

Anna lowered her hands, her head still shielded against Jack's shoulder. The jumper smiled at her.

"Why would you *do* that?" she asked.

The boy's eyes crumpled, and his defensive lineman shoulders slumped. "I really didn't mean to scare you. You can't get hurt here, you know. It's not possible. One time Little Tom—"

"Really?" Anna interrupted. She punched Jack's arm as hard as she could.

"Ow! What did I do?" Jack rubbed his biceps.

"That hurt?"

"No."

"Then why did you say ow?"

"Because you punched me. What the hell?"

"Just checking," Anna said. She turned to the boy. "I'm glad you're okay."

The boy smiled, showing a lot of white teeth. "I'm Ricky. It's great to meet you guys. We're always happy to see new people. It gets dull around here with the same old faces, if you know what I mean."

He held out his hand for them to shake. He had clammy hands. Anna tried to wipe her palm on the leg of her shorts without anybody noticing, but Ricky caught her and gave her a rueful smile.

"Sorry about that." He spread his hands. "The sweaty palms came with me."

Jack's scrunched his eyebrows. "That doesn't make any sense at all."

"I know, but what can you do? My whole life I had sweaty palms. Looks like I'll have them for my whole afterlife, too. Everybody used to give me grief about it. When my sister and I were little, Dad tried to get us to hold hands to cross the street, but my sister wouldn't. She said she didn't want sweaty stink hands." He paused. "Sorry. I ramble. It's a thing I do. Anyway, come on. The others will want to meet you."

"Others?" Anna asked.

"Not everyone stops here, but some people do, and some of them stay."

"Why?"

Ricky turned away from them. "Lots of reasons," he said, his voice flatly controlled. There was a moment of deep silence, and then he said. "Come on, I'll introduce you and you can ask them. I think you'll really like them. They're good people. Weird, but in, you know, a good way."

They followed him to the cargo doors of the factory. Even before Ricky slid the door open on its track, Anna could hear the machinery rumbling and clanking on the other side. It made her realize how silent the afterlife had been thus far: no far-off traffic or people shouting in the distance, no planes overhead, no birdsong.

"What do they make here?" Anna asked.

Ricky answered her as he opened the door, but the words were lost as the grinding noise of the machinery hit them.

"What?" Jack and Anna said together.

Ricky responded with a follow-me gesture. The factory floor was dark, lit only by the shreds of light arcing through the window vents. Huge pieces of machinery squatted in the shadows. Their motion created a rumbling pulse that thumped up through the soles of Anna's feet and into her chest. She could almost imagine she had a heartbeat again. It was a good feeling.

Ricky strode through the center of the room, hands behind his back, comfortable as a foreman inspecting his workers. Jack and Anna followed close behind him, much less confident than he was in the dark, echoing space.

Anna leaned toward Jack and spoke into his ear. "I'm waiting for something to jump out from behind those machines and rip our heads off."

Jack nodded and responded in a slightly louder voice. "Or the machines will move and stretch and we'll realize they're not machines at all, but giants waiting to eat unsuspecting travelers."

"Don't worry." Ricky stopped them in the middle of the floor. "There's nobody in here but us. The others don't like to come down here. They think it's creepy."

"And they would be correct," Anna said. "What are these machines doing?"

"Honestly, I have no idea. They make a lot of noise and things come out of them. Like, all kinds of things. One time I even found . . . well, you'll see. It's pretty awesome."

They watched a huge mechanical arm swing high above their heads, pluck something off of one conveyor belt, and deposit it onto another across the room. Then Ricky gestured them forward. They walked through a small door into an enormous warehouse. It was stuffed to bursting with piles of what appeared to be miscellaneous junk that towered almost to the ceiling. Anna stopped to stare. She saw an ancient car, and a sad pull-string doll with yarn for hair, and a pink tricycle with handlebar streamers.

Anna picked up the doll and pulled the string on its back. "Let's brush our teeth," the doll said. Anna examined it more closely. The pattern on its dress was not white polka dots as she had first thought, but tiny teeth, and the broken thing it was holding in its hand might once have been a toothbrush.

Jack called for her. He was waiting at a metal ladder, with one foot on the bottom rung. Ricky was already halfway up. Anna set the doll down gently on top of a typewriter case the color of burnt orange and followed.

The ladder ended on a mesh catwalk. Anna could look down between her feet and see the mounds of stuff below her. She felt a wave of vertigo and clung to the rail, forcing herself to look straight ahead. Strange, she'd never had any problem with heights before. Somewhere far in the distance there must be a wall, because there was a ceiling overhead and something had to be holding it up, but all she could see were shoes and mirrors and calico dogs.

Anna caught movement out of the corner of her eye and turned, expecting nothing more interesting than a pile of junk shifting under its own weight. Instead, she saw a man in a black robe standing on the side of a peak, like a mountaineer resting on his way up Everest. She yelped. Jack and Ricky both looked at her.

"There's a man," she said, by way of explanation.

"That's Professor Haggarty," Ricky said. "He's studying the warehouse. It's a pretty strange place." He cupped his hands around his mouth and called, "Professor." The man turned, waved, and started to work his way toward them.

Ricky continued. "Nobody knows much about this. What all of it is. Why it's here."

"Who's running the machines," Jack added.

"Whoever they are, they'll have to stop soon," Anna said. "There isn't room for much more."

"Look again," Ricky said.

Anna's gaze followed his pointing hand to the wall where one of the conveyor belts from the factory dumped through a square opening into the warehouse. She watched boots and VHS tapes and rocking chairs tumble from the conveyor belt to the pile. She blinked. "It's moving, the whole pile is moving. Isn't it?"

Jack leaned over the railing to get a closer look.

Ricky said, "Yeah, it's moving. There's a belt that rolls under the piles. The room seems to go on forever, as far as I can tell. Not even Professor Haggarty has ever seen the back wall, and he went away for a long time once, trying to find it."

"The building didn't look that big from the outside," Anna said.

"It isn't. I've walked around it a bunch of times. But from in here, you can start walking and never reach the end."

"So it's bigger on the inside?" Anna said.

"Anna, look at this!"

Jack plucked a red-and-blue action figure from the pile. It was plastic and missing its head. He gazed down at it, cradling it in his hands. "It's Optimus Prime. I had one of these."

He touched the broken plastic where the head had been. "I think Ella has it now." His eyes, when he looked up at Anna, were scrunched and sad. "Why is this here?"

Anna shrugged. "Why is any of this here?"

"That is the question of the hour," said a British-accented voice. They turned to see Professor Haggarty laboring up the side of the closest mountain. When he was high enough, Ricky put out an arm to help him clamber over the guardrail and onto the platform.

"Thank you, my boy. I see you have some new friends."

"Professor, this is Jack and Anna."

"Yes, yes," the professor said. "I have been studying the warehouse for some time, but have hit upon no satisfactory conclusion as to why all of this is here. Though the objects ostensibly appear to be created by the machine, a physical inspection indicates that they are of great age." He plucked something out of a nearby pile. "Take for instance this blanket. It is stitched and patched in several places. The tag is so faded as to be illegible."

He proffered the blanket for their inspection. Anna took it from him and rubbed the silky edging between her fingers. "It looks like a kid's blanket," she said. "Like the kind Linus carries around all the time. Someone must have really loved this blanket."

Professor Haggarty continued as though she hadn't spoken, "And therein lies the conundrum, new objects that look old. Why? I thought to answer the question by cataloging the items. For the most part, they can be broken up into five categories: toys, clothes and shoes, vehicles, tools, and household goods. These categories are not mutually exclusive, but nearly every item falls into at least one."

"That seems to cover pretty much everything," Jack said.

"On the contrary," the professor said, tucking his hands into his wide sleeves. "There are no fine artworks, food items, books, or writings of any sort. Everything is factory made, and nothing is larger than an automobile. And then there is the room itself, which is a puzzle in its own right. It is functionally infinite, which raises many interesting questions, such as, if a room contains infinite space, can it in fact be called a room? As I'm sure you have noticed, the room is growing. It would be safe to assume that it grows at a rate equal to or greater than the fill rate, since it never runs out of space. But what governs this growth? And what form of physics allows a building to be infinite on the inside and finite on the outside?"

He rubbed his temples. "It seems the more I know, the more questions I have."

"The joys of science," Ricky said. "We won't keep you, Professor. I know how busy you are."

"Quite. Yes. If you'll excuse me."

He climbed carefully over the rail and onto a pile, precipitating a small toy-slide. As soon as the movement settled, he struck out toward the elusive back wall.

"You have to stop him somehow or he'll go on like that all day," Ricky muttered. "He's not bad company, though, if you can get him to think about something else for three seconds at a time."

Anna asked, "How long has he been here?"

"Longer than me," Ricky said. "Probably a lot longer. Why?"

"He was wearing a robe."

"I guess they did that—professors, I mean—back in his day."

"It was all the rage in 1902," Anna said.

"How long have *you* been here?" Jack asked.

Ricky turned away from them, toward a plain metal door. Anna thought maybe he wasn't going to answer, but then he said quietly, "I died in 1989—March 1989." There was another one of those heavy pauses while Ricky got lost in his own thoughts, and Anna didn't have the courage to interrupt him. Ricky shook himself free of the past.

"Oh, well, it's a pretty okay place to be if you have to be dead. Come this way. There's a public room I hang out in a lot, and everyone there always loves meeting new people."

He opened a plain metal door that led out to the skywalk. The walls on both sides were glass, but someone had strung a series of blankets across them like curtains, blocking the view to the outside. They walked across.

There were people in the halls of the office building. Anna could almost pretend they were regular people going about their regular workdays, except that they all seemed to be dressed for some sort of historical reenactment party. She saw short breeches and bustles, mobcaps and bell-bottoms, fedoras and leather jackets.

Ricky greeted almost everyone who passed, calling them by what Anna hoped were nicknames.

"Hey, Tall Pockets, where's the beef?" he said to a pockmarked man in a black frock coat. The man smiled and tipped his hat.

"Little Tee, where have you been hiding?"

"Do you know everyone here?" Anna asked.

"Pretty much. Only about two hundred people stick around."

"And you know all of them?"

"Well, yeah. It's like a town. Hey, Dead Jim." He high-fived a middle-aged man with a gap-toothed smile.

"Aren't they all dead?" Jack said.

"Well yeah, but he's Dead Jim. There's a good story behind that one. So one time—"

Ricky stopped in midsentence as an older woman with a sour expression swept past them. "Hello, Mrs. Rosenbloom."

The woman sniffed, "Young man."

When she had passed, Ricky grinned at Jack and Anna. "Remind me to tell you that story later." He stopped outside of an office. "This is it." He opened the door.

Chapter Seven

Ricky led them into a room large enough to accommodate a full-length conference table. The chairs were scattered in clusters around the room, and the table itself was propped against the back wall, blocking out the lower half of the windows. Anna wondered why they hadn't put it against the other wall; at least then the light wouldn't have been so dim.

Just inside the door, a man was juggling using three high-heeled shoes. He nodded to Ricky.

"Working on a new act, Bruno?"

"Always I practice," Bruno said. "But without my brother . . . is no act."

"Were you in the circus?" Anna asked.

Bruno let two of the shoes drop to the floor, thunk, thunk. He caught the third by its spiked heel and gestured with it as he spoke. "The Brothers Barabas. We are pride of sideshow. All little children come to see us juggle fire. Ooh, they say, and aah. We are very famous."

"What happened?" Jack asked.

"I have buttered fingers." Bruno bent to pick up the shoes. "But I practice, practice, and when brother comes, I show him."

"I think you're doing well," Anna said.

Bruno smiled, and then, in one fluid movement he bowed and set them in motion again. Ricky led Jack and Anna deeper into the room.

In the shadow of the conference table, two men were sitting with a cribbage board on a card table between them. The older of the two had gray hair and a face like a porcelain doll that had been dropped one too many times. His opponent was much younger. He was wearing a three-piece suit with a gold pin in the lapel.

The younger man threw his cards down onto the board. "Blast, skunked again. I swear you cheat, old man."

"Don't need to cheat when I'm better'n you. Give over one of those marbles, Harry."

"What are the marbles for?" Anna muttered to Ricky, but Ricky wasn't listening. He'd drifted over to the window and was staring out at the sand.

The old man answered. "Scorekeeping, young miss. We've been playing this tournament for a long time, y'see. I'm ahead six hundred and some games to Harry's five hundred and sixty-four. Every time he loses, he has to give me one of his marbles."

"And every time Carver loses, he has to give me one of his," Harry said. He bent down to a briefcase lying open at his feet, plucked out a marble, and handed it to the old man.

"On the rare occasions when such a thing occurs," Carver said, and dropped the marble into a giant plastic Coke bottle that might once have been a novelty bank.

"So Harry is losing his marbles?" Jack said.

The old man snickered.

Harry grimaced. "Oh yes. You slay me." He pressed his hand to his heart. "You wait until Haggarty finds a mah-jongg board down there."

Carver reset the pegs on the board. "That mad old philosopher couldn't find the moon with a telescope," he said.

Ricky turned away from the window long enough to say, "He is my friend, you know."

The sound of running feet approached them. Anna turned. An auburn-haired girl in a frilly white nightgown and a hooded robe was pelting toward them. She stopped suddenly and narrowed her eyes at them. Anna realized that the robe was actually a hooded sweatshirt, unzipped down the front.

"It's okay, Little Vee, these are my new friends, Jack and Anna," Ricky said. "Jack, Anna, this is Violet."

Violet moved forward more cautiously. She hugged Ricky, but her eyes stayed on Anna. Anna tried to tell herself that it was nothing—the girl was just curious—but she couldn't shake the feeling that Violet was somehow reading her.

"I'm going to go talk to Grandmother," Violet said. She turned and marched out of the room.

That was weird. "Who's Grandmother?" Anna asked.

Ricky watched Violet leave, his eyebrows furrowed in confusion. "She's, well, she's everyone's grandmother, more or less. She keeps track of things, helps people sort out disagreements. One time Long Legs Len and Davey Jones got into an argument about—"

"She's been here as long as anyone can remember," Carver interrupted.

Ricky added, "I'm sure you'll meet her soon."

"Why don't you kids pull up a chair? This is a slow joint and we don't get much gossip," Harry said.

"And Harry's tired of losing," Carver said.

"I'm tired of listening to you beat your gums, old man," Harry said. "At least the young people have some news of the world, not babble about the damned City that no one wants to go to anyway."

"Harry, everyone wants to go to The City," the old man said. This had the timbre of an old argument.

"Except me," said Harry."

"Yes, of course," Carver said in a tone that suggested "give it time" in subtext.

Ricky dragged a chair across the carpet and set it behind Anna. "Thanks." She sat down. "Why don't you want to go?"

"I did not choose to die," Harry said, with a significant look at Ricky.

"I know I'm an idiot, Harry. You don't have to harp on it," Ricky said.

"And now that I am dead," Harry continued as though he hadn't heard this, "I plan to exist here for as long as possible. People go to The City and never come back."

"Grandmother came back," Ricky said.

"But she didn't enter the gates. If she had gone in, they might not have let her out again."

"It's not a conspiracy, Harry," Carver said. "It's a place."

"A place that everyone wants to go to, but no one knows why. I'm not having this argument with you again, old man. We're supposed to be talking to the young people."

Jack pulled up a chair beside Anna and sat with his right ankle on his left knee. "What do you want to know?"

"Everything," Carver said. "Has that whole internet thing died out yet? Seemed daft to me, all these strangers talking to one another in chatter rooms."

Anna turned her laugh into a cough, and then realized that didn't really work in the afterlife.

Jack raised his eyebrows at her. "Not quite," he said. "Everyone has the internet. I had it on my cell phone."

"What's a cell phone?" Harry asked.

"It's kind of hard to explain. When did you die?" Anna asked.

"The year 1928. I was rowing in Newport Harbor with Hazel Temple when the boat overturned."

"You didn't know how to swim?" Anna asked.

"Not after that much bathtub gin. Besides, it was November."

Anna bit her lip. "I'm sorry. What about Hazel?"

"No need to apologize. That's old news. Hazel made it ashore okay, the dumb Dora. What does this have to do with cell phones?"

"Nothing, really," Jack said. "A cell phone is like a telephone, but it doesn't have any wires and it's small enough to fit in your pocket."

"Baloney," Harry said.

"No, it's true," Carter said. "I remember my daughter had one of them. What else has happened since I died?"

"I don't know, when did you die?"

"In 1994."

Anna and Jack looked at each other. Neither of them was great with recent history. They didn't teach this stuff in school. "Remember President Clinton?" Anna asked.

"Nice guy with an easy smile. Democrat, but you can't hold that against him," Carver said.

"He was impeached."

"Like old Tricky Dick? What did he do, wiretap the White House? Bomb Cambodia?"

"No, he was . . ." Anna interlocked her fingers and then dropped her hands, embarrassed to be having this conversation with a man as old as her grandfather, "you know . . . with his secretary."

"I think she was an intern," Jack said.

"And they impeached him for that? I doubt he's the first president to yard on his wife."

"Arthur Carver. What are you saying to these young people?" a woman's voice said from the doorway.

She was nearly as old as Carver and was carrying a set of knitting needles. With her was a middle-aged woman, maybe sixty years old on the outside. She had a skein of yarn and a partially knitted something under her arm.

"Just catching up on live-side politics, Hannah, don't you worry your old gray head about it."

Hannah pursed her lips and narrowed her eyes. "Now you listen here, Carver," she said, shaking the knitting needles at him. "I may have died six months earlier than you, but I was five and a half years younger when I did it. Don't go talking to me about old gray heads."

The other woman crossed the room to a grouping of chairs. "Why don't you children come and chat with us for a bit?" she said.

"You might as well," Carver said. "Otherwise we'll never hear the end of it."

Jack and Anna looked to Ricky for guidance. "You two go ahead," Ricky said. "I'll stay here a bit longer. I can keep an eye on Mr. Carver and make sure he isn't cheating." But he was glancing out the window as he talked.

Anna watched him. His face was sad, distant. She shrugged one shoulder. "Well, let's go meet Ms. Hannah and knitter number two."

"Ms. Jean," Ricky said without turning. Anna hesitated a moment longer. "Don't worry," Ricky said. "They won't eat you." He smiled, but there wasn't much heart in it.

Anna dragged her chair over to where the ladies were sitting. There was a moment of silence while the two women sorted out their knitting. Anna pulled her foot up onto the seat of her chair and hugged her knee to her chest. Without Ricky standing beside them, she felt like a child cornered by a bunch of her parents' friends at a party.

"Now that we're all settled," Hannah said, working her knitting needles, "tell us about yourselves."

"Um," Anna said.

"Best begin at the beginning," Jean said, working her needles just as quickly. "How did you die?"

"Well, we were on our way to the beach when we got into a car accident," Anna said.

"A car accident," Jean said. "That's how my brother Stephen died."

"And Meredith on the third floor," Hannah added.

Jean nodded. "Drunk driver."

"How does she know?" Hannah asked.

"My dear, it was obvious. The man was all over the road," Jean said.

Hannah tut-tutted at this, then said, "And before the accident? Tell us about your lives."

"We're students at this crappy high school in the middle of nowhere," Anna said. "But I'm going to apply to Rice and Syracuse and Virginia Tech." She saw pity on their faces. "I mean, I was going to."

"I was going to be an engineer," Jack said. "And maybe write science fiction in my spare time." He held on to the seat of his chair, as though afraid it might buck and throw him off.

"And how did you two meet?" Jean asked, her voice low and gentle.

"In middle school," Anna said. "And to be honest, it took me a year to warm up to him." She glanced at Jack, then away before he could read her expression. She didn't know what her face was saying right now. Her mind was a mess.

Jack picked up where she'd left off. "We made friends during the sixth-grade play. It was *A Midsummer Night's Dream*, but set in the seventies—better costumes that way."

"Anyway," Anna said. "We were always in the same home room because our last names start with the same letter. We were about to start our senior year. I turn eighteen next week."

"Would have turned eighteen," Jack said. They both fell silent—not looking at each other, not looking at anyone.

"It is good," Hannah said, "that you have each other."

Anna let this go unanswered. Their knitting had caught her attention. They seemed to both be knitting on opposite ends of the same scarf, but that couldn't be right. It wasn't how knitting worked. Besides, even though both sets of needles were flashing rapidly, the scarf never seemed to get any longer than about five feet. It was the shadowless building all over again—one minute she couldn't see it, the next minute it was unmistakable.

She pointed at Hannah. "You're undoing her work."

Hannah's needles paused. "It's called tinking, dear. Like *knit* spelled backward. Usually you do it only to fix mistakes, but we find it saves on yarn since a full skein is hard to come by here."

Anna slumped back in her chair. All of this was too freaking weird for her. She wanted to go home, wanted it with that deep stomach-gnawing ache that you get when you're away at overnight camp for the first time. She glanced across the room at Ricky, still standing by the window. Ricky noticed her looking and came over.

"Why is that table in front of the windows?" Anna asked.

"Well, dear, we got a bit tired of the view," Hannah said, without looking up from her knitting. Her tone implied that she hadn't completely answered the question.

"What's out there?" Anna asked.

"Nothing," Ricky said. He pulled over a chair and sat backward on it, with his arms folded along the back.

"And somewhere past that is the forest," Hannah said, "which you can't see from here, of course, and somewhere farther on, The City."

"So they say," Jean said.

"They're there," Ricky said. "Grandmother has been to The City—well, to the gates, at least. And you've all heard Violet talk about the forest."

Nearly everyone had mentioned The City at some point. But this was the first time Anna had heard of the forest. "What forest?" she asked.

"They say," said Jean, "that between here and The City, the path cuts through a great forest, and in the forest your body will become real to you again. You will feel pain and fear. There you will face your memories, your nightmares, the dark things that kept you up at night . . ."

Jack's face was stricken. Anna remembered her worst nightmares, and they didn't come close to what she knew of his. She shifted her leg so that her knee touched his. He flinched.

". . . Some people never make it through. They get trapped." Jean seemed to take an unreasonable amount of pleasure from this idea.

"There's no other way?" Anna asked.

"None," Ricky said, "but after that there's The City."

The mood changed instantly. "It's the gate to heaven," Hannah said.

"They say it's the most beautiful thing you've ever seen," Jean added in a singsong tone. "People of every nation, living together. Where nothing can hurt you and all sins are forgiven and the streets are paved with gold."

Anna broke in, "That's what they used to say about America, isn't it?"

"And it's as accurate now as it was then, I'm sure," Jean said.

"You don't believe it's there, do you?" Jack asked.

Jean's knitting needles flashed. "It sounds like fairy stories to me. First you are judged. Then you are rewarded. It's all too neat. I'll stay here, thank you, and talk to the new people as they come in, and do my knitting, and not worry about what may or may not be out there."

Hannah looked disapprovingly at her friend. "Jean's quite the skeptic. I don't know what got into her generation. It's all science and data and provable hypotheses and I don't know what else."

"You believe it's there then?" Anna said. "The City and the forest and all of it?"

"I see no reason why Grandmother would lie about such things," Hannah said.

"Then why are you still here?"

"Well, when I first got here, I thought I'd wait for my husband. I thought he'd be right along behind me. Old men like him don't often live long after their spouses die. I was right. Took him a bit longer than I expected, but he never could be on time. And then we thought maybe we'd wait for our children, because, well, there isn't any rush, is there?"

"Mr. Carver is your husband," Jack said.

"Of course, dear."

"So much for death do us part," Carver said just loudly enough to be heard on the other side of the room.

"Arthur, if you would like to go on up the road alone, you be my guest. I've had enough of your bellyaching to last me two afterlives."

The words were harsh, but her tone was light and she never looked up from her tinking.

Ricky stood up.

"Are you leaving, dear?" Hannah said.

"I thought maybe I'd show Jack and Anna my room—if you guys want to see it," he said.

"It was nice visiting with you, dears," Hannah said. "If you decide to stay, do come visit us again."

Out in the hall, Ricky said, "I thought it was about time we got out of there. Once Mr. and Mrs. Carver get started on an argument, it can last for days. Well, metaphorically anyway."

Anna said, "Can I ask you something?"

"You're going to ask me if I killed myself, right? Because of what Harry said."

"Sorry, that's probably out of line."

"Nah, like he said, it's old news."

"Why did you do it?"

"I guess it seemed like a good idea at the time."

~

The room was dark, but Death didn't mind. He always saw what was there. Right now, what he saw was a Ping-Pong table and a stereo on a stand and a teenage boy. The boy was sitting in an armchair in the middle of the game room. He held a framed photograph in one hand and a pistol in the other. If Death had been human, he would have tried to stop what was about to happen.

Death waited. He was good at waiting.

The boy's soul tore out of his body a millisecond before the bullet did. The soul stood staring at the hole in the back of his own head.

"I didn't mean it," the soul said. He scrambled around in front of the body and crouched down. The head was bowed as though he had fallen asleep sitting up. The soul touched the gun where it had fallen onto the floor.

His eyes settled on Death for an instant and then slipped away. "I didn't mean it," he told the body. He let one knee touch the ground to steady his balance as he turned to look at Death. "I didn't mean it. I thought I meant it, but I didn't. I . . ." He stopped. "You're Death."

"Yes."

The soul's other knee hit the floor. He raised his hands toward Death. "Fix it," he said.

"I can't."

"If you give me another chance, I'll do it better. I won't stay inside my own head so much. I'll be a better person."

"There's nothing I can do."

The soul reached up and held the body's face in his hands. He tilted the head back and looked into the body's vacant eyes. He stood, suddenly, and looked down at the body. "I feel like crying. Why am I not crying?"

"You can't."

The soul nodded, as though this made some sort of sense to him. "What happens now? Am I a ghost?"

"Only for the moment. Come over here and shake my hand and we'll be on our way."

"Shake your hand?"

"To seal the deal."

"What deal?" The soul stepped back until he was standing next to his body.

"When you shake my hand, you are accepting my guidance for your journey into the next life. I will be bound to protect your immortal soul until such time as it has been delivered, unharmed, to your destination."

"Unharmed by what? Why do I need a guide?"

"A human soul cannot navigate alone between the worlds. Unprotected, you would be blown by the winds of fate and entangled by the web of time. You would find yourself trapped, a lost soul doomed to wander the rifts for all eternity."

"No, it's bad enough I took my life. I'm not throwing my soul away, too."

Death held out his hand. The soul reached out, but stopped. "Can we wait? Is there time? My dad will be home any minute. I want to see him."

"You don't," Death said.

"I really do."

Death said nothing. The silence built up around them.

Downstairs, a voice called, "Ricky, are you home?"

The soul tried to run out of the room, but the door was closed, and he couldn't work the handle. He had stood talking too long, and already he was being pulled toward the next world. Death watched the soul become more and more frustrated, until finally, he slammed one shoulder against the door and fell through it, into the next room. Death followed in a more sedate manner. He simply decided that he should be standing beside the soul, and he was. He arrived in the room—a bedroom, if he was any judge of furniture—just as a man threw open the bedroom door.

"Ricky!" the man shouted. "Turn down that music!"

This man was clearly the soul's father. They looked even more alike than humans usually did. The soul, still on the floor, rolled out of the way so his father wouldn't step through him. He whimpered quietly and sat up as the man opened the door to the game room.

Death put his hand on the soul's shoulder. It was the kind of gesture that humans found comforting. "Are you ready to go now?"

"No. No, not yet," the soul said.

The father adjusted something on the shelf. Probably the radio, though death couldn't hear any difference. The man approached the body in the chair, obviously frustrated that his son hadn't acknowledged him. "Look, I know you're angry, but—" He stopped. If Death were the betting type, and everyone knew that he wasn't, he would have put money on the man having just noticed the gun on the floor.

The soul got to its feet and walked up behind its father. "Dad, I'm sorry. I'm really, really sorry. You're always telling me to think, but I couldn't stop thinking, that was the problem. I couldn't shut it off. I couldn't make it stop, the worrying, the wanting . . ."

His father paid no attention. He was busy pulling the body to the floor. He tried to stop the bleeding while yelling at someone named Karen to call 911. When Karen appeared at the door, he shouted at her to stay out. "Use the phone in the bedroom."

The soul was still talking ". . . so I got the gun from your safe, but you can't think it's your fault. It's not your fault. You're a good dad, the best. I should have told you that. I should have—" He stopped. His father was sobbing as he held a blood-soaked blanket against the body's head.

"He can't hear me," Ricky said.

"No," said Death.

"He can't save me either, can he?"

"No."

The soul turned to look at Death, his expression pleading. "Can I stay here, just watch over him until he dies? Then we can go on together."

"No, your soul has instincts. You will cross soon whether you have a guide or not. Alone you will have no path. You could wander the afterlife forever and never find The City." Death held out his hand.

The soul stared at it. "Just a little longer?" he said. "Please?"

Death would have sworn on the Scale of Justice that he was incapable of pity, but he stared into the boy's face for a moment and then dropped his hand. "I will ask you only one time more," he said. "Do not refuse me again."

"Thank you."

The soul walked into the bedroom and sat down on the bed. It watched through the door as its father tried to save its life. Death stood next to a shelf of sports trophies, watching the soul for signs of fading. He remained fairly solid, and probably would for a while longer, at least until they removed the body from the house.

There were new voices downstairs. "Up there. The first door on the left," Karen said. The soul stood up quickly. Seconds later, two EMTs were in the room. The first one, a short-haired woman, rushed straight through and set to work on the body. The second one hesitated in the doorway. For an instant, his ice-blue eyes fell on the soul standing next to the bed, and then he followed his partner into the game room.

Death looked after him, wondering what exactly he had seen. Humans rarely saw souls in transit. Was there something special about this one?

"Let's get out of here," the soul said. He held out his hand.

Chapter Eight

When Ricky threw open the door to his room, it bounced against a pinball machine wedged in the corner. Across the room, a futon without legs rested next to a desk stacked high with comic books. A mismatched pair of beanbag chairs took up most of the middle of the floor, the indentations in them suggesting that Ricky had lain across them, playing the vintage Sega Genesis that was hooked into an ancient CRT television.

"Where did you get all this stuff?" Jack asked.

"The warehouse obviously, genius," Anna said.

"The pinball machine was the hardest," Ricky said. "It took four of us to get it up the stairs." He went to the window and looked out.

"What are you looking for?" Anna asked.

"I'm just . . . looking." He fiddled with the pull cord of the window blind. The muscles of his neck were tense. He was holding something back. Anna checked to see if Jack had noticed, but he had crouched down beside the TV and was flipping through Ricky's video game collection. "You have *Altered Beast*!"

"You can play if you want," Ricky said.

"Your TV isn't plugged in."

"Oh, it doesn't have to be." He bent down and spun the dial. The screen filled with snow.

Jack collapsed backward onto a beanbag chair. "How?" he asked.

"Oh, that's weird," Anna said.

Ricky shrugged. "No idea. If it has an On button, it turns on. It doesn't matter if it's plugged in or not. Also, nothing wears out. Don't get me wrong,: if you threw the TV against the wall, it would break, but it will never just die."

"It's already dead," Jack said.

"I guess so, yeah."

Jack picked up the Sega's plug in one hand and pushed its On button with the other. The start screen flared to life on the TV. "Yup, that's creepy."

There was a knock on the door. Jack started, dropping the plug to the floor with a thump.

"Ricky!" It was Professor Haggarty's voice. "Are you there, boy?" The door rattled with the force of his knocks. "Ricky!"

Ricky went to the door and opened it. "I'm here, Professor. What's up?"

"Oh good, your friends are with you." He strode into the middle of the room, his black robe whipping around his legs. "I've had an epiphany, thanks to this young lady." He flung his arm toward Anna. Anna stepped backward until her calves hit the futon.

"It was your statement about someone's love for that blanket." He began to pace, kicking one of the beanbags out of his way. Jack scooted the one he was sitting in closer to the wall.

"It made me think," Haggarty said. "Perhaps I was basing my investigations on the wrong set of assumptions. Instead of looking at the individual components, I should have been looking at what all of these items had in common."

He stopped and pounded his fist into the palm of his hand. "Human sentimentality. That's the common link, or so I believe. Consider." His finger stabbed the air. "These are all precious objects, not monetarily, but sentimentally. I postulate that just as people leave the world and come to this place when they die, so do things from our world, when they are destroyed beyond repair, come to the warehouse. In short"—he spun to face Anna again—"the factory is a delivery system for the warehouse, which contains every beloved object in the history of humanity."

His shoulders slumped. "I only wish that I could prove it."

"It's a good theory, Professor—probably your best theory yet," Ricky said, patting the professor's arm.

Haggarty rewarded Ricky with a thin smile. "But there are . . . complications. People love books, paintings, sculpture, but none of these things exist in the warehouse." He sagged down on the futon. "Perhaps I'm wrong."

"Well, maybe . . ." Anna began.

Professor Haggarty's head jerked up. "Yes?"

"No, it's probably stupid."

"Speak, child." He jumped to his feet. "Scientific inquiry is about bold ideas."

"Okay." Anna let her eyes settle on a magenta lava lamp glooping in the corner of the room. She tried to think her idea through as she said it aloud. "Suppose there's another place for things like books and art. I mean, *Starry Night* isn't the same thing as a—as a lava lamp, for example. You wouldn't want to dump it into a warehouse. Maybe there's like a museum somewhere along the way, or inside The City itself."

"And a library for the books," Jack added. "That actually does make sense."

Anna glared at him. "So glad you approve."

The professor was nearly bouncing with excitement. "Yes, yes, what a theory. And so easily proved. I must set out at once to find them."

"You're leaving?" Ricky said.

"Yes, yes, right away, in fact. There's no reason to hesitate. Thank you, Miss Anna, you've been immensely helpful." Haggarty seized Anna's hand and shook it.

"Of course," Ricky said. He plodded across the room and sat down on the futon.

Anna looked into Haggarty's eyes, and then, deliberately, at Ricky, who was staring at an unremarkable patch of carpet. The professor followed her gaze. "You know, boy," he said. "I could use a research assistant."

Ricky straightened up. "You want me to be your assistant?" His expression didn't light up with happiness as Anna had expected. He looked, if anything, more unhappy than he had a moment earlier.

"I do," Professor Haggarty said.

"I would love to, Professor, I really would, but I can't leave yet," Ricky said.

Professor Haggarty sat down on the futon and put a hand on Ricky's shoulder. "There's a whole world to explore out there. I am certain your father would understand."

Anna felt like a tardy theatergoer who had walked in halfway through the scene. She was missing something.

Ricky stood up, dislodging Haggarty's grip. He shook his head. "I can't."

Professor Haggarty stood up too. "It has been a pleasure knowing you, young man."

"You too, Professor."

They shook hands. Haggarty said, "I'm going to gather up a few things, and then I'm off."

"We'll go up to the roof and wave goodbye if you'd like," Ricky said.

"I would like that. Very much."

Professor Haggarty nodded to Jack and then to Anna. "Please excuse the interruption."

"I hope you find what you're looking for," Jack said. Professor Haggarty left the room, closing the door gently behind him.

"Why didn't you go with him?" Anna asked.

Ricky glanced out the window. He rubbed the back of his head. "Come on, we'd better get up to the roof or Professor Haggarty will be gone before we get there."

He led them down the hall and up a flight of stairs to the third floor. There were people up there, too. Anna heard voices through half-open doors, and once, a man in a frock coat ran from one room to another, slamming doors behind him. With his small round glasses and long hair he reminded her of Ben Franklin.

She nudged Jack. "Hey, I thought of a perk to being dead."

"Oh?"

"No more assigned reading. No more *Autobiography of Benjamin Franklin*."

"Or *Walden*," Jack said.

They had reached the end of the hall. Ricky pulled back a curtain to reveal a window empty of glass. Someone had cleared it out carefully, leaving only a few glittering shards in the upper sill.

"Come on," he said. He sat down on the windowsill, swung both legs out, and let himself fall.

Jack groaned. "I had hoped we wouldn't have to jump off any roofs today."

Ricky's head appeared at the window. "It's not far, five feet or so."

"Ladies first," Jack said, sweeping the curtain back and extending a hand toward Anna.

"Gee, thanks." Anna ignored his hand, clambered over the windowsill unassisted, and dropped onto the roof of the catwalk. She looked around. They were just about where Ricky had been standing when they first saw him. Red desert stretched in all directions. Above it was the empty sky, cloudless, sunless, but somehow bright. Paradoxically, all that emptiness made her feel profoundly claustrophobic.

"Are you guys seeing a desert with a single path?" Ricky asked.

"Why wouldn't we?" Anna asked.

"You've heard that saying, everyone experiences the afterlife differently? Well, there was a guy down on the first floor who said that we were all crazy talking about deserts and paths, because clearly the afterlife was a shopping mall. He was very annoyed that Sears was closed."

"What?" Anna had follow-up questions, many of them, but Ricky interrupted her.

"There he is."

They looked down. Professor Haggarty was standing on the sand below them. He had a small brown rucksack on his back. He waved. Ricky waved back. The professor turned and headed off into the desert. He wasn't on the path, but then, maybe he was on a path that only he could see. There was no way to be sure. Anna glanced at Ricky. He was turned in on himself again. His eyes were looking past Haggarty, at something no one else could see.

"There you are," a voice said. Anna flinched. She hadn't heard anyone approach, but there was Violet, leaning out of the window.

Ricky said, "Hey, Little Vee. What's up?"

"I checked your room. You weren't there." Her hands disappeared inside her sleeves. "Grandmother wants to meet Anna."

"You'd better take her then," Ricky said. He didn't seem surprised by the summons. "What about Jack?"

"No, only Anna."

"Why?" Anna and Jack asked together.

"Grandmother said."

"Violet." Ricky's tone was a warning that Violet completely ignored. She didn't even look at him. Her eyes were on Anna, which wasn't creepy at all.

"Grandmother said," she repeated.

Anna looked at Ricky and raised her eyebrows. He shrugged.

"I don't think—" Jack began.

"It's okay," Ricky said. "Violet will bring her back to my room when they're done. Right, Vee?"

"To your room, yes." She zipped her sweatshirt up to her chin, then down to her waist, then up again. "Let's go now," she said.

"I'll see you soon," Anna said. She squeezed Jack's hand and let go.

She went to the window and pulled herself up. It was surprisingly easy. Either she had gotten stronger or she wasn't as heavy in the afterlife. Jack came to the window behind her. "Be careful, okay?"

"I'm always careful."

"No you're not." He didn't mention the incident on the river. He didn't have to. Anna had known him long enough to hear what he wasn't saying.

"I'll see you soon." Anna ducked away from the window before Jack could say anything else.

The hallway Violet led her to was quiet. In other parts of the building there had been voices, and doors slamming, and occasionally laughter, but here it was just their footsteps, hushed by the industrial carpet. Violet stopped in front of a door at the end of the hall. "You're ready?"

Anna shrugged. She didn't know why she was here, so it was hard to know if she was ready or not. Violet knocked softly on the door.

An elderly but firm female voice told them to come in. Violet opened the door.

~

Jack and Ricky sat in beanbag chairs playing *Virtua Racing.* Jack was losing. Anna being gone distracted him. He couldn't help but imagine all the awful things that might happen to her in this crazy place. She might lose her way in an endless maze of corridors. She might drink a potion that would cause her to forget he existed. She might stumble into a room without a floor and fall forever like Alice through the rabbit hole. He would never know where she had gone, and if he somehow found out and went after her, he could never, ever catch up to her.

He overshot a turn and ended up on the shoulder, hurling sixteen-bit spears of simulated grass in all directions.

"I'm sure Anna will be back soon," Ricky said.

Jack was embarrassed. He hadn't realized his worry was so obvious.

"Yeah, I know. It's just, this place is really strange. What does *soon* even mean in a place without days and nights and clocks and stuff?"

"Good point." Ricky passed through a checkpoint, earning a time bonus. "It's hard to believe I've been here for decades. It doesn't seem that long."

"Why have you stayed here all this time?"

Ricky was way ahead now. There was no way Jack could beat him, so Jack was surprised when Ricky threw his controller on the floor and stood up.

Jack tensed, ready for Ricky to yell at him or kick him or throw a lava lamp at his head while shouting that it was none of his damn business what Ricky chose to do with his afterlife. Ricky did none of those things. Instead, he went to the window and looked out.

"You know, when I killed myself, I instantly regretted it. My soul left my body and I thought, *Oh shit, why did I do that?*" He shook his head. "I couldn't take it back. I couldn't apologize. I saw my dad come in before Death took me away. He tried to save me. But there was no way back."

Jack sat in the beanbag chair, controller still clutched in his fist. He didn't know what to say. All the comments about Ricky's dad. All the times Ricky stared out the window. It all made sense. Ricky was waiting for his dad so he could apologize.

"I had an uncle who killed himself," Jack said. "He set himself on fire in the parking lot of his high school. Do you think he regretted it?"

Ricky looked down at Jack with eyes that saw right through him. "Yeah, man, I'm sure he did."

Chapter Nine

A white-haired woman was sitting in an ancient recliner with her back to the open blinds. Her arthritic fingers stuck out at uncomfortable angles. Anna noticed because she was counting the beads of a crystal rosary. On the wall to her left was a small watercolor of a little girl kneeling in prayer beside a bed. She looked like Violet minus the overlarge sweatshirt.

Grandmother smiled, revealing teeth so perfect, they had to be false. "Anna, is it? Welcome."

"Yes, um, ma'am, you wanted to see me?"

"There's plenty of time for that," Grandmother said. "Sit down, please."

Violet pushed a small upholstered stool into the rectangle of light cast by the window.

"I left my friend back there . . ."

"That is what I wanted to talk to you about, in fact. Sit down." Her tone did not invite argument. Anna considered arguing anyway, but what would be the point? She was here. She might as well listen to what the old woman had to say.

Violet sat down on the floor next to Grandmother's chair and leaned her head on the armrest. Grandmother petted her hair with the hand that wasn't holding the rosary.

"I got married when I was sixteen," Grandmother said. "Over the years, I had three children and six grandchildren and seventeen great-grandchildren." She held Anna's gaze. "They cried at my funeral and laid flowers on my casket."

Anna had to bite back the urge to ask how she could possibly know that.

"I had lived a full life. I was ninety-four when I died." Anna waited. Grandmother leaned forward and pushed the recliner closed so that her feet rested on the floor. "How old are you, Anna?"

"Seventeen."

"So much life left to live."

"I thought so yesterday." Anna hoped she sounded more overwhelmed than sarcastic.

Grandmother smiled. "You may think so tomorrow. You're not dead yet."

Anna sat up straight. "How did you know?"

"It is easy enough to spot, once you've seen it a time or two. You shine a bit brighter than other people at the moment. Your friend . . . ?"

"He's fine. We're both fine."

"My dear, I believe you may be mistaken."

"He's not dead." Anna gripped her knees, leaving tiny indents in her flesh. "You don't know Jack like I do. He wouldn't just go and die on me."

Violet leaned forward, resting her chin on her hand. She seemed entertained.

"You can't go through your life, or your afterlife, terrified of losing," Grandmother said. "We all lose things along the way—our youth, our memories, our friends—but nothing's ever lost forever."

"I'm not going to lose Jack." Anna stood up. She was done here. She had been done before she came here. She didn't even know why she was listening to this crazy old woman and her creepy-doll sidekick.

Violet looked up at Grandmother. The two shared a meaningful look—meaningful to them, at least. Anna was still in the dark. Some part of her—the part that wasn't frustrated and enraged and, let's be honest, a little bit frightened—wondered what their relationship was.

For once, it was a good thing that Anna couldn't cry. She didn't have to worry that her fear and frustration would spill out onto her face.

"The truth will come out in the forest," Grandmother said.

Anna bit the insides of her cheeks to keep from cursing at this stupid old woman. It didn't hurt. She wondered what would happen if she just bit right through them. Would they bleed? Could she even do it? Why would she want to?

"That place is the playground of the fallen one," she said, in the same tone of voice Anna's own grandmother might have used to tell her that her grandfather was in the garage. "He will take your fears, your misdeeds, and your secrets, and he will use them against you."

"Thank you for the advice," she said, "but this isn't Salem."

"No, it's purgatory."

"Ah," Anna said, and fell silent. She had no argument for that. She'd read somewhere that it was a bad idea to argue with crazy people, because when you're doing it, no one can tell which of you is crazy. After a pause she added, "I don't believe in the devil."

Grandmother shrugged, as if to say, *That's okay, he believes in you.*

Anna had tried to be polite. She'd tried to hear Grandmother out, but clearly the old bat was insane. Anna didn't say goodbye, she just walked out. Grandmother let her go without protest, but Violet caught up to her in the hall.

"Does she tell everyone what to do?" Anna asked when the girl fell in beside her.

"She knows a lot. You should listen to her." Violet zipped her jacket up and down.

"Why thank you, but I don't need advice from a seven-year-old."

Violet darted in front of her and stopped dead, forcing Anna to either stop or go through her. Anna stopped.

"You still don't understand, do you?" Violet said. "Look at me. How long ago do you think I died? You talk about Salem like it's a fairy story. I remember what you've only read about. I remember the hysteria and the fear of good women. One wrong step, one wrong look, and you might be called a witch. And then what? We had no way to defend ourselves. The church itself turned away from us and let the devil take us."

The little girl drew herself up tall, looking Anna square in the eye. Those eyes looked ancient. They knew much more than they were telling, but Violet had more to say.

"I died and I thought it was over, but it wasn't. I saw the devil in the wood. I saw him with these eyes. I saw him tempt my sister and pull out my mother's hair in clumps. I saw him dance his evil dance. Listen to your elders, child." She spit the word at Anna's face. "The forest is a dangerous place. You should stay here as long as you can. And if you love your friend, living or dead, you'll persuade him to stay here, too."

Anna's mouth opened, but she didn't know what to say.

"Don't bother," Violet said. "I can see you're a fool, and fools don't listen to reason." She spun on her heel. "Third door on the left," she said.

"What?" Anna said, but Violet was already walking away. She didn't answer, and she didn't look back.

Anna went to the third door on the left and knocked.

"Come in," someone called.

Anna opened the door cautiously. Who knew what new madness might be lurking here?

Jack and Ricky were sitting on the beanbags playing *Donkey Kong* on an original Nintendo system.

"Hey," Ricky said without looking up.

"You're back," Jack said.

Anna was ridiculously happy to see him. Of course he wasn't dead. Look at him sitting there playing video games like old times. He was fine. They were both fine. "No shit, Sherlock." Anna sat down on the floor between the two beanbags.

"Screw you, Watson," Jack responded.

On the screen, Ricky's character missed its grip on a vine, fell, and died. Ricky handed the controller to Anna.

"So I was thinking, you guys are going to stay, aren't you? It would be nice to have people my age around."

Jack said, "No," at the same time Anna said, "Maybe."

"What do you mean, no?" Anna said.

"What do you mean, maybe?" Jack said.

Ricky clambered out of his beanbag chair. "I'm gonna—I'm gonna go beat my high score on pinball," he said, and retreated to the pinball machine on the other side of the room.

Anna set the controller on the floor and picked up a Rubik's Cube that had been left there. She hated arguing with Jack. She hated arguing with anyone, but she really hated arguing with Jack. He had this you-kicked-my-puppy expression that always got to her.

"You don't actually want to stay here?" Jack said.

She spun two sections of the Rubik's Cube so it was all spiky angles. "Why not? There's plenty to keep us occupied here. Besides, what else have you got to do?"

"Can't you feel it?"

Anna shrugged. "The pull? I can live with it. I mean, it's a feeling. I don't have to do anything about it. There are people here, and things to do." *And this way I keep you safe. We don't have to walk into the woods alone and face your nightmares. We can just stay where the people are, even if some of them are bat-shit crazy.* She couldn't seem to make herself admit out loud that she was scared, not right now, and certainly not with Ricky pointedly not listening on the other side of the room.

Anna could feel Jack's eyes on her face, but she kept her gaze on the Rubik's Cube, spinning the sections around and around, not even trying to match the colors. "I mean," she said, "did you ever wonder what's actually pulling us forward? Maybe it's like a black hole sucking us in until the gravity is so strong that we collapse into a singularity."

"Are you okay?"

Anna looked up sharply. Her eyes searched Jack's face. He looked back at her, his eyes open and blue and guileless.

"Besides being dead, you mean?"

There it was, kicked puppy. She hadn't needed to say that, especially because she knew it wasn't true. She wasn't dead. She was going to be fine. Everything was going to be fine. They just needed to wait this out. Anna stood up quickly and put all her attention into inspecting a poster for some movie called *Time Bandits*. It showed an expanse of blue ocean with a giant's eyes and forehead sticking out. He was wearing a three-masted ship on his head, or maybe it was a really ornate hat.

"You could go on without me," she said. That wasn't fair either. She knew he wouldn't go.

"Yes, or—now bear with me here—you could come with me."

She turned. Jack was staring at her. There was worry in the scrunch of his eyes and in the furrows of his forehead.

"Why can't we stay here?" She let her eyes flick toward Ricky and back. The rhythm of the pinball flippers had slowed. He was listening.

"He can come with us if he wants, but I can't stay here. I need to keep going. *We* need to keep going."

"But the forest—"

He grasped her arm above her elbow. "I'll protect you."

She started to laugh. She couldn't help it. He looked hurt again but tried to hide it. Anna bit her lip and made herself take a breath. "And who will protect you?"

Jack let go of her arm and picked up a controller as though trying to pretend he had never touched her in the first place. "We'll take care of each other," he said. The tension between them thinned.

Ricky drifted over. "You're going, aren't you?"

"Yes," Anna said. "We're going. But you're welcome to come with us." Safety in numbers. "Actually, we'd really like you to."

"Yeah," Jack said.

Ricky shook his head. "I can't. I'm waiting for my dad, remember?"

"Why are you waiting for him?" Anna asked.

Ricky didn't answer. He sat down and picked up the second controller. He offered it to Anna. "Want to play one more round of *Donkey Kong* before you go?"

~

Later, Ricky walked them out to the edge of the path. He shook Jack's hand and hugged Anna. "When you get to the forest, remember to keep moving. You can only get stuck if you stop."

"Stuck?"

"They say it happens. But it won't happen to you. You have each other."

Anna took his hand and squeezed it. "I hope your dad comes soon."

He squeezed back. "Me too," he said. "Take care of each other, okay?"

They walked away from him, away from the factory, back to the path. Anna looked back once, to see if he was still watching them. He was. He lifted his hand to wave at her, then turned and walked back toward the factory.

Anna forced herself to sigh. It made her feel better. "I wish he would've come with us. I liked him."

"I could tell," Jack said.

"Jack?"

"Yes, Anna."

"Shut up."

He grinned. "Onward to the forest."

Anna looked over her shoulder. The factory had turned into a dark smudge in the distance. How had they gone so far so quickly?

"Oh, yay," Anna said, her voice flat. "What new adventure awaits?"

"I've got a pretty good idea," Jack said.

Anna looked at Jack out of the corner of her eye. His face had tightened. He was looking out over the sand.

"Are you going to be okay?"

"Oh yeah, fine. I wonder if he'll be cruel today or just incoherently crazy."

"Maybe he won't be there at all."

"If my nightmares are in there, then that's exactly where he'll be."

"Maybe the stories aren't true."

Jack shook his head. He didn't believe it.

Anna looked back over her shoulder one last time. The factory had disappeared.

Chapter Ten

There was no natural fading of one landscape into the other, just a regiment of trees stretching endlessly left and right as far as Anna could see. The path had narrowed to a crumbling trail, barely wide enough for them to walk side by side. They stopped and looked up at the arching trees, which met over the path, casting deep shadows. It would be dark in there.

When Jack spoke, Anna twitched, startled.

"Can't go over it, can't go under it, can't go around it," he said in a singsong voice that didn't match the mood at all.

"Have to go through it," Anna answered in a monotone that did.

Jack offered Anna his arm. She took it, slipping her hand through the crook of his elbow. They entered the forest together. Only a few steps in, Anna stopped again. It was almost involuntary. The shade of the trees had fallen over her, and she had frozen like a field mouse caught in the shadow of a hawk.

Jack tugged gently at her arm. "Ricky said we shouldn't stop," he reminded her. "It's just like going for a walk in the woods back home."

The sentiment got her moving, but she knew it was wrong. This was nothing like the Maine woods. Comparing the two was like comparing a kitten to a mountain lion. They shared a basic similarity of form, but that was as far as the comparison would stretch.

At home, she would have touched the tree trunks as she passed, imagining she could feel the sap running under the bark, imagining a tiny stir of warmth that recognized the fleeting human life reaching out to it.

Here she kept her arms close to her body to avoid the touch of questing branches. She imagined that the trees, if aware of her at all, were resentful of her presence—resentful of the way that she could walk through this place while they were trapped forever by roots that sucked no nutrients from the soil, with limbs that reached stiffly toward an absent sun.

Leaves shivered despite the lack of wind. The sound only gave shape to the unnatural silence. It drew attention to the lack of birdsong and squirrel rustlings and faraway traffic noises that were so much a part of the modern Maine woods.

Anna's steps slowed. Jack refused to stop. It was walk or be pulled. She walked.

"Lions and tigers and bears, oh my!" Jack said, obviously trying to cheer her up. He spoiled the effect by glancing over his shoulder, as if expecting to see someone, or something, following them.

"There's no place like home, there's no place like home, there's no place like home," Anna chanted. "If only I had a pair of ruby slippers." She tried to remind herself that she might well be going home, but it was harder to believe here.

"You know," Jack said, "in the book, the shoes were silver. They changed it in the movie to show off the Technicolor."

Anna made an effort. "Is that why?" she said. "I always wondered. My mother loves that movie. She used to make me watch it with her whenever it came on TV. We owned it, but she still got all excited when it came on once a year. She'd call me down out of my room and make popcorn and we'd sit on the couch. I always complained, but by the time Dorothy met the scarecrow, I'd be hooked . . ." She paused, remembering. Jack tugged her back into motion.

"I was going to show Ella *The Nightmare Before Christmas* this year," Jack said. "She's finally old enough not to think it's scary."

They walked in silence for a while. Anna didn't even have the sound of their breath to keep her company. She tried to shake the feeling that the trees were watching her. Jack glanced around again. She didn't have the courage to ask him what he was looking for.

This is his fault, you know. The leaves chattered, as though they heard her thoughts and agreed. *You should be at the ocean by now, climbing the rocks around Sand Beach, pretending you're the only person on earth.* Anna tried to push the voice away. It was the same voice that tried to tell her she could fly when she was standing on the edge of a cliff. She was fairly certain everyone had the same tiny mad voice inside them. It just talked, with no sense of self-preservation. *He almost killed you, and now you're staying here for him,* the voice continued.

She tried a rebuttal. *It's not like I even know how to go home.*

The voice snorted. *You could if he wasn't here, holding you back. He's always trying to trap you in his craziness.*

Anna spoke loudly to shut the voice up. "I may never watch a movie again. Or go to a Halloween party, or play cars with my brother, or go to school."

"Lucky us." Jack tried to smile. "No more pop quizzes, or lectures from Ms. Bird."

Anna said, "Or drama club, or stupid dances or skipping class with a note from the gym teacher." A branch dragged across Anna's arm like a ragged fingernail. She swatted it away.

"I'm sorry."

He killed you, the voice said. "You killed us," Anna echoed.

"It was an accident."

She uncoupled her arm from his. "You should have been more careful."

"I didn't put the truck across the road." They were still walking, but slowly. The forest had gone silent. Anna was certain it was listening.

"You were driving too fast."

"You distracted me."

Anna stopped and turned to face him. She was suddenly furious. The silence pounded in her ears. "Don't turn this around on me." Her voice was rising. "You were driving too fast. You crashed into that truck. You killed us."

Anna shoved him hard. He stumbled backward into the deeper darkness, and bounced against a tree trunk. Twigs splintered around him. The leaves were roaring now. His eyes flared.

"What the hell is wrong with you?" Jack shoved her back. "Get away from me. I'm sick of your shit."

"My shit! My shit!" Her voice took on a whining edge. *"I'm Jack and nobody understands me. I'm so smart but everybody thinks I'm weird. Boo hoo."*

He shouted over her. *"I'm Anna, look at how gorgeous and wonderful I am. All the boys are in love with me . . ."*

"You've only stayed my friend this long because you want to get into my pants."

"Shut up," Jack yelled. "You broke up with me. I loved you, and you didn't give a shit."

"We were fourteen!"

"You wrote me a fucking note!"

"You killed me!"

"Good."

Anna slapped him. The sound of it echoed off the trees. She paused, one arm poised to hit him again if he said another word. Her chest heaved. Her hand stung.

Jack touched his own cheek. "That hurt. Oh my God. That hurt!"

"Good," Anna said. She still felt ready to murder him. The trees were rustling again, filling her head with their static, making it difficult to think clearly.

"No, Anna, listen to me. That hurt."

He pinched her. She smacked his hand away. "Ow, what the hell?"

"See? Pain. Don't you get it? Something's weird here."

Anna pressed both hands against her chest. "I'm breathing, and my heart is beating. What's happening? Are we alive?" She clutched his arm. "Maybe we're hallucinating. Maybe I'm lying on a gurney somewhere and the paramedics just restarted my heart. I'm going to wake up and this will all be a dream."

"I don't think so."

"Why not? It's a good thing to think." Tears stood out in her eyes. "Look, now I'm crying."

"I know." Jack unlatched her hand from his arm, but kept hold of it. "Remember what they said. We have to face our demons in the forest. Maybe that's what's happening."

Anna blinked and looked away from him. "I *am* mad at you. A little."

"I know."

Anna took her hand back and used it to tug at her braid. "But I know it wasn't really your fault," she said.

"It was mostly my fault."

"I could have told you to slow down."

"You shouldn't have had to."

She acknowledged this with a shrug. "So what now?"

"Now I think we keep walking," Jack said. "And we are very careful about what we say and do."

"Do you think we could have hurt each other? I mean really hurt each other."

"In this place? Maybe," Jack said, "if we were mad enough. The rules that apply out there don't seem to work in here."

"Great. As soon as I start to understand what's going on, they change things on me."

They walked on. Anna tried not to notice that the trees seemed to have drawn in closer during their argument.

"Jack? Do you think this is where the whole hell concept came from?"

"I don't know. I don't see any flames."

"Maybe flames are a metaphor. Maybe hell is being surrounded by what frightens you."

"Are you afraid of trees?"

"Not generally." These particular trees, though, were giving her the creeps.

"Then as long as we don't run into any clowns, I'll assume this isn't hell."

Anna patted his shoulder. "Don't worry. I'll protect you from any clowns we come across."

There was a thoughtful silence. Jack said, "You don't think there will really be any clowns, do you?"

"No." Anna tried not to laugh. She didn't want to start another argument. "Why do they scare you so much?"

"Have you looked at a clown? Seriously freaky."

"I think they're sort of sad, really," Anna said. "With their faces all painted and their huge shoes. Kind of like strippers."

"Aw, jeez, clown strippers. Now, *that's* a scary image."

Anna held an imaginary microphone to her mouth and said, in a fake announcer voice, "Gentlemen, please welcome to the stage the beautiful Bimbo." The rustle of the trees was like distant applause. If Jack noticed this, he said nothing about it.

"You know what's worse than clown strippers though?" he said. "Stripper clowns."

"What's the difference?"

"Well, clown strippers would be strippers who dress as clowns, but stripper clowns would be clowns who strip."

A picture of this popped into Anna's mind. She shook her head to dislodge it. "Oh. Ew. Yes, that's worse. Why are we talking about this?"

"What do you want to talk about?"

"Anything to occupy our minds so we don't start thinking about the fact that we'll never go to a strip club, or order a drink in a bar, or graduate from college, or travel to Australia—"

"Okay, okay. I get it."

Anna continued. "Or learn to play the guitar, or buy a house."

"Or become a famous inventor," Jack added. "Or find out what happened at the end of the Gunslinger series."

Anna inched closer to Jack to avoid an outstretched branch. "You really never finished it?"

"The book said if you think the story should end here, then don't turn the page. So I didn't."

"But it makes so much more sense when—"

"I didn't want to know."

"I read it. I could tell you."

"Nope. I'll have to live with it. I mean . . . You know what I mean. Hey, I think the trail splits up there." Jack pointed.

Anna squinted into the distance. She could almost see what he was talking about. There was a difference in the texture of the shadows ahead of them. "Can it do that?" she asked.

"I guess so."

As they approached the fork in the path, Anna drifted to the left, Jack to the right. They stopped. Both of the new paths were blocked by heavy wooden doors hung between tree trunks.

"You've got to be kidding," Jack said. "They're bathrooms."

The door in front of Anna had a plastic silhouette of a woman stuck to it. The other door had a silhouette of a man.

"Apparently," Anna said.

"Well, that's not weird at all," Jack said.

"At the risk of asking the obvious, why?" Anna said.

"I bet you can't go through here," Jack said.

"It's a door. Who's going to stop me?" Anna pushed against the Men's door. It didn't budge. She jammed her shoulder against it. Still no movement, but now her shoulder hurt.

Jack pressed the palm of his hand against the door. The door swung open. "Try now," he said.

"This isn't going to work, is it?" Anna said, but she tried anyway. It didn't work. She hit something invisible but solid, and bounced back. "Like walking into a sliding-glass door."

"Can't we walk around it?" Jack said.

"You mean leave the path?" Anna asked. She looked at the forest. The tree trunks stood close together, closer really, than such large trees should have been able to grow. The narrow gaps between them were filled with brush and interlocking branches. Anna reached out and pushed at a branch. The thicket shifted like worms poked with a twig, wriggling together to form a thicker wall where her finger had touched. She snatched her hand away.

"Not going around," she said. "Definitely staying on the path."

They retreated to where the trail forked. Anna sat down cross-legged. Jack flopped down beside her. Both were careful not to touch the trees.

"What do we do now?" Jack said.

"I guess we have to split up." It wasn't fair. She had come into this damn forest so he wouldn't be alone. Now the forest was trying to separate them. She couldn't let it happen. Out loud, she said, "Or we could stay here forever and ever."

They looked around at the trees crowding close around them.

Jack said, "I'd rather not, thanks."

"Well then . . ." Anna hugged her knees to her chest and looked back the way they had come. "We could go back to the factory, find Ricky and Grandmother . . ."

"Going backward isn't easy. Besides, I don't think we should. These are our paths. We're supposed to walk them."

"Supposed to? . . . What's all this supposed to? You're usually the one who's all anti-establishment. Who cares what we're *supposed* to do? I was supposed to live to be eighty-nine like my great-grandmother. I was supposed to graduate from high school and go to college and study architecture and get a job working for a big agency and live in a bright apartment with a view of the ocean. I was supposed to find something more fun to do than go to my goddamn high school prom . . .”

She was crying again. She tried to stop, but couldn't. Jack scooted over next to her and put his arm around her. Anna knew she should pull away, stand up, wipe her eyes, but she couldn't find the energy. She collapsed against him. Jack pressed his cheek against her hair. He rocked her gently. After a moment, Anna felt tears falling on her head. Jack was crying too.

There was no way to tell how long they sat there. It could have been ten minutes or ten years. The light never changed to show them the passage of hours, and they never got thirsty or hungry or ran out of tears.

Jack shifted slightly and looked down the path as though watching something. Anna wiped her eyes and tried to see what he was looking at, but she was almost immediately blinded by tears again.

“Anna,” Jack said. “Anna, I have to keep moving.”

She wiped her tears on his sleeve. “Why? What's the point? What's the point of doing this if we can't do it together?”

Jack tugged gently at her hair. “Something is pulling us forward. Something wants us to get somewhere. Remember The City? Cities have buildings and people. Besides, anything's better than sitting here feeling sorry for ourselves.”

“But I'm supposed to protect you.”

He laughed, but it sounded sad. “No, I'm the one who should be protecting you. And I've done a less-than-awesome job of that so far.” He sighed. “At least we can't die twice,” he said, half to himself. He stood up.

Anna tilted her head back to look at him. “We may never see each other again,” she said.

“I don't believe that. Remember the year we decided to have our palms read at the fair?”

Anna sniffed, smiled. “I remember.”

“Remember what the psychic lady called us?”

"Soul mates. We laughed at her."

"We did, but I sort of thought . . ." He looked away, embarrassed.

Anna wondered if that was why she was here. Could two people actually connect so deeply that when one died, the other went along for the ride? She had heard of old couples who had been married for decades, dying within hours or days of each other. But that didn't exactly apply to them.

Jack reached down a hand to help her up.

Once she was on her feet, she felt better. "Okay, fine," she said. "Walk as fast as you can and don't stop for anything, okay?"

Jack nodded once, but firmly. "Okay.

Anna wished she had a tissue. She sniffled again, feeling childish. Her door pushed open easily. She looked back at Jack. He was standing at the fork in the road, watching her. She twiddled her fingers at him. "See you on the other side."

~

Optimus Prime was dead.

He had been sitting on the shelf in Ella's bedroom, where he always sat when he didn't want to play with the girls. Ella and Barbie were having a contest to see who could jump the farthest. Barbie was winning, but Ella thought she could catch up. She made one extra-big jump, and her shoulder hit the shelf where Optimus Prime was sitting. The shelf shook. Ella's big book of fairy tales fell over and hit Optimus Prime. He fell from the shelf to the floor.

Ella had a rug on her floor, but he fell in the place where the rug wasn't. Ella closed her eyes tight so she couldn't see that he was broken, but she already knew that he was. She opened her eyes again.

His head had snapped right off.

"We have to have a funeral," she said.

All her friends started crying, but Ella didn't because she was the biggest and the bravest, just like Michael. She knew it was up to her to make a funeral for Optimus Prime.

First, he needed a coffin. Jack's had been a big wooden box. Ella didn't have a wooden box, but she did have an old shoe box. She dug it out of the closet and dumped out the crayons that had been inside it.

Then she went back to where Optimus Prime was lying. She reached down and picked him up carefully. It wouldn't hurt him, because he was dead and dead things can't hurt. But she picked him up carefully anyway because she was sad. She put him in the box. Then she put his broken-off head in the box too.

She set the box in her wagon and then loaded in all of her friends, even baby Sarah. Usually it took a long time to load everyone up because they all wanted to tell her a story or bring something along. Today she did it very quickly. Everyone was sad, and nobody wanted to talk.

When her friends were all settled, she pulled the wagon down the hall. Mom didn't even say anything when she went bump-bump-bump down the stairs. Mom was sad too.

Ella pulled the wagon out the back door. It was gray and drippy outside. It wasn't raining, but it had been. The ground was all squishy.

Ella looked around the yard. Optimus Prime needed flowers. There were dandelions, lots and lots of them. But Ella didn't think they were pretty enough. Mom's garden had lots of flowers. Normally, Ella wasn't supposed to pick the flowers in Mom's garden, but this was a special occasion. Besides, if she was careful, Mom might not even notice. Ella picked and picked. She stacked flowers in the cart until her friends almost disappeared under the blooms.

Ella dragged the flower-topped wagon to a spot near where the grass ended and the trees started. She would have to dig a hole to put the coffin in.

"Everyone be good. I'll be right back."

She ran into the shed, being extra quick and trying not to look too closely at anything because lots of spiders lived in the shed and Ella didn't like spiders. She found a trowel through half-squinted eyes. As soon as she picked it up, she went running back to the wagon. Then she wiggled around to make sure there were no spiders left on her that she couldn't see.

Once she had gone into the shed to put away her jump rope and then she'd gone right into the house to have lunch. She'd been sitting at the table about to bite into a bologna-and-cheese sandwich with the crusts cut off when a great big spider crawled off of her arm and onto the sandwich. She'd screamed and thrown her sandwich across the room, and Jack had laughed and picked up the spider and taken it outside. Ever since then, Ella had been really careful when she went into the shed.

She knelt down in the grass and dug a hole. At first it was hard to dig, because the grass tried to hold the dirt together, but once she got down a little bit, it got easier. She put the box down next to the hole and then arranged the flowers in bunches all around it. She wished she knew how to make all the flower shapes she'd seen at Jack's funeral.

"These look like piles of flowers," she said to her friends, "but they're really fancy shapes in disguise."

One by one, she pulled her friends out of the wagon and set them up in rows facing the hole. Some of them didn't sit up well on their own. They had to lean against each other. Ella didn't even try to make Sarah sit; she just held her under one arm.

Ella heard the back door open. She turned to look. Mom came out onto the back steps and said, "Ella, what are you doing?"

"I'm having a funeral for Optimus Prime. He fell off the shelf and now he died."

"Okay," Mom said. "Okay." She went back inside without saying anything else, not even about all the flowers that Ella had picked.

The before Mom would have come out to see exactly what she was doing, or at least would have yelled about the flowers. But this was a new mom. A sad mom. Ella missed the old one.

She looked down at her friends gathered around the little grave, and at the flowers mounded there, and at the box. It had the name of a shoe company written on it. That was okay: it was a transformer box. Just like Optimus Prime transformed from a robot to a car, this box had transformed from a shoe box to a coffin.

She nodded to Legs the Frog-man, who was the closest thing her friends had to a priest. And then she bowed her head and listened to what Legs had to say.

"Friends, Optimus Prime was a good robot. Sometimes he fought with us and sometimes he played with us, but he loved us. And we loved him. He was a good robot and a good friend. Even though he's dead, he loves us just as much as always. Remember that."

Ella nodded. She started to hum "Amazing Grace" but couldn't remember it very well, so she hummed "Twinkle Twinkle Little Star" instead as she placed the box in the hole. She covered it up with dirt, and then she shifted all the flowers to the top of the dirt pile.

Her friends talked quietly amongst themselves while she loaded them into the wagon. They said what a good friend Optimus Prime had been, and how sad it was that he was gone and how nicely Legs had talked about him.

When they were all loaded, Ella stopped and looked at the grave. The flowers looked pretty there. She hoped Optimus Prime liked them.

Then, dragging the wagon behind her, Ella went inside. Mom didn't say anything to her when she came in. Ella left the wagon by the door and went looking for her.

She was in the living room sitting on the couch. The TV was on, but she wasn't really watching it. She was looking past it, at the pictures on the wall. One was of Ella and one was of Jack and one was of Mom and Dad on the day they got married, and one was of Uncle

Steve, who Ella had never met. She'd met lots of other uncles and aunts and cousins, but Uncle Steve had died. Maybe that's why Mom was looking at his picture. He had died too, just like Jack, except a long time ago, before Ella was born.

"I'm inside now," Ella said.

Mom turned her head. "Okay, sweetie. Are you hungry?"

"Not yet. I have to feed my friends first."

"Okay," Mom said.

Mom's fingers brushed one of Jack's white shirts that had never gotten put away. All the rest had disappeared somewhere, but this one stayed on the arm of the couch, neatly folded. Ella wondered if it was the same one Mom had put over her eyes the day she thought they were going to the beach. She wished Mom wouldn't look so sad.

"Mom, I have a joke for you."

"What's that, sweetie?"

"What did one muffin say to the other muffin?"

Mom didn't say, "I don't know, what?" She just waited, so Ella kept going.

"It said, 'Aah, a talking muffin.'" She giggled at her own joke, but Mom didn't. She just smiled a very small smile.

"That's very funny. Let me know when you're ready for lunch, okay?"

"Okay." Jack would have laughed.

She went back to her friends. They were all sad, too, from the funeral. She wished people wouldn't be sad all the time.

Very carefully, so none of her friends would fall out, Ella dragged the wagon back up the stairs. She had to walk past Jack's room to get to hers. The door was shut. It had been shut for days. Mom had shut it after Jack died and never opened it again.

Ella looked up and down the hall. Nobody had told her she couldn't go into Jack's room. Well, except Jack, over and over again, sometimes very loudly. But she wasn't going in. She was just going to peek. Besides, no one was looking.

She turned the knob and pushed open the door. It smelled like Jack in there. His clothes were on the floor. His action figures were all in a line on the shelf. His blankets were all scrambled together on his bed. It looked like he'd never gone away at all, or like he'd be back again any minute.

Ella remembered watching him get ready to go to the beach. She'd given him Octavius. Was Octavius dead too? Ella didn't know who to ask. If he was dead, he must be with Jack. And Optimus Prime must be with Jack. And Uncle Steve too. That made her feel better, knowing Jack wouldn't be alone wherever dead was.

"I'm sorry I broke Optimus Prime," Ella said to Jack who was not there.

She shut the door and took the wagon back to her room.

Chapter Eleven

Anna stepped through the door. It swung shut. Twilight closed in around her. Overhead the trees were infested with thick vines that dropped trailing tendrils. With every step she took, the darkness seemed to deepen, until she felt she wasn't seeing trees, but the shadows of trees making stripes of darker darkness. The path was a narrow crumbling strip, barely wide enough for her to stand on. She felt afraid.

Once, when Anna was five or six, she had been staying with her family overnight at her grandparents' house. Sometime in the night, a bad dream had driven her from her bed in search of the room where her parents slept. She had stumbled around, half asleep in the dark, growing more and more terrified in the unfamiliar house.

Finally, her dad had found her huddled in a corner a few feet from his room, crying. He had made up a story about how dreams come from your pillow, and gave her one of his own so that she couldn't have any more bad dreams. Anna wiped tears on her arm. She wished her daddy would swoop in to rescue her now. "You're a big girl now, Anna Evelyn," she told herself aloud. "There's nothing to be afraid of." The trees seemed to shiver at the sound of her voice. She wrapped her arms across her chest and pushed forward, ducking now and then to keep the vines from touching her.

It was one of those things you were supposed to grow out of, fear of the dark, fear of shadows. But Anna hadn't, not really. At home she had a blue light bulb in the lamp on her bedside table. That way, she could leave the light on all night, without it being so bright that it kept her awake. No one knew that. Not even Jack.

Out of the corner of her eye she thought she saw a woman in a white gown with long, tangled black hair spilling down her back—the woman from the nightmare that had frightened her all those years ago. The woman's face was pale, and her eyes were black. She raised one long finger and pointed at Anna.

"I don't believe in you." Anna almost succeeded in preventing her voice from shaking. She tried not to think about the incongruity of telling something you didn't believe in it.

The woman's ghostly face contracted in confusion. Tree branches trembled. A vine fell from the canopy and whipped across the path between them.

"Go away," Anna said as forcefully as she could.

The woman stood for a moment, wavering. Anna clenched her jaw and walked past. Something picked at Anna's sleeve—the woman or a branch, Anna didn't stop to find out which. She moved as quickly as she could, fighting the urge to run.

A few steps later, a gibbering demon swung from a branch above Anna's head. Anna kept walking. "I remember you," she said. "You hung from my fan."

She walked under the branch without pausing. Anna's newly reanimated heart was beating madly. Every nightmare she had ever had was here. But she could handle this. All she had to do was keep walking.

All at once she was hit by the crushing realization that her little brother, only two years old, was lost in the mall. This was worse than any nightmare. It felt like it was happening all over again. Anna could almost see it, the nervous employees, her mother's face red from crying, the horrible moment when she heard the description of Nathan over the store's intercom system. She felt her older brother, Michael, clutching her hand, saying, "It'll be okay" over and over until the words lost meaning.

But they'd found him, wandering around with his hands in his pockets. *He's okay. None of this is real.*

She almost believed it. The dizziness was back. She tried to take a deep breath, and couldn't. She realized suddenly that her legs felt heavy, and her eyes hurt inside her skull. Her chest constricted. She was having trouble breathing. It felt like the time she had fallen off a swing and gotten the breath knocked out of her. She'd been lying there, gasping, with tears leaking from her eyes, and then Michael had been by her side, rubbing her back and speaking calmly. She wished he were here now.

She leaned against a tree, trying to breathe and swallow at the same time. She knew she had to keep going. Ricky had warned her not to stop, but maybe she could sit down for a second, just long enough to catch her breath. She melted to the ground. The forest seemed to be getting darker, but no, that was her eyes closing.

~

Somewhere nearby someone was saying her name over and over. It was a familiar voice.

Another voice, young, also familiar, said, "What is it? Is she awake?"

"I thought her eyelids twitched. There, see?"

Fingers gripped her hand. Anna opened her eyes. The light was blinding. There was something on her face—a tube—in her nose and across her cheeks. She tried to pull it away with her free hand, but someone grabbed that one as well. She tugged. The grip tightened. The first voice said her name again, and this time she was certain she should recognize it. She blinked three or four times, trying to clear her vision.

"She's awake. Thank God, she's awake. Anna, can you hear me? It's Michael."

Michael. It was Michael leaning over her, clutching her hand. Had she fallen off the swings? No, that had happened a long time ago, when Nathan was a baby. As though thinking of him had brought him there, Nathan was suddenly beside her, too. She had barely enough time to catch a glimpse of his face, looking pale and tired but excited, before he threw his arms around her. She could smell his shampoo and the musky smell she had always thought of as "boy." It obscured, but didn't quite cover, the antiseptic sting of the hospital. She was in a hospital.

Over Nathan's head she could see a TV mounted on a wall and an ugly framed print of the type found only in hospital rooms and cheap motels. It showed a narrow stream and a bridge with entirely too many pink and blue flowers around it. The metal bed frame squeaked as Michael tried to pry Nathan off of her.

"Don't overwhelm her, Nathan. We need to call a nurse."

Nathan bounced up, almost knocking Anna in the chin with the top of his head, and jammed his thumb six or eight times against the call button attached to the rail of the bed. He was crying.

"You were dead, for like five minutes," Nathan said. "But they brought you back and they thought you'd never wake up. They said if you did wake up, you might have brain damage. Do you have brain damage? Mom and Dad didn't want me to come, but I made Michael bring me because it wasn't fair. I had to be here because I knew you would wake up. And you did, so I was right. Are you—"

Michael plugged the flow by reaching up and putting his hand over Nathan's mouth. He jerked it away again quickly.

"Gah, you licked me. Nasty." Michael wiped his hand on Nathan's shoulder. "Be quiet for a minute, okay? She just woke up."

Anna's head felt sticky, as if someone had been using it as a cotton candy spinner. "What happened?" she asked.

Michael took her hand—not, she was relieved to note, with the hand that Nathan had licked.

"You were in an accident."

She remembered bits of glass, twisting metal, pain, but that was it. "I don't . . . remember."

"The doctor said it might take a while for your short-term memory to come back."

Anna sat up slowly. She felt okay, except for the sticky feeling in her head, and her leg—her leg was stiff and heavy. She reached down to touch it and felt something solid under the sheet. She knocked on it.

"A cast?"

"Your leg was broken in the accident."

Anna remembered that. She remembered that clearly. The sudden pain, the bone bursting through the skin. It was more or less the only thing she remembered. Everything else was hidden behind a dark fog.

"Where is . . ." She waved her hand. "Parents?" she finished. It wasn't really what she had meant to say.

"I finally convinced them to eat something," Michael said. "They went down to the cafeteria." He looked at Nathan, who had stayed miraculously silent for an entire minute. "Why don't you go get them? They'll want to know."

Nathan tore out of the room. Anna could hear his sneakers squeaking as he ran down the waxed floor of the hallway. The sound reminded her of something. As she turned her head, she caught a flash of color in the corner of her eye. A vase of gerbera daisies in orange and yellow and rocker-girl pink stood on the bedside table beside a standing army of get-well-soon cards. Anna picked up the one closest to her. It had a picture of a bunny, obviously drawn by Nathan. He liked to draw bunnies with one ear folded over. The speech bubble coming out of its mouth said, "Get Well." She opened the card. Inside it said, "NOW!" Nathan had signed the bottom with his first and last name, a quirk he'd developed in third grade after the teacher started throwing away papers without last names.

As she returned the card to the table, her hand brushed something that made a crackling noise. She picked it up. It was a fifty-cent bag of sour gummy worms. A name burst like a bubble in her brain. *Jack.* Jack had been driving the car.

She looked up at Michael. Something in her eyes must have warned him what was coming. He started to back away. "That nurse is taking a long time," he said. "Maybe I should go find her."

"Michael." Her voice was low. Michael froze with his hand on the doorknob. He wouldn't look at her.

"Where's Jack?"

"I'll just be gone a second," Michael said. "After the nurse checks on you, we can talk."

Crackling filled the silence between them as Anna tightened her hand around the bag. "Michael, where is Jack?"

Michael turned, his face a nervous mask. "I'm sorry," he said, so quietly she barely heard him. She closed her eyes.

"I'll only be a second," he said. She heard the door click shut behind him.

Left alone, she weighed the bag in her hand, trying to puzzle the meaning out of this familiar clear packet with its red-and-yellow paper label. She opened the bag, reached in, and selected a blue-and-orange gummy worm.

For a long moment she stared at it, trapped there between her thumb and forefinger. She thought about how worms can survive if you cut them in half, and realized that it couldn't be true. If you take away half of a living thing, the other half shrivels and dies.

As she raised the candy to her lips and smelled its fruity sweetness, a flash of memory cracked through her mind. She smelled gasoline and tasted blood. *Enough.* Anna jerked open the drawer on her bedside table, threw the gummy worms inside, and closed it with a bang that echoed in the empty hospital room.

A moment later, the door opened and her brothers walked into the room with her parents behind them. Her mother rushed the bed and threw her arms around Anna. Her father took one look at her and melted into a chair. His eyes were bloodshot. She watched, bewildered, as he began to cry.

Chapter Twelve

Jack waited for Anna's door to shut behind her before opening his. Everything was exactly the same on the other side except that Anna wasn't with him. But if what Ricky had said about the forest was true, he wouldn't be alone for long. Jack tamped down a rising feeling of panic. He could do this. He'd met his uncle night after night in dreams. It was only a matter of time before he showed up here as well. Jack knew how to handle him.

The dark forest shuddered around him. Jack looked up into the canopy. He couldn't see the sky. A branch brushed his shoulder. He jerked away, and then laughed at his own skittishness. It was only a tree.

Soon, he realized that the path was widening. The trees seemed to be drawing away from it, leaving patches of sand exposed between their roots. Jack thought it might even be lighter up ahead. Maybe the forest had decided that it was pointless to try to frighten him. He tried to tell himself that a forest couldn't think, but the trees above him shivered as though they didn't believe it either.

It was definitely lighter up ahead. He hadn't reached the other side of the forest. It was a clearing, a perfect circle, with a shaft of light stabbing down through the trees. Someone was sitting cross-legged in the ray of light, staged for the most dramatic visual effect. The figure was wearing a black hooded sweatshirt, the hood pulled up to hide its face.

Jack sighed. "Hello, Uncle Steve."

Steve looked up, but his face remained in shadow. Jack was grateful for that.

"Jack! I've been waiting for you."

Jack hesitated at the edge of the clearing. He would have to get past his uncle to reach the other side of the forest. He wondered if Steve would follow him. There was only one way to find out. Jack walked into the clearing.

Steve bounded up and blocked Jack's path. "Not leaving yet, are you? Stay and visit with your old uncle."

Jack sighed. "You aren't real, Uncle Steve." Jack tried changing direction, but Steve sidestepped, blocking him again.

"Aren't real?" The voice rose in pitch, sounding affronted. "Are too. Real as you. Real as me. Real as anyone. If I'm not real, why are you yellow?"

"I'm not afraid," Jack said, inching sideways.

His uncle snorted and mirrored his movement.

"Why are you here?" Jack said.

"Have to be somewhere. Everything is somewhere. Might as well be here. Here, there, everywhere. Focus!" The shout made Jack glance at his uncle. He looked away quickly.

Uncle Steve said, "More important. Here are you. Ask why."

"I died today."

Steve applauded.

"It was an accident," Jack said.

"Crash, squish, boom. Good job."

Jack spoke slowly, enunciating. "It was a car accident. I didn't kill myself. I'm not like you."

Uncle Steve giggled and put his arm around his nephew's shoulders. Jack panicked. His uncle had never actually touched him before. He'd talked and talked, yes. Followed him from dream to dream, often. But never, ever touched him. Jack tried to squirm away, but the hooded figure held on.

"I've waited a long time." Uncle Steve's voice was suddenly serious. "You waited too. Don't lie to your old uncle. I know how you feel."

"It doesn't matter now."

Steve grabbed Jack's shoulder and spun him so that they faced each other. The hood fell back, and Jack suddenly stood eye to eye with his uncle.

The face looked like Jack's: wiry blond hair, blue eyes, the occasional dark freckle on otherwise pale skin. They could have been brothers, except for the flap of charred skin hanging from the right cheekbone, the forced half smile caused by lips that had burned away on one side, and the oozing pustule where the right eye should have been.

Bile burned Jack's throat. He'd seen it a thousand times, but now he could smell charred flesh and rotting meat. Another first. It made him sick. He tried to pull away. His uncle caught a handful of his shirt. "Tag, you're it!" he shouted. Then he shushed himself. "No time for games."

"Let go," Jack said.

"Let's go," Steve countered.

"Go where?"

"Go and see, go and see." He giggled.

Jack struggled, but Steve's grip was unbreakable.

"Ready now, let's count to three," Steve said.

"One!"

"Let go."

"Two!"

"No!"

"Three!"

~

Anna lay on her back in the hospital bed. She was wide awake but felt like she was dreaming. Her mother was curled up on the window seat, snoring softly. Anna didn't remember it getting dark. She didn't remember her brothers and her father leaving. She must have slept for a while, then, even though she had been certain she wouldn't. How could she sleep, when Jack was dead?

The blinds were drawn over the window that looked out into the hall, but the door was open a crack. Anna looked up when she heard a steady squeaking and the swift movement of many feet. She watched through the crack as a gurney flashed by, surrounded by a crowd of white uniformed doctors and nurses.

The squeaking brought to mind the image of a bearded man holding a broom or a pole of some sort. The memory slipped away. That had been happening to her all day. Unconnected bits of memories bobbed on the surface of her mind. She'd catch a glimpse of something, the echo of a sound, and then it would wink out. The doctor said it was normal, her brain sorting itself out. She would be back to her old self in a few days.

My name is Anna. I am seventeen. I am at Eastern Maine Medical Center. I was in a car accident. Jack is dead, she told herself. *I was dead.* Nathan had said that when she'd first woken up. She had been dead for minutes. It felt like longer, much longer. Hours, at least. Days. But maybe that was the coma playing tricks.

And yet, she could almost remember being dead. Jack had been there. They were walking, trying to get . . . somewhere. She remembered Jack telling her they were soul mates. But Jack hadn't said that. The psychic lady at the fair had said it. Jack had been there, of course, and they'd laughed about it. A dream, then. It must have been a dream.

~

Uncle Steve let go as Jack lunged forward. Jack sprawled face-first into grass. He sat back on his heels, too startled to panic. "Where are we?"

"Same place, different view," Uncle Steve said.

"We're by the highway."

Steve held one burned finger to his lips. "Shh! It's coming."

Jack looked nervously up the road and saw an eighteen-wheeler hauling toward them. It looked familiar. "No. No, I don't want to see this."

~

Anna sat up in bed. She'd heard something—not a memory, but a real thing, a voice. She held her breath, straining to hear. There it was again. It sounded like Jack calling her name. Maybe there had been some kind of mistake. Maybe he wasn't dead after all.

She glanced at her mother to make sure that she was still asleep and then tried to get out of bed. Her left leg refused to move. *Broken*, she remembered, in the accident.

~

Jack couldn't look away from the approaching truck. As the big rig passed them, a pair of deer bounded into the road. The truck swerved, brakes hissing. The trailer jackknifed, overbalanced, fell on its side.

Jack grabbed the front of his uncle's sweatshirt and screamed into the charred face. "Take me back."

His uncle giggled. "Can't go back, haven't gone. Look who's coming now."

Jack heard the car approaching, heard the music pouring through the open windows. He turned without wanting to and saw the blue Chevy speeding toward them. He could see his own face through the windshield. He saw the moment of terror as the version of him in the car saw the truck ahead, and then the face hardened. The car sped up. He could hear Anna screaming. The him in the car smiled. In the last moment before they crashed, he smiled, and his smile looked like Uncle Steve's.

Over the sound of tearing metal, Jack, the real Jack, shouted, "No, that wasn't how it happened."

~

Anna sat still, listening. The sound came again, louder. This time she was certain it was Jack's voice. A wild thought occurred to her. *Maybe it was a mistake. Maybe they lied to me. Tried to protect me. Jack isn't dead. He's here. In another room. Hurt. Dying.* She had to get out of bed—now. Carefully, carefully, she dangled her right foot toward the floor, then put her hands on either side of her left leg and shifted it off the side of the bed. The weight almost pulled her down. She'd never broken a bone before. She hadn't realized a cast was so heavy.

~

Uncle Steve snapped his fingers. Suddenly they were sitting in the back seat of the car as it sped toward the overturned truck. The radio was blaring. Anna was screaming. Jack saw himself in the front seat, watched as his foot failed to hit the brake and instead pressed the gas pedal.

"It wasn't like that."

Snap. The scene reset. Jack was inside his own head, listening through his own ears to the radio, and Anna, and the voice of his thoughts. The voice said, "Finally."

They crashed.

~

The cast hit the floor hard, and Anna grabbed at the bed to regain her balance. Behind her, the snoring stopped. She held her breath as her mother shifted position. The snoring resumed, slightly louder than before.

~

Jack was thrown from the car and landed on his face in the forest. He scrambled to his knees. "I didn't do that. I didn't think that."

His uncle stood over him, arms akimbo. He was smiling.

"I don't remember that," Jack said, the certainty fading from his voice.

"Remember, remember the fifth of November. Nephew Jack can't remember." The branches above were thrashing, making a noise like a distant crowd shouting for the death of a gladiator.

Uncle Steve dropped to one knee, putting them eye to eye. For once Jack didn't even try to look away. "What do you remember?" Steve asked, his voice strangely level.

"There was a truck, a truck up ahead, and Anna was screaming, and I knew we were going to crash. I had to stop the car . . ."

"And?"

"It wouldn't stop."

"You didn't want it to."

"I would never hurt her."

Uncle Steve giggled. "Watch again." He grabbed the front of Jack's shirt. Jack's stomach lurched. They were beside the road. An eighteen-wheeler was approaching.

Jack screamed.

~

Anna heard her name clearly this time. Jack was calling for her. He sounded hurt, frightened. She reached for the IV rack. It rolled toward her on tiny silent wheels. If she was careful, maybe she could use it as a crutch to get out into the hall and find out where they were keeping him.

With one last glance at her mother, she took a deep breath and hopped forward. There was a moment of panic when the IV stand tried to go one way and her foot went the other, but she righted herself. The door was close. Four or five hops at the most. And then she could rest against the door frame. She could do this.

~

The deer ran. The truck swerved. The car approached. Anna screamed. The brakes squealed.

"No more, no more."

~

Anna inched forward bit by bit. Her broken leg ached. Her chest felt tight. She fought to keep from gasping. Just two more steps. One . . . T—. In her haste to get to the door she had tried to move too fast. The IV stand rolled too far to the left. Unable to touch her left foot to the ground, she realized there was no way she could catch herself. Anna tried to break her fall with her hands, but her forehead cracked against the floor. Pain spiked through her head. She shouted.

~

"Please stop, please!"

~

Anna's mother was on one knee beside her, trying to keep her from moving while shouting for the nurse. Anna struggled against her arm. She could hear Jack's voice clearly now.

"Let me up. Mom, let me up. He needs me."

"Nurse, nurse!"

"Let go! I hear him. I hear him." She clawed at her mother's arm.

A swarm of people in scrubs appeared at the door, enveloped her, and lifted her into the air. She struggled against them. They were holding her arms, holding her legs, crushing her torso so that she couldn't scream, could barely breathe. Worst of all they were shouting orders at each other, making so much noise that she could no longer hear Jack's voice.

~

Jack fell down on the grass and sobbed. He closed his eyes, but he could still hear the scream, the brakes, the crash.

~

Someone must have turned on the overhead light, because it blazed suddenly in Anna's eyes. She closed them. Her lungs were aching for lack of air. She had to get them off her. She gathered all her strength, heaved against the arms that held her down, and opened her eyes . . .

She was in the forest, propped against a tree. The restraints stopping her breath were vines. They had wrapped around her torso and left arm. Her left leg was completely invisible beneath the tangle. How long had she been here? Something moved against her right ankle. She looked down and realized with horror that she could see the branches growing, trying to wrap themselves more tightly around her. She kicked out with her foot, dislodging the creeping thing, and then tore at any branch she could reach.

She could still hear Jack, screaming a wordless, sobbing cry that made her heart pound. Anna clawed at the branches, screamed at them, swore at them. They tore her skin, ripped her fingernails from their beds. But they bent and broke in her hands. Others seemed to slither away. She managed, eventually, to climb to her feet.

She cupped her hands on either side of her mouth and called Jack's name. He called back, sounding so lost in the land of panic that he couldn't have found calm with a GPS-enabled Range Rover.

"I'm coming, Jack! Keep yelling."

No problem there. He didn't seem to be able to stop. *Maybe he really has gone crazy,* she thought. But this was Jack she was thinking about. He was probably imagination deep in some dream or other. The screaming, though—that was really getting to her. He sounded so frightened.

She looked at the barricade of trees lining the path. "Can't go over it, can't go under it, can't go around it. Have to go through it," she chanted to herself, and plunged into the brush. The trees tried to keep her out. She heard them creak and snap. She forced her way off the path and into the depths of the forest.

She held up her arms so that they shielded her face, leaving a sliver of a gap for her to see through. Even so, branches raked her arms, clawed at her hair, and tore her legs. She could feel the sting of a thousand small cuts opening, and then a disconcerting itch as they began to close again almost instantly. The wounds on her hands were healing too. She put that aside in her mind to freak out about later.

A mound of tangled vines tripped her. She scrambled to keep her balance, trying to avoid touching the trees around her. It was impossible. The trunks were close together, the spaces between them filled with vines and branches. She was on her feet again and moving forward before she thought to wonder what was under the mound. Had someone else been trapped the way she was? She couldn't stop to look. Jack's voice was fading. She was getting closer, but he seemed to be running out of pain, or breath. Maybe the trees had him too. She pushed herself to move faster.

She was running so fast that she nearly fell when the path opened up and the trees let her go. Jack was lying facedown in the center of the path, his hands folded over his head as though bracing for impact. He was crying more softly now, repeating the same phrase over and over. "I'm sorry, Anna. I didn't mean it. I'm sorry, Anna. I didn't mean it."

Anna knelt down and gently touched his shoulder. He screamed as though she had pressed a branding iron to his neck and tried to shimmy backward on his knees and elbows. As soon as the scream faded, he filled the clearing with the sound of "I'm sorry, Anna. I didn't mean it." The trees were laughing at him.

Cautiously, Anna looked around. The vines seemed to be spreading toward them. She had to get Jack out of here. He was covering his head again. "Jack," Anna said softly. "It's me. Anna. I'm here. Everything is okay."

He didn't seem to hear her. She leaned down beside him and tried to pull his arm away from his head. He jerked away from her.

She stood up. It was the forest that had done this to him. If she could get him out, he'd be okay, she hoped. But how? He wouldn't listen. He wouldn't let her touch him. He hardly seemed to know she was there. She covered her mouth with her hands, trying to think what to do.

"Jack Xavier Pratt, you look at me right now."

Nothing. He mumbled to himself. The vines were definitely closer now, and above them, the branches seemed to be reaching toward each other, closing the clearing in around them.

In desperation, Anna dropped to her knees beside Jack, leaned down, and kissed him on the corner of his mouth.

His eyes popped open. She smiled. "Hi."

"Hi," he said in a sleepy voice. "Did you just . . ."

"Nope."

He seemed to wake up all at once. She could almost swear she saw consciousness flood into his eyes. "Anna!" He sat up, grabbed her around the neck, and hugged her tightly. "I'm sorry, I'm sorry, I didn't know."

She tried to pull away, but it was like being hugged by her little brother. No matter how you squirmed, his arms were still around you.

"What are you talking about, Jack? Sorry for what?"

"I killed you."

"We've been over this already. You didn't mean to."

"I did, though. I went crazy and I pushed the gas instead of the brake. I wanted to die. I wanted both of us to die."

"Jack, that's insane."

He let go of her and buried his face in his hands.

Anna shuddered at her own carelessness. "No, I don't mean . . . Sorry, that was a bad choice of words. You're not crazy."

"I am. Uncle Steve showed me what happened. What *really* happened." He started to tell her, but she interrupted.

"Uncle Steve? Crazy Uncle Steve?"

"Yes."

"He was here?"

"Yes, and he brought me to the road. He showed me the accident. I didn't even try to stop."

Anna patted his back. "It wasn't real." She glanced at the creeping trees. They were running out of time for discussion.

Jack let go of her. "You should probably go on without me. You won't be safe as long as we're together. I don't know when I might snap again and try to hurt you."

Anna clasped his hands. "One: we're dead. There's nothing you can do to hurt me once we get out of this forest. And B: you would never hurt me."

"I already have."

"Jack, let's walk." She levered him to his feet. It was difficult. He hardly had the strength to stand. She led him forward, talking the whole time, trying to distract him. "Do you remember when we were in middle school and Andre Booker insulted me and you backhanded him so hard, he fell down the stairs?"

"Yes."

"And the time I fell out of the tree at your house and you thought I hit my head on that rock and you cradled my head in your lap until I could sit up?" Anna pulled her arm out of the reach of a branch.

"I didn't know you remembered that."

"And the time I came to you crying because I found out that Danny had taken Jenna to the movies over the weekend and then his car keys mysteriously went missing and turned up the next day in the fish tank in the biology room?"

"Nobody ever proved that was me."

"It was you."

"Okay, so maybe I happened to find his keys on the ground and while I was bringing them to him, I tripped and they flew out of my hand and landed in the fish tank. I couldn't stick my arm in there and get them. I might have gotten my shirt wet."

"The point is . . . you would never hurt me on purpose. Even if you were as mad as the hatter, the dormouse, and all the little teacups, you would never hurt me."

"But Uncle Steve said . . ."

She stopped him by taking his arm. "Uncle Steve is a nightmare. I'm real." She caught his gaze and held it. "I trust you, Jack."

There was a long moment of silence. Finally, Jack licked his lips nervously. "Anna? Back there, did you—"

"No." She walked away quickly.

He followed her. "You don't even know what I was going to say."

"I plead the Fifth." She hoped he would leave it alone. She didn't have the energy to explain herself. She barely had the energy to keep walking forward. But she had to. There was no going back now.

Chapter Thirteen

The line of trees broke suddenly, revealing the desert sands that had become so familiar. Jack sighed in relief when they finally stepped out of the shadow of the trees. He had been trying to convince himself that his experience with his uncle had been a hallucination, that his terror had been the product of an ominous setting combined with his overactive imagination. Believing himself seemed easier out in the open.

He felt no need to breathe in again. Everything was back to normal. Except something was going on with Anna. She was too quiet. Somewhere under the whispering trees she had stopped talking and had never started up again. Jack wondered what had happened.

He looked over his shoulder at the dark line of trees, which seemed too far away. It must be an optical illusion. He crashed into Anna, who had stopped in the middle of the path. "What are you stopping for?"

"The path split."

"But we're not in the forest anymore."

"Yes, genius, I can see that."

Jack looked down. The path had separated into three prongs. The paths to the left and the right were wide, curving off into the distance in opposite directions. The center path was narrower and continued along the same line as the one they'd been walking on. Jack could feel the pull guiding him forward. "Just keep walking straight," he said.

"No."

"What do you mean, no? This one is literally straight and narrow."

Jack stared at Anna, who shook her head. There was definitely something going on with her. She had drifted over to the far edge of their path and was looking out over the distance. There was nothing there.

"What are you doing?" he asked.

"Nothing." She set one foot down in the lighter sand to the left of the path.

Jack reached for her. "You shouldn't . . ."

"Why?"

"Because—because it's not the right way."

"I'm done with this, Jack. I'm done with rules I don't understand and landscapes that make no sense. There's got to be something else out there."

"What are you talking about?"

She strode away across the sand, away from all the paths.

"Anna!"

Jack ran to catch up with her. It was difficult for a moment, as though a strong gust of wind hit him as he stepped off the path. But once he was through it and rushing after Anna, he wasn't even sure he'd felt it.

"Where are you going?" he asked when he reached her side.

"Where's your sense of adventure, Jack? Remember when we were little and we would have given anything to set off across an unexplored world with no one to hold us back? Well, here it is." She threw her arms out, encompassing the entire hereafter. "Let's go."

"There's nothing out there."

She dropped her arms, turned, and walked away from him. "There has to be."

He followed. "Why?"

"Video-game rules again. Either there's something out there, or we'll blink out of existence for a second and end up on the other side of the world."

"That's *Pac-Man*! You can't base life choices on the mechanics of *Pac-Man*."

Anna shrugged. "That's all right then. I'm dead."

"You're not making any sense." Jack had to speed up to keep pace with her. "Whatever happened back there . . ."

Anna froze. Jack continued another step out of sheer momentum before he turned to face her. They stood that way for a moment, a pace apart, Jack looking at Anna, Anna looking at the ground. When she spoke, it was in a low voice, barely controlled.

"Would you like to tell me all about what happened to you?"

Jack would not.

Anna started walking again. "Then let's agree right now not to talk about it, okay?"

"Okay, but—"

"Turn back if you want."

"You know I won't."

"I know," she said, her voice angry.

Jack wondered what she was mad about. He was fairly certain he hadn't done anything to make her mad. The forest must have really gotten to her. But they were out of that now. Everything was fine. At least, it would be if they were on the path. Why had she made them leave the path?

"How will we find our way back?"

"How do you know we'll want to go back?"

Humoring her seemed the only option here. "Okay, so supposing we do want to go back, how do we find our way?"

"It's easy, genius." She pointed down at their footprints, a simple-enough trail to follow.

Jack looked over his shoulder. Anna hadn't stopped. He hurried to catch up with her.

"Anna?" he said.

She made a grunting sound in response but didn't turn to look at him.

"Why do you call me genius all the time?" he asked.

"Because you're one of the smartest people I know."

Jack looked sideways at her. "Okay, what's wrong with you?"

"What do you mean? I'm fine."

"That was nice. You're never nice."

Anna glared at him and increased her pace.

Jack watched her walk away from him. He didn't know how to deal with this new, quiet Anna. She should have hit him and made a sarcastic remark. Then he would have said something clever back. In three minutes she'd have been laughing and would have forgotten all about whatever was bothering her.

Instead, she was staring into the distance, through the ghost people into the sand and emptiness beyond. Her brow was furrowed, her jaw tight. Jack thought that if she could have remembered how, she might have started to cry. He reached out, took her hand, and squeezed it. She didn't pull away. That worried him. He let go.

"Maybe we should go back. There's nothing out here." But even as he spoke the words, he realized he was wrong. There was something farther on. He couldn't tell what it was from this distance, but a long gray shadow lay ahead—another art installation, maybe.

When they got closer, he realized that something was in fact nothing. What he had seen on the horizon was a long hole in the earth, so broad that he couldn't see the other side.

He followed Anna right up to the edge of the cliff and stood beside her, looking down. Tendrils of mist swirled, reaching. Like pale shades of the trees in the forest. The certainty seized Jack that if they somehow reached him, they would pull him apart until no atom of his body remained bound to another. He would cease to exist, and then this mist, this grasping, tearing ghost, would rearrange the world as though he had never existed. It would consume the very memory of him.

Anna leaned precariously over the edge. Jack grabbed the back of her shirt to keep her steady.

"Careful," he said. "You'll fall."

She settled back on her heels. Jack let her go, but his arm stayed raised. She was in a weird mood.

"Did you ever go up to the top of Cadillac Mountain and stand on the rocks there?" Anna asked.

"Yeah, Mom and Dad drove us up last summer."

"Whenever I go up there, I stand on the rocks looking down at the blue ocean and all the puzzle-piece islands and think, *I could jump right now and I wouldn't fall. No. If I jumped from this spot at this time, I couldn't fall. In this moment, and only in this moment, gravity would fail, and I would soar out over the ocean and the islands and never stop until I got to the edge of the world.*"

She was standing close to him, her eyes filled with such fervor that he forgot for an instant that they were standing on the edge of a cliff in the afterlife.

"Do you know how that feels?"

Jack only had time to say, "I—" before Anna stepped backward. He grabbed for her. She caught his arm, pulling him off balance and over the cliff. They plunged into the mist. It didn't destroy him, but everywhere it touched went numb. Terror clawed up Jack's throat. He screamed.

He pulled Anna closer and clung to her like she was the only thing in the universe. She *was* the only thing in the universe. Her body was shaking with sobs—no, with laughter. She was laughing. He found a single brain cell with time to be amazed. The others were all busy panicking at the prospect of falling to their doom.

They'd been falling a long time. Jack looked down. The mist had thinned enough that he could see the ground far away but rushing toward them. How deep must this pit be, that it took so long to reach the bottom? They spun slowly in the air until he was looking back up at the sky. The cliff top had disappeared, consumed by mist.

His back hit the ground hard enough to shatter every vertebra. His head bashed against the edge of something hard. Anna rolled away from him. Still lost in terror, Jack clung to the last bit of her he could reach, the tips of her fingers.

He should have been shattered, his skull smashed to fragments, his organs burst and leaking into the sand. He didn't feel any pain, but maybe he was in shock. He'd read about soldiers during World War II who had been blown in half and hadn't noticed until they looked up and saw their legs standing up beside them.

"Why would you do that?" he screamed, staring wide-eyed at the bits of blue sky between the clouds above. It made him dizzy to think that they had been up there seconds before.

"We can't get hurt. We're dead," Anna said in a calming tone. She was already sitting up. She removed her hair elastic and combed out her braid with her fingers. Jack started to sit up too, but stopped when what he had seen finally sank in through the terror.

"The sky is blue."

"Good job, Captain Obvious. They tell me it's done with light refraction."

"No, right now, the sky is blue. It's never been blue before. Hell, there's never really been a sky before."

Anna glanced up and shrugged. "So?"

"So? So! You don't think this is a big deal?"

"We're dead," she said as though it meant something.

"You keep saying that."

"It keeps being true."

Jack sat up and looked at her. Her eyes slipped away from his. There was almost no expression on her face, and that in itself was worrying. Jack had known Anna a long time, and her eyes alone could tell you the story of her life with footnotes. Something was bothering her. It would do no good to ask her what. She wouldn't tell him the truth anyway.

Instead, he looked around this new place. There wasn't much to see—at least, not much worth looking at. The landscape seemed to consist entirely of mounds of trash stacked as tall as houses. Anna wandered over to one and stirred the refuse with her toe. A beetle the size of an Oreo scurried toward Jack. He stood up quickly.

"It's like the factory," he said.

"Not quite. This is all trash."

"That was all trash too."

"No, that was stuff. Used stuff, but—but loved stuff, I guess. This is trash." She used her foot to excavate the edge of a pile: tin cans, nylons, bits of glass, old newspapers.

Jack heard something roll down the pile behind them. He turned. It was a green glass bottle. He looked up to see what had dislodged it, but the top of the pile was lost in clouds, which seemed to be creeping closer. He moved nearer to Anna.

"So what does it mean?" he asked, soliciting another shrug from Anna. "What's all this for?"

"It's trash," Anna said. "It's not *for* anything." She set off between two piles.

"Where are you going?"

"I don't know. There's not really any point in staying here, though."

"We could go back."

Anna stopped and looked up at the cliff. "How exactly?"

Jack turned to look. It was a sheer rock face with only the smallest bits of broken ledge that might serve as handholds if you were really desperate. He wasn't that desperate. Not yet. Besides, Anna seemed in no hurry to get back to the path. Now that he was thinking about it, Jack realized that he couldn't feel the pull that had guided them all this way. He closed his eyes, trying to sense it no matter how weak it was, but there was nothing to sense. That set a mustard seed of fear growing in his stomach.

"Are you coming or what?" Anna called.

Jack jumped. At almost the same instant, a Christmas ball bounced down the pile next to him and shattered against the fender of a car. Jack looked up. The piles were shifting, like an old house in spring.

"Coming," he said, and he went after Anna. He followed her around the mountains of trash. The wind was picking up. There was no wind in the afterlife. Not in the afterlife he knew. Which raised the question Where were they now? Maybe they'd never really left the forest. Maybe it had all been an illusion and they were still trapped there, surrounded by the laughing trees.

A newspaper skittered by, and he trapped it under his foot. It was the obituary page of some newspaper he had never heard of. He picked it up and read. *Sienna White Probert, 17, daughter of Brian Probert and Sharyl White and student at Hampden Academy, died on May 11* . . . Jack opened his hand and led the wind drag the newspaper away. He wondered what his obituary would say: *Jack Xavier Pratt, age 17, of Newport, died Thursday along with best friend Anna Evelyn Poplin, 17. Both died instantly when the car Pratt was driving slammed into an 18-wheeler on Route 1 near*... No, that sounded more like the news report.

For the first time, Jack wondered what had happened to the truck driver. Did he remember them dragging him to safety? It would be nice to think that his last act on earth was to save someone's life. There had to be some value in that, didn't there? Maybe it could go some distance toward making up for killing his best friend. A small distance.

Jack caught up to Anna. She was standing in a clearing between trash piles, her head cocked to one side, listening.

"What is it?"

"I can't tell," Anna said. "It almost sounds like . . . waves."

"It's probably the wind."

"They don't actually sound anything alike." She took off in the direction of the sound. Jack followed, paying more attention to the gathering clouds than to where he was going. It almost looked as though a storm were coming. Again, he nearly crashed into Anna, who stopped suddenly as she came around yet another pile of trash.

"We made it," she said.

Polluted water rolled as far as the eye could see. Every wave churned up plastic bottle caps and string and candy wrappers, but it was definitely the ocean. Anna stepped closer, until a high-flung wave covered her feet with water and a half-dissolved hamburger wrapper.

"Don't go in there," Jack said. "It's dirty."

"So? It's not like we can catch diseases. We're dead, remember?"

"Stop saying that."

Anna took his wrist and drew him toward the water. "We're dead. Get over it."

He stepped back, away from a floating piece of rubber that he sincerely hoped was a deflated balloon. "*You* get over it. You're the one who keeps saying it. We're dead, we're dead." He flailed his arms at each repetition. "I know we're dead. It's not the kind of thing you can forget."

The wind had picked up even more. It whipped the waves into whitecaps and scattered tin cans and other bits of trash across the few empty scraps of land. Already a sort of rubbish drift was forming against the nearest mound.

Anna strode deeper into the sea, until the water reached her knees. Jack tried to pull her back, but she swatted him away.

"What's that?" she asked, pointing at a dark mass in the distance.

Jack raised his eyes. It looked like a low cloud bank, or maybe fog, moving quickly over the water.

"If I didn't know better," he said, "I'd say it was a storm."

"Do you know better?"

While he'd been looking away, she'd waded even farther into the water. Now she was standing waist-deep. Her palms turned down over the tops of the waves as if she were trying to bless the sea.

He had to raise his voice to answer her. "I thought I did, until just now. Anna—"

She disappeared below the waves. Riptide. Jack dove toward the spot where she had been. In that moment, he did forget that they were dead. He forgot everything. Fear crowded out his thoughts. She was going to drown. He had to save her.

He grabbed at a smudge of purple that might have been her sleeve. It turned out to be an empty soda can. He struck out deeper, until he was treading water. The storm was well and truly coming now. He could feel it. Something caught his arm. He tried to pull away and saw that it was a hand. Anna's hand. She bobbed to the surface, spitting water and swearing more fluently than he had known she could.

"Anna!"

"Well, that was unpleasant," she said, as soon as her mouth was clear.

"You-you . . . argh!"

"It's okay, I'm fine. Let's swim to shore."

He grabbed her sleeve and held it, to keep them from drifting apart. The waves seemed to be actively trying to drown them. "Which way is that?" he said.

Somehow, during his brief search for Anna, the shore had slipped away. They were out on the open ocean.

Chapter Fourteen

Jack fought to stay above water. He'd never been a good swimmer, and with the steadily growing waves, it was a struggle to tread water and keep hold of Anna's sleeve. He looked around desperately for some sign of land. It was useless. A steady rain had started, and driving wind promised worse on the way. The sea tossed them up and down. Half the time they were in the trough of a wave and couldn't see more than a few feet. The other half they were spitting brown water and clawing it out of their eyes.

"It's a good thing—" Anna said.

A wave crested over their heads. Anna's sleeve almost pulled out of Jack's hand. He clutched until he could feel his fingernails digging into his palm through the fabric of the shirt. When he came up, a bit of soggy cardboard clung to his shoulder. He plucked it off and hurled it away.

Anna batted a milk carton away from them. "I said, it's a good thing we're already dead."

"We can still sink, you know." He imagined sinking to the ocean floor. It would be littered with trash—rusted refrigerators and bent bicycle frames and discarded cans of paint leaking pigment into the current. They could walk along the bottom, held back only slightly by the press of water around them. They wouldn't be crushed by the pressure—even that couldn't hurt them here—but they'd have to walk in silence, sound waves turned to meaningless noise. And there'd be no way to tell which way the shore was. They could walk for years without ever speaking, no arguing, no jokes, no laughter.

"Jack, what's that?"

"What? Where?" Every time he opened his mouth, water filled it. He spat and resisted the urge to scrape his tongue with his fingers. It wouldn't matter. The polluted water was everywhere, in his ears, in his eyes, down his throat. He wondered how much of it he'd swallowed.

"Over there." Anna pointed as a wave broke over them and doused her.

Jack tried to keep his hand on her sleeve and his eyes on the thing. It was flat, with a single long post or something sticking out of the top. Anna thrashed to the surface, pulling away from him.

"Who cares what it is?" Jack had to raise his voice to be heard over the sound of the storm. "It floats. It might even float with us on top of it."

Fortunately, the thing seemed to be drifting toward them on its own personal current. Anna snagged it when it got close. It was a table floating upside down. All the legs were broken off except for one, which stood straight up from the corner like a naked mast. Anna climbed aboard first, careful not to swamp the thing, while Jack clung to the side.

"Never let go, Rose," Jack said.

Anna shifted to the far side of the table so he could pull himself up without tipping it. "What?"

"You know. *Titanic*. Jack and Rose, the raft." He climbed aboard. A sheet of water skimmed after him and drained away again. "You made me watch it."

Anna shrugged.

Jack tried not to read too much into that. "What do we do now?" he asked.

"Wait for the storm to pass, and watch for land, I guess."

Jack edged over until he and Anna were sitting back to back in the middle of their makeshift raft. He looked out over the thrashing waves. This was not the ocean he'd had in mind when he'd gotten into his car this morning. At least he probably couldn't get seasick. That was a good thing anyway. Except that as soon as he thought about it, he did feel seasick. Which was crazy. He closed his eyes to block out the sight of the churning coffee-and-cream water and the bobbing bits of trash. He wished he could throw up. He'd feel better—probably.

Anna said something, but the wind whipped the sound of her voice away.

"What?" he shouted.

"Do you remember the storm?"

He squeezed her hand. Of course he remembered the storm. It had been last summer. They'd heard the storm coming and gone outside to meet it. The air had been electric, making Jack's arm hair stand on end. Wind had torn at their clothes and whipped Anna's ponytail away from her face.

When Anna had nudged Jack, a spark had jumped from his bare arm to hers. She'd laughed. Jack had thought he'd never felt so alive, so profoundly happy as he did at that moment with the electricity of the storm coursing through him.

Lightning had flashed over the rain-veiled trees, a photo-perfect shard of electricity. Then the rain had hit them. It had damped down their wild hair and pulled some of the electricity from their blood. There'd been a crack as a second snap of lightning found its mark among the trees.

Anna's mother had called them in then, and given them towels. She'd gone back into her office, but Jack and Anna had stayed by the windows, towels wrapped around their shoulders, watching the storm pass.

Now, floating on a tabletop in the middle of a polluted sea somewhere in the land of the dead, Jack closed his eyes and wished for home. He wished for towels and a door to shut out the rain. He had never in his life felt so homesick. He hadn't even known he could feel homesick for a whole reality. Homesick not just for the house he'd grown up in, not just for his mother and father and sister and dog, but homesick for towels and doors and television and chairs and endless rows of corn.

He didn't notice that the storm had quieted, not until Anna spoke and he realized that he could hear her even though she wasn't shouting.

"'. . . and he sailed off through night and day, and in and out of weeks and almost over a year . . .'" she quoted.

"Let's hope we don't find an island full of monsters," Jack said.

"Do you see that?" Anna scrambled to her feet, causing their makeshift raft to bob and spin. She grabbed the lone table leg to keep herself from falling. Jack sat still, wishing she would learn not to jump around in boats.

"Land ho!" Anna pointed at a low cloud way off in the distance. Jack squinted. It might be land, or it might be another storm. It was hard to tell. He said so and then added, "And what is up with you? Ever since the forest—"

Anna went rigid. "I don't want to talk about the forest."

"Neither do I. But if there's something wrong . . ."

"I think we're getting closer."

Now they could see an island dominated by a low, ideally dormant, volcano. Boulders dotted the narrow sloping beach around it. Jack could see people moving around the stones.

"Jack, those are people."

Jack didn't feel as excited as Anna sounded. He wondered what kind of people would be out here in the middle of this sea of garbage.

Now and then a person on the beach bent and straightened, like a crane catching fish. They seemed to be picking up pieces of trash that had washed ashore.

Anna shouted and waved. On the beach, a woman looked up, shading her eyes against the sun. Anna called out again, but the woman didn't respond. She just stood, watching as the raft drew closer. The same tide that had carried the junk was carrying them as well.

Jack realized he was afraid. He had no idea where the feeling had come from, but Anna clearly didn't share it. She dove off the tabletop and struck out toward the shoreline. For half an instant, Jack contemplated not following.

This close to the volcano, the water was warm, almost hot, like dishwater that had only just cooled enough to stick your hands in. It was so different from what he had expected, so foreign to the icy waters off the coast of Maine, that at first he flailed in place, shocked. But Anna was nearly halfway to the shore, and he needed to hurry if he wanted to reach her before the people did.

While Jack dog-paddled, Anna swam smoothly, arm over arm. She reached the shore before Jack was a third of the way, making him wonder if perhaps staying on the table-raft might have been a better option.

By the time he reached the shallows, Anna was standing in ankle-deep waves, speaking to a woman holding a dented hubcap.

The woman responded in what might have been Spanish, or possibly Portuguese.

Jack looked across the beach. Other people were shambling toward them, expressions vacant. They did nothing to dispel his fears.

"Please excuse Celia," a man said. "She doesn't speak English. My name is Lars." He held out a large hand for them to shake. He was built like—well, like an extremely large man, and he wore an eye patch, leaving Jack wondering where he had hidden his parrot. "Welcome to the island. It is always a pleasure to meet other believers."

"Believers?" Jack asked.

"You did come here to escape the siren song of The City, did you not—that so-called goal that all the ghosts are striving toward?"

"No," said Jack.

"Yes," said Anna at the same time.

Lars seemed to hear only Anna. "Well, you will not be disappointed. We have built our own city here on the island, where we can await the final judgment."

Jack wanted to ask what judgment, but Lars was already striding across the beach toward a dark spot in the base of the hill.

"Anna, I'm not so sure about this place."

Anna didn't answer. She followed Lars. The workers on the beach were already returning to their tasks. None of them met Jack's eye. Lars led them to the mouth of a cave. Anna and Lars paused in the dark opening. Jack stopped a few feet behind.

"Your city is in there?" Jack asked. "Why not out here in the sunshine? You have sunshine," he added, as if pointing out an amazing but as yet unused feature of a new sports car.

"The weather gets bad here, with storms that show the wrath of God, sent to test our faith," Lars said. "Long ago, the first comers to this island sheltered in the cave to escape the storm, and we have been here ever since."

Jack watched Lars bow his head to step inside the cave. There was something strange about this man, but Jack couldn't figure out what it was. It gnawed at him.

Lars led them deep into the cave, where a sort of passageway sloped downward into the heart of the hill. It got darker the deeper they went, but not as dark as it should have. Light was filtering up the passage.

"There's an actual city down here?" Jack said. "With streets and houses and stuff?"

"A town, really. We call it Haven."

"How creative."

Anna elbowed him in the ribs.

They were coming to the end of the passage. Lars stopped, sighed, and tore down a piece of newsprint that had been stuck to the wall. Someone had written on it in thick black ink. Jack only had time to catch the words *abandon* and *hope* before Lars crumpled it and stuck it in his pocket.

Fear crawled up Jack's back like a hairy-legged spider. "What was that?"

"A waste of paper."

"The people here," Jack said. "Are they all believers?"

"Of course. The weak waver now and then, but the community guides them through their trial."

When the cave opened up, they were on a ledge halfway up a wall. The space below was large enough to hold a football stadium. The middle third of the space was filled with a town laid out in a perfect grid, with the rising spire of a church marking the exact center. Neat shacks were built out of cardboard and corrugated metal. From Jack's vantage point it looked like the play village of a giant who had scavenged a dump for building material. Jack saw all this by the light of a moat of molten lava that bubbled from a crack in the far wall and wound around the outside edge of the town.

"Oh, hell no," Jack said. He caught Anna's arm and pulled her back toward the entrance. "Come on, Anna, time to go."

"We just got here."

"So?" He dropped his voice. "We are underground, in a cave full of molten lava. In. The. Afterlife. Do you see a problem here?"

Anna shrugged. "It looks nice enough to me."

Jack spun to look again at the red glow. "Nice?"

Anna pulled away.

"Seriously?" Jack said.

Anna looked over her shoulder at him. "It's not like it's going to kill us," she said, and shrugged—again. That shrug was getting on Jack's nerves. It made him want to shake her.

"You're so certain that I'll follow you, aren't you?" he said.

She might have paused for an instant, in the space between putting a foot down and picking it up again. But then again, it might have been his imagination. Jack watched for a few more steps, waiting without much hope to see if she would turn back. He sighed, and followed her across the sloping ledge and over the wooden ramp that connected it to the cavern floor.

People worked among the houses, patching roofs, mending walls. No one looked up as Jack's group walked by. They were all intent on their work—intent and silent. Jack's creepiness meter clicked up another notch.

The only person who seemed to notice their existence was a woman standing next to a rickety scaffold housing a cracked and tarnished bell. She was holding the bell cord in one hand. Her other hand rested on top of a large hourglass set on top of a flat stone. She glanced at Jack and Anna and then looked away, as if she didn't want to be caught looking.

Jack was unsurprised when Lars brought them to the church. The door was a tattered curtain that might have been made from an old bedsheet. As Lars raised his arm to pull the curtain back, Jack realized what had been nagging at him.

"You're breathing!"

"Of course. The breath is vital. A man's soul is nourished by his breath."

Jack clapped one hand over his mouth and pinched his nose with the other. Anna rolled her eyes at him. Jack counted to thirty and felt no urge to exhale. He dropped his hands. "I'm not breathing."

"You will learn. The elders will teach you. It is one of the many lessons you will learn here."

Lars opened the curtain and, before motioning them through, handed Anna a tattered piece of cloth, about the size of a wide scarf.

"What is this for?"

"Women's heads must be covered inside the church."

"Why?"

"It is written."

Jack expected an argument. Truthfully, he hoped for an argument. It would prove that the old Anna was still in there somewhere, that the forest hadn't killed her. Anna raised her eyebrows, but draped the piece of cloth over her head and shoulders.

Maybe she wasn't even Anna. Maybe a ghost had taken her place and was fooling him into believing that she was Anna, while the real Anna slowly went mad under the forest's dark influence. But no, that was ridiculous. If he needed any further proof of his own insanity, thoughts like that would certainly go a long way toward convincing him.

The inside was barely illuminated by red light through the open window frames. Rows of makeshift benches filled most of the room, leaving an open area in the front no larger than a parking space. A man was standing there, hands raised, apparently praying. Lars waited until the man finished his prayer and looked up.

"Elder Matthews, these are two new arrivals to the beach. They floated here on a tabletop."

"A wooden tabletop? Has it been reclaimed?"

"Yes, Elder."

"God is good. Brother Lars, return now to your good work. I will look after these two until the evening service. If you would step into my office, brother, sister."

He led them through another curtain into a tiny room barely large enough for the furniture inside it. Really, though, what was inside could hardly be called furniture. There were two overturned plastic crates that could be used as seating. In front of them was a table with a top made from a door and makeshift trestles for legs. The only piece of furniture that really deserved the name was a dramatic wingback armchair, upholstered in a crushed velvet that had seen better millennia and was now faded to a sort of sickly pale magenta. Elder Matthews sat in it.

"Can I take this thing off now?" Anna asked.

"Of course." The elder's smile reminded Jack of a used-car salesman.

Anna pushed the cloth back from her shoulders until it hung like a shawl.

"Now, I must ask, have you both been baptized?"

"Yes," said Anna.

"Yup," said Jack.

Anna turned in her seat to look at him. "Really?"

"Yes. Really. My mom was a Lutheran."

"You don't go to church."

"Not since we moved to Maine, but we used to, every Sunday."

Anna was still staring. "Really?"

"You don't know everything about me."

Anna bit her lip. "I never said I did."

"Yes, well," Elder Matthews broke in. "That is good. All that remains, then, is for you to be accepted into our community."

"Do we want to be?" Jack said.

Elder Matthews looked angry, but he covered it quickly.

Anna shrugged. "Why not?"

"Young brother, the Lord has brought you here for a reason. You and your friend are clearly believers. You see through the lie of this so-called afterlife and hunger for something more."

"A grilled cheese," Jack muttered.

Elder Matthews ignored this. These people seemed to be masters of ignoring things they didn't want to hear. Jack wondered if that was something else the elders would teach him.

Elder Matthews was trying to sound sympathetic. "I understand that you are feeling lost and confused. I was the same when I first arrived." He leaned forward on the desk, which rocked. "I died and there were no angels. Saint Michael did not appear. Even Jesus was suspiciously absent. Instead, there were doctors and clipboards and fields of hell-blasted sand. I was told that I should follow the pull of The City, follow my path, and all would be revealed. But through prayer and discernment I saw this for the lie it was, a ploy by the

Father of All Lies to waylay my soul. I left the Evil One's path and returned to the bright light of God's favor.

"You see, I had been a good man. I had lived my life in accordance with God's law. I would not allow the idol of The City to seduce me and rob me of my just reward. I was carried through the storm by the grace of God to this island." His voice rose and seemed to pull his hands up with it. "When I arrived here, I heard a voice, mighty as the wave crashing on the beach. It said 'Hush' and the storm faded, and I knew that I had heard the voice of God."

Elder Matthews leaned back in his chair. "There were others living inside the mountain, protected from God's rage. We recognized the folly of our former lives. All of us—Christians, heathens, Jews, and Muslims—realized that we had been led astray by our earthly churches and temples. Our religions had failed us. But together— together we built Haven, and here we pray and fast and follow the laws revealed to us in prayer.

"Here, we await the coming of our Lord. Here, we remain faithful until the true afterlife begins." With each *here* he jabbed the tabletop. "For it is written that in the last days, the Lord will come to us and bear us up to heaven while the unbelievers burn in their City of Ghosts."

"Where exactly is that written?" Jack asked.

"Here." Elder Matthews picked up from the desktop a folded-up newspaper that turned out to be a book made of yellowed newsprint and written in thick marker. The words *The Book of True Knowledge* were written over a news story headlined "Murder-Suicide Shocks Springfield."

Elder Matthews cradled the book in both hands. "Here is the accumulated knowledge of the afterlife as revealed to the true believers."

Jack opened his mouth to say something that he would probably regret later, but was interrupted by a bell ringing outside.

"Please excuse me," Elder Matthews said, standing. "I must go prepare for the evening service. I will return to guide you soon."

When he had gone, Jack whispered to Anna, "You don't believe any of this, do you?"

"Don't you believe in God?"

"Of course I do. You know I do. But this isn't God. This is crazy."

"They have a point, you know. Is this what you thought the afterlife would be? Has any story or myth or parable you've ever heard prepared you for a post-mortem that included an intake exam and a factory that went on forever and a phone booth to contact afterlife support?"

"Well, no, but I'm pretty sure the forest shows up in the *Inferno*. I only saw the *Wishbone* episode, but I'm fairly certain they mentioned some sort of evil forest that messed with your mind. And I know Charon is straight out of Greek mythology."

Anna waved all that away as if it were unimportant. "And where are the angels?"

"In The City, maybe? I don't know. Maybe there aren't any. How could any living person be certain what will happen in the afterlife? It's a one-way ticket, no survivors."

Anna sighed like an adult trying to explain causality to an overly inquisitive child. "We are dead. The people here are nice and they have weather. Haven't you missed weather? Besides, if it turns out to be too awful, we can always leave."

Inside a volcano with a bunch of religious fanatics who've built a city out of trash. What could go wrong? Jack winced, because he knew as well as anyone that thinking *what could go wrong* was like spitting in the face of a large, angry bully. Someone was going to get hurt, and it was going to be you. At least he hadn't said it out loud.

"Besides," Anna said. "What could go wrong?" Jack groaned and collapsed forward, until he was supporting his head in his hands.

"Jack, are you okay?"

Anna put her arm across his shoulder and rubbed the back of his neck, the way she used to when he got motion sickness on carnival rides. He slumped there, pretending they were sitting on a bench at the Bangor State Fair, and that he would open his eyes to the flashing lights and dirty asphalt of the midway.

Chapter Fifteen

Feeling Anna's hand drop away, Jack looked up to find Elder Matthews standing in the doorway, staring at them.

"Follow me, please. It's time for your presentation to the community."

Elder Matthews led them back into the church. A hundred and fifty or so people had gathered for the evening service. The women with their patched headscarves sat on the left. The men, bareheaded, sat on the right. There were no children—at least, none younger than Jack and Anna.

Elder Matthews brought Jack and Anna to the front of the room while the people watched, unmoving. He planted Jack on a stool facing the men and Anna in a chair facing the women. Standing between them, he addressed the congregation.

"We gather here together to welcome Jack and Anna into the arms of our community. Like us, they saw through the glamour of the world above, and like us, they will hasten the coming of the Lord by following his commands. To that end, the reading today will be the words of the Law."

Elder Matthews opened the newspaper book and began to read.

"'A lie is the work of the devil. Do not lie. Do not tell false tales. Engage not with works of fiction.

"'God is the only creator. Forgo mere copies of his great works. Do not paint. Do not sculpt. Do not build what is not needful.

"'Your body is pure; keep it so. Do not eat. Do not drink. Do not engage in sexual acts.'"

The voice droned on. In his head, Jack catalogued the do-nots: no eating, no drinking, no sex, no art, no stories. What did these people do for fun? He envisioned a group of believers sitting in a circle playing a game of never-have-I-ever. "Never have I ever taken the Lord's name in vain," someone would say. Those who had done it would raise their hands. Then, instead of getting a point, they'd be pelted with rocks.

Jack turned his attention back to Elder Matthews, who was still reading. "'Those who transgress must be punished. Accept your punishment willingly as judgment from the Lord. A sin by one is a sin by all. Speak out, that the sinner may be punished and the community cleansed.

"'Your life before is but the memory of a dream. Cling not to the past, but look to the future glory of the coming Lord.'"

Elder Matthews closed the book. "Do you, Anna, and you, Jack, affirm your commitment to follow these rules, now and to the end of days?"

"I do," Anna said.

"Do I?" said Jack.

He looked at Anna. She seemed unbothered by the litany of rules she had agreed to.

"I do," Jack said, even though he knew he didn't.

Elder Matthews spread his hands. "We welcome you, then, brother and sister, into the Community of the Law. May your lives here be filled with the love of the Lord."

The congregation said, "Amen." But to Jack, it sounded like a curse.

"Jack, you will go with Brother Joseph. Anna, you'll be staying with Sister Doris."

"You mean you're splitting us up?" Jack said. Anna, as was usual lately, seemed serene at the prospect. Her face was blank.

"Men and women do not live together in our society. It reduces temptation," the elder said. "You will see each other at prayers."

Anna waved to Jack as her new housemate led her out of the church.

~

Jack's new home was a ramshackle hut with a cardboard roof and rag curtains in the door and window. Joseph ushered Jack inside. The shack was a single room maybe ten feet square, with a few woven rugs on the stone floor. Joseph nodded to one of them. "You sleep there."

"Can I sleep?"

"It is time for sleep," Joseph said. He tromped over to his own rug, sat down, and began to take off his shoes. Another man ducked through the door. "Welcome, new brother. I am Alfonso." He was younger than Joseph, with an accent that Jack couldn't place. He proffered his hand for Jack to shake.

"Hi," Jack said. "Does this happen a lot? People coming to live with you?"

"God has provided plenty for all. We willingly share what we have with you." Alfonso closed the ragged curtain. The room dimmed, but Jack could still see outlines of red light around the doors and window.

Jack didn't feel sleepy, not at all, but homesickness was hitting him hard. He thought about his bedroom back home, with the hideous wood paneling and the weird ceiling slants that made him unable to stand upright in half the room. He thought about his closet, remembering the year when a family of birds had found their way in from the cold and built a nest in one of his old sneakers. He had found them only when the babies hatched and started chirping.

He passed the night that way, eyes wide open, staring into a personal hell of memories. His old life, his actual life, seemed perfect and beautiful and so very, very far away.

~

Eventually, a bell clanged in the distance. When Alfonso and Joseph both sat up and began to put on their shoes, Jack sprang up gratefully.

He followed his housemates into the streets. They led him to the church, which was once again packed with the faithful. Jack saw Anna sitting on the women's side, her head covered by a mostly blue scarf. Jack caught her eye. She gave him the tiniest wave.

"You okay?" Jack mouthed. She nodded in response.

Alfonso clasped Jack's shoulder. "You should pay attention. The service is about to start, and you don't want to miss anything."

A different elder led the prayers. "Hear, believers: the Lord our God, the Lord is one." He paused. The people echoed him.

"Holy be his name. The Lord is most great." Again the echo. Alfonso was declaiming the words loudly, his head thrown back, his eyes bright. Clearly he was a true believer. Jack sat beside him in silence. He didn't know the words. He didn't want to know the words.

At long last, the people answered, "Amen." Some of them stood up and began to leave the church. Jack stood, happy to follow them. Alfonso grabbed his wrist and pulled him back into his seat.

"We must stay a while longer, new brother."

"Why?" Jack asked.

"You must learn to breathe."

Jack closed his eyes for a second. This day was getting better and better.

A woman stood and moved to the front of the room. She had short gray hair and a smile that wouldn't have looked out of place on a cartoon villain.

"For the benefit of our new brother and sister, let me reintroduce myself. I am Elder Salma, and I am here to teach you about the breath.

"In our former lives, breathing posed no challenges. In fact, when something was described as 'easy as breathing,' it was understood that this was an easy thing indeed. However, the Lord in his wisdom sees fit to test us in this new world, and breath has become a challenge. It is not needed by the body, so the body does not bother with it. It is, however, needed by the soul. And so we begin by breathing in-two-three and out-two-three and in—"

This place seemed designed to drive you insane, Jack thought. If Anna was right and he wasn't already crazy, he would be after another day or two of this.

After breathing class, the bell rang again. The church filled. It was time for prayers. While everyone else prayed along with the elder, Jack prayed that breathing class was over for the day.

His prayer was granted. Alfonso led him outside, where a man in a blue jacket assigned Jack and Anna to a work group. Apparently, some of the townspeople had forgone the thrills of breathing to sort through the material that had been gathered from the beach the day before. The work group's job was to wander around the place, fixing broken or unstable shacks.

As he worked, he stole glances at Anna. She had pushed her headscarf back onto her shoulders, but she was wearing a ragged piece of fabric around her waist like a skirt. He wondered where she had gotten it, and why in God's name she would wear such a thing.

When no one was looking, he sidled up to her.

"Hey, how are you?" he said.

"Great. My housemates are really nice. That's one of them over there, Laura."

She didn't look great.

"What's with the dirty bedsheet?"

"It's a skirt. The girls thought it would be better for me not to flaunt my legs in public."

"Flaunt your legs?" Jack ruffled his fingers through his hair, trying to rearrange his thoughts. He couldn't deal with this right now. "Did you sleep?"

Anna shook her head. "I don't think anyone really sleeps. I don't think we can, but it was nice to lie in the dark for a while and think about things."

"It was?" Jack said.

"Yeah. I mean, I guess around the middle of the night it got kind of boring, but—"

"Hey, you two." Their supervisor strode toward them. "You don't need to talk to fix that window frame. In fact, Sister Anna, go help the girls with the roof project."

Anna started away from Jack. He grabbed her wrist. "Anna, wait."

Something whipped through his line of vision and smacked his forearm. It didn't hurt, but it startled him, and he let Anna go. She slipped away.

The supervisor lowered her stick. She said something, but Jack wasn't listening. He was staring after Anna. She'd run away, left him, because someone had told her to. He felt like he was lost at sea again, only it was worse this time because Anna wasn't there. She'd swum away and left him floating on the tabletop all alone, and he had no idea how to get back to shore.

"Brother Jack, are you listening?"

Jack dragged his attention back to the supervisor. "What?"

"I said, it might be best for you to go and see Elder Matthews. He can be a great help to new members as they adjust to the community."

Here one day and he was already being sent to the principal's office. Maybe he'd be lucky enough to get expelled. That was a comforting thought. He only hoped Anna would come along with him if that happened. The thought chilled him. He'd never before had to wonder if Anna would stick with him. He didn't like that he was wondering about it now.

On his way to Elder Matthews's office, Jack stopped to watch the man standing next to the bell tower. He held the bell pull in one hand. The other was resting on the hourglass. He was watching it closely. At the instant the last grain of sand fell through to the bottom, he flipped the glass.

"What are you doing?" Jack asked.

The man glanced briefly at him, then back to the hourglass. "I'm keeping the hours, so we know when to pray and when to sleep."

"You stand here all day?"

"There are other timekeepers. We each take our turn. Is there something you wanted, Brother?"

"No, I just wondered."

"You're the new one. Jake."

"Jack."

The timekeeper's eyes flicked toward him and away. "Right. You came with the girl. Be careful that she doesn't lead you into wickedness. A sin by one is a sin by all."

"I'll, um—I'll do that. Sorry to bother you." Jack hurried into the darkness of the church.

Inside, he stopped outside Elder Matthews's curtain. He didn't know what the protocol was here. He couldn't knock on the door, because there wasn't one, and he was afraid to knock on the wall in case the whole building came down. He cleared his throat. "Excuse me, Brother Matthews."

"Come in. Ah, young brother Jack. You should be at work with the repair crews, I believe. Have you had some trouble? Do sit down."

Jack took a seat on one of the overturned milk crates. "I was talking to Anna, and my supervisor hit me with a stick."

"I see. There's no need to be upset, Brother. New members to our community often have a difficult time adjusting. The spirit is willing, but the flesh is weak, as we used to say." Elder Matthews smiled. "That is why you have those set above you who are wiser and more experienced.

"Your supervisor is merely trying to help you let go of your previous relationships. It is better that you not concern yourself with a female even though you once called her friend. As the Book of the Law says, 'Temptation is all around you. Be on your guard. Let no sin enter your heart.' Do you understand?"

Jack understood. He understood that this place was poison. He'd give Anna another day or two to snap out of it, and then they were leaving, even if he had to carry her.

~

Another night came. At least, they said it was night. Jack had no way of knowing, since he hadn't been allowed outside. Allowed? Was that the right word? Was he being kept here, like a prisoner? Surely he could go outside if he wanted to. He sat up.

As far as he could tell, Alfonso and Joseph were both contentedly faking sleep. At least, they were lying on their backs with their eyes closed. As quietly as he could, Jack eased his way over to the door. He almost expected Joseph to jump up and grab him, but he was able to slip outside without anyone apparently noticing.

Already he was getting used to the red light of the cavern. He could see clear down the street, almost to the church. He could even see the timekeeper, a black form against the red glow. Damn. Jack ducked between two shacks. If he had seen the timekeeper, maybe the timekeeper had seen him.

He looked both ways. There was no one around. Still, he walked as quietly as he could, letting only the balls of his bare feet touch the warm rock of the cave floor. He was almost to the end of the line of huts when he heard a noise. He stopped and tilted his head, waiting for the sound. There it was. A swish. Like a broom across a tile floor.

Jack leaned carefully around the corner of the nearest hut and came face-to-face with a man. Jack swallowed a shout, muffling it to a hollow squeak. The man's eyes widened. He pressed his finger to his lips and motioned at Jack to follow him.

When they were well away from the huts, and presumably out of the earshot of any counterfeit sleepers, the man whispered, "Who are you?"

"I'm Jack. Who are you?"

"I am the groundskeeper. I sweep the streets."

Jack inspected the man. He was bald and clean shaven, making his head look like a jack-o'-lantern with a broken stem, and he was indeed holding a broom.

"At night?" Jack said.

"I don't want to disturb anybody. You shouldn't be out and about at this hour. If the elders find out . . ."

"You won't tell, will you? I only wanted to go outside for a minute. Just to see what it's like."

The groundskeeper smiled. He was missing at least three teeth. "All right, then, but let's go quietly. Someone might be snooping." He put one finger on the side of his nose, a ridiculous gesture that Jack had seen only in illustrations of *The Night Before Christmas*.

"These believers love to play spy on your neighbor," the groundskeeper said.

He led Jack up the ramp, through the low cave and out onto the beach. It really was nighttime. The beach was dark and silent, with only a distant moon to cast a ray of silver across the waves. "No stars," Jack said.

The groundskeeper grimaced. "The stars are dead. Long dead." His voice was low and pained.

"They say," Jack said, "that because the stars are so far away, the stars we see from earth could be dead, and we would never know it, because the human race will be gone before their last echo reaches us."

The groundskeeper said nothing, but swept some sand off a rock with his broom and sat down.

Jack continued, still looking up, "You'd think they'd be up there. Wouldn't you? This is the afterlife. What better place for dead stars."

"Oh, they are up there," the groundskeeper said. "But dead stars can't shine. They're up there, cold and silent and invisible."

"That's awful." Jack paused, and then said, "What about the sun? The sun is a star."

The groundskeeper shrugged. "You saw a light in the sky. How do you know it is the sun?"

"It looked like the sun."

"You look like a believer, yet you are not one of them."

"Yes I am."

The groundskeeper smiled at Jack's nervous expression. "I'll tell you a secret." He leaned closer. "Neither am I."

Jack slumped down on a rock. "My friend Anna, she brought me here. But it isn't right. We shouldn't be here."

"But you are here, and this is where you are."

All the protests Jack had been swallowing down for the last two days came out at once. "Dead stars can't shine. Dead humans can't die. Heaven, hell, punishment, reward." He flung his hands out. "Why does it matter now? No one's playing tricks on us. No one's testing our faith. The path was right there, and we stepped off it, all on our own."

The groundskeeper rocked back and put his hands on his knees. "You can go back if you want. No one is watching."

"I can't leave her."

"You love her."

"What? No, I . . . I mean yes, sure, she's my best friend."

"She's your soul mate."

"That too," Jack said. He looked up at the sky, imagining the dead stars looking down at him. Each one was a tiny dark core of emptiness, aching for the good times when it was burning and alive. Now, it could only suck dust from the darkness, like a bitter old woman slurping the last sludgy dregs of tea from the bottom of the cup.

"Time we went back inside." The groundskeeper stood. He put his hand on Jack's shoulder. "People come here, and yes, people leave.

But they all come for a reason. Sometimes the best thing you can do for a person you love is allow them the time to find their reason."

~

The next day, as Jack left the church to join his work crew, Elder Matthews stepped out of the shadows. Reflexively, Jack shied backward away from him.

"I didn't mean to startle you, young brother. I merely think we should have a conversation. Could you come with me, please?" He led the way into the building without waiting for an answer.

Jack trailed along behind. Second time to the principal's office in two days. That had to be a record.

Anna flashed him a worried look as he passed her. Jack smiled and opened his hand in a placating gesture. She bit her lip.

In the office, with the curtain drawn shut behind them, Elder Matthews motioned for him to sit. As the elder settled into the big armchair on the other side of the desk, Jack wondered how the thing had gotten here. It couldn't possibly have floated.

"Young brother Jack, I have heard that you went out on a midnight excursion."

So the timekeeper had seen him. He'd have to be more careful next time. Jack deployed his default talking-to-authority-figures strategy, which consisted of agreeing with anything they said but giving nothing away. "Was that okay?"

"We have a curfew for a reason, Brother Jack."

Jack wanted to ask what reason that was exactly, but instead he said, "I'm sorry, I didn't realize."

"Alone in the dark, in the night, men's thoughts turn to . . . unwholesome things. It is best to remain at home, where you will not be tempted."

"I'll keep that in mind."

"You were alone, Brother?" The elder paused. "Not meeting anyone."

Somehow Jack thought Elder Matthews would not approve of his conversation with the groundskeeper. It was possible that he didn't even know the man existed. If that was true, Jack wasn't going to be the one to out him.

"Who would I be meeting?"

"You came here with a— a female."

Jack was surprised. This wasn't at all what he'd thought he was getting in trouble for. Maybe Elder Matthews wasn't as on top of things as he thought.

"Yes, but I'm not sneaking out in the night to see Anna," Jack said. "I was curious to see if it was really dark outside. Where we were before it never got dark."

Elder Matthews leaned forward. He looked skeptical. "That is good to hear, Brother. Please understand, we do not wish to infringe on your freedom in any way, but we must protect the community. A sin by one is a sin by all."

"Yes, sir, I understand."

"Very well, Brother, you may go."

Jack made it to the door before Elder Matthews added, "And Brother? Stay away from the groundskeeper. He is essentially harmless, but a little . . . I believe the kind word is *slow*. One never knows what he might do."

Jack nodded, not trusting himself to speak. He had no idea if Elder Matthews actually knew he had spoken to the groundskeeper or if he only suspected. Strange that Jack hadn't even thought to ask the man's name. Maybe he would let another night or two go by to give things time to settle down, and then he would go and find the groundskeeper again.

~

Michael showed up his usual fifteen minutes early for the morning shift at the doughnut shop. The overnight guys, the ones who actually made the doughnuts, had already gone home. That was fine with him. Michael liked the shop best when it was empty. Nobody had burned any coffee yet, so the air was full of the smell of doughnuts. And the music hadn't been turned on, so the only sound was the hum of the refrigerators. It was peaceful.

The only other person in the shop was Trevor, the manager. Generally speaking, Trevor wasn't a big talker, which Michael liked. He also trusted Michael to show up and do his job, which Michael liked even more.

After two months, Michael knew the opening procedures by heart. Normally, he and Trevor didn't bother to say more than hello to each other until the pre-commuter rush. But not today. Today, Trevor spoke to Michael as soon as he walked through the door.

"Michael, you didn't need to come in today." He was standing behind the cash register reconciling the drawer before they opened.

"I'm on the schedule."

"I got Cassie to cover for you."

Michael sighed. That would be the day. Cassie couldn't cover for anyone. On any team you cared to mention, every other person in the group would be covering for her. Not only was she chronically late, but she tended to get overwhelmed and let the coffee burn anytime they had more than three people in the line.

"You really didn't have to do that. I would have called if I wasn't coming in."

"I just thought . . ."

Michael didn't let him finish. He ducked into the back room to put his stuff away and get water for the coffee. Trevor got the hint and shut up.

They did their opening work in silence. When it was done, and just before Trevor unlocked the front door, he said, "I was sorry to hear about your sister. If you need some time off . . ."

Michael winced. He didn't want people making a big fuss about everything. He was fine. Everything was fine.

"I'm here to do my job. The quality of my work isn't going to suffer. I promise."

"That's not what I'm worried about," Trevor said, but he dropped the subject. He opened the doors one minute late.

Five minutes after opening time Cassie showed up. She and Trevor had a whispered conversation. Michael couldn't hear what they were saying, but he saw Cassie looking at him. He wished Trevor had left well enough alone.

Michael handed his customer a perfect chai latte. He put on his best customer service smile to show Trevor how completely fine and not in need of any sort of special treatment he was. Trevor was being dense on purpose.

"Michael, why don't you let Cassie take over the register?"

"You want me on drive-through?"

"No, I've got it. You just make the drink orders."

Michael didn't argue. This was fine. Everything was fine. He was better at dealing with customers than Cassie was, but at least if he was mixing drinks, the coffee wouldn't be so strong you could chew it.

Cassie managed to hold it together until Josh came in at ten thirty. Again, there was a whispered conversation with glances in Michael's direction. This time he clearly heard his own name and Anna's.

He wished they'd shut up. It was none of their business. His life was none of their business. But he was just going to ignore them. He focused on getting the drink orders exactly right. It wasn't hard. He had all the recipes memorized, and he knew better than to rush. He was faster overall when he did each step deliberately.

He handed an iced coffee with cream across the counter to a girl with a pair of Ray-Bans perched on her head.

"Um, does this have milk in it?"

"Yes."

"I asked for whipped cream, not milk."

"Oh, sorry." Michael started to take the cup back from her. "Let me just add some."

"No, you can't just add some. I'm lactose intolerant. I can't have milk. You'll have to make it all over again."

Michael blinked at her. He wanted to scream. He wanted to throw the drink in her perfectly made-up face. He wanted to explain to her very slowly and with pictures that whipped cream and milk both came from a cow and that therefore, she was a brain-dead bimbo who didn't deserve the life she was currently wasting on self-entitled bitchery.

He took a deep breath. "Of course," he said. "Let me just fix that for you."

She released the cup. Michael pitched the whole thing in the garbage and started over. Even with her glaring over the counter at him, he didn't rush. He did each step deliberately. Rushing got you into trouble. He handed her the fresh drink.

She pulled her sunglasses down over her eyes. "It's about time." She left.

Josh sidled over. "Holy shit, man. What a bitch."

"Josh, language," Trevor said.

"Seriously?"

"What if another customer overhears you?"

"They'd probably agree with him," Cassie said.

"There's nobody in the shop," Josh said.

"Still," Trevor said. "But Michael, you handled that very well. Why don't you take your fifteen-minute break now?"

"Yeah, okay."

Normally, Michael took his break at the table in the back room. That way he was within earshot if things got busy and they needed him. Today, he went out the back door. There was a picnic table there.

Theoretically, it was for employees to eat lunch on, but it tended to be used more commonly as a smoking area.

Michael sat on the bench with his back to the table and set his lunchbox down beside him. He was facing the outer wall of the shop. It was better than facing the road. There weren't very many cars passing. But those that did flew by so fast.

The traffic was getting bad around here. This morning, when he'd tried to turn onto Route 7, it had taken him forever to find a break in traffic wide enough for him to turn safely. He'd actually worried he might be late to work. And then when he finally had turned, a car had honked at him, as though going the speed limit was some sort of inconvenience for them.

He pulled a yogurt out of his lunchbox. When he tried to open it, the foil lid refused to separate from the plastic cup. He pulled extra hard. The two separated with force, sloshing yogurt over his hands.

Michael looked down at the mess. He hurled the cup full of yogurt at the wall of the shop. The yogurt splattered in a sunburst pattern. The cup thunked to the ground. Michael smashed it flat with the heel of his shoe.

Then he went inside to wash his hands. When he came back into the shop, Trevor said, "That wasn't fifteen."

"It's fine," Michael said. "Everything is fine."

Chapter Sixteen

After a fun-filled day of breathing practice and repairing houses, Jack retired to his hut. For a change of pace, he lay down on his stomach and ran his fingers over the woven pattern of his sleeping mat. Finally, driven by boredom, he attempted conversation.

"Alfonso, where did you live before?"

"Idle chatter is wasteful. There is no need to talk about things long past," Alfonso said. He was smiling as he said it, but it was not his usual friendly smile.

"I lived in this tiny town in Maine," Jack said. "It used to be a mill town, but they closed it, and the government gave us millions of dollars to clean up the filth it left behind."

"It is time for sleep now," Joseph broke in. He jerked the curtain closed.

"I was only—"

"Now."

Jack heard him stomp across the room and lie down with an unnecessary amount of huffing for someone who didn't have to breathe. Jack rolled over and clasped his hands behind his head. He wondered if he should go find the groundskeeper tonight. What was the worst Elder Matthews could do to him?

He sat up. Joseph shifted on his mat. Jack lay down again. He obviously couldn't leave yet. Joseph was sure to shout the hut down if he noticed Jack sneaking out. Not that it would take much effort; it wasn't particularly sturdy to begin with. He wished he had a pillow—not that he actually needed one. He wasn't uncomfortable, but he felt awkward, like if he could see himself, he would look uncomfortable.

He folded his arms behind his head and set his mind free to wander through his memories, nudging it now and then to keep it away from the more unpleasant bits. If he let himself, he could still picture the version of the accident his uncle had shown him over and over. But he wasn't going to let himself. Instead he thought about the first time he had gone to a dance with Anna. It was the eighth-grade semiformal, and his dad had decided that the only appropriate thing to do was rent his son a tux for the occasion. He had been so proud to see Jack going to a dance with a real, live, and actually pretty, girl.

Anna had a picture of them somewhere, middle-school Jack and Anna, round-faced and oh-so-young-looking, standing arm in arm in front of the school, dressed up like grown-ups in a tux and gown. He had even given Anna a corsage, which had made her laugh in surprise. She'd been happy then. He missed seeing her happy.

He sat up again. He had to get Anna off this island. Maybe the groundskeeper could help smuggle them away. He seemed to have more or less free rein over the place at night. Alfonso and Joseph didn't stir as Jack crept outside.

This time he kept away from the center of town, out of sight of the timekeeper. Every few steps he stopped to listen for the sweep of the groundskeeper's broom. Eventually, Jack sighted him at the outer edge of the town, close to the cave mouth.

The groundskeeper smiled when he saw Jack, and beckoned him closer. Jack looked around to make sure no one was watching and then cut across the street. The bell began to ring. Jack jumped. They'd caught him. He was going to be punished with double breathing practice or forbidden from seeing Anna or— The groundskeeper grabbed his arm.

"You must return to your home, quickly."

"I'm in trouble."

"No. Someone else is. Go now." He pushed Jack back the way he'd come and darted away in the opposite direction. Jack ran for his shack, reaching it at the instant Joseph pulled aside the curtain. They stood eye to eye for a moment.

"Where have you been, Brother?"

"I—I wanted to pray, and I didn't want to bother you, so I went outside. What's going on?"

Joseph looked as though he didn't believe the lie, but he didn't press the issue. "Another night alarm," he said.

The bell was still ringing. Jack didn't know what a night alarm was, but it had to be better than sleeping. He followed Joseph and Alfonso away from the hut.

When they reached the church, the entire town was crowded around a small tableau outside the doorway. The timekeeper had both hands on the bell pull. To her left, Elder Matthews stood between a pair of large men. The heavies were more than six feet tall and built like football players, not exactly low profile, yet Jack had never seen them before. He wondered where they'd been hiding.

Each held a struggling captive. One was a man, sans pants, his smiley-face boxers exposed for all to see. The other was a woman, her top three buttons undone, her hair escaping from her ponytail.

Elder Matthews gestured, and the ringing, mercifully, stopped. "Brothers and sisters," he shouted. "These two stand accused of breaking the Law of the Lord."

The crowd murmured. Jack tore his eyes away from the scene to search for Anna. He found her far on the other side of the semicircle, between her housemates. She hadn't seen him yet.

"They were caught in the act of sexual congress." The crowd groaned. "Who will bear witness to their sin?"

Two women and a man stepped into the open space before the crowd. "I will," they said together. This was clearly a well-practiced ritual.

Jack shuddered. He felt as though he had wandered into an open-air performance of *The Crucible*. He started to inch his way through the crowd toward Anna.

"Their sin has been witnessed, and they must be punished," Elder Matthews said.

Jack fought to keep Anna in sight through the jostling crush of people. Everyone was trying to get closer to the action.

"A sin by one is a stain on us all. Bring the stocks," Elder Matthews said.

Jack didn't like the sound of that. He didn't like the sound of that at all. The two heavies disappeared into the church, leaving their captives standing beside Elder Matthews. Jack wondered why they didn't try to run. He thought he would have.

"Do you confess your sins before this, your community?" Elder Matthews asked.

The woman shouted, "I do, I do."

The man answered so quietly, Jack barely heard him. "I do."

A hand closed over Jack's. He jolted. It was Anna. She didn't look at him—her eyes were on the scene—but her hand gripped his tightly.

"Then bear your punishment for the good of the many," Elder Matthews said.

The heavies were back, each carrying an armful of wooden planks. Elder Matthews placed his hand on the woman's head. She sank to her knees on the stone floor of the cavern. The heavies closed in around her.

Anna squeezed Jack's hand tighter and tighter. When the heavies stepped back, the woman was wearing a yoke that enclosed her neck and wrists. A smaller piece of wood was locked around both ankles. She might have been able to stand if she'd tried, but walking would have been impossible.

As the heavies converged on the man, Jack leaned close to Anna and whispered, "Have you seen enough? Can we leave now?"

She looked at him, her face inches from his. Her eyes were sad and frightened. At least they weren't blank. She opened her mouth to say something but stopped when Joseph dropped a heavy hand on Jack's shoulder.

"Come away from her now," he said in a low voice, "or it'll be your punishment we come to see tomorrow."

Jack didn't say anything. He didn't have to. Anna had already scurried away into the crowd.

~

Back in his hut, Jack lay awake, staring at the ceiling. It was all he could do to keep himself from fidgeting. He'd seen the look in Anna's eyes. If he could find a way to get to her, he was almost certain she'd leave this place with him. He wished he could be completely certain.

Someone pulled aside the curtain and looked in on them. "Brother Jack, come with me, please."

Jack sat up. He couldn't see the man's face in the dim light. "Who are you?" he asked.

"Elder Matthews sent me. He wants to speak to you before morning bell."

Jack glanced at Joseph. Had he tattled to Elder Matthews about Jack's conversation with Anna? Joseph lay still on his mat, as though he were actually asleep and hadn't noticed a stranger walking into their hut without knocking. Alfonso rolled over to face the wall.

Jack got up and followed the other man out of the hut and toward the church. They passed the prisoners, kneeling by the church's front door. The man glanced up for a second, but the woman didn't even move as they went by. Jack's guide ignored them and walked through the church and into Elder Matthews's office without knocking. Apparently, privacy wasn't a big concern around here.

"Thank you, Brother Shamus," Elder Matthews said. "You may go back to your duties now. Sit down, Brother Jack."

The smile Elder Matthews wore this morning was even less convincing than usual. It reminded Jack of the guidance counselor from his elementary school, the one who'd talked to him about fitting in and the difference between fantasy and reality. Every time Jack had been sent to him, his smile had become more and more brittle, until Jack imagined it would explode into tiny shards if someone said one more word about dreams.

Elder Matthews leaned his elbows on his desk and steepled his fingers. "I'm sure you remember our conversation about the groundskeeper. He is not a suitable companion for a young brother of our community."

Jack said nothing.

Elder Matthews went on. "I'm also sure you remember that you took a vow when you joined our community. You promised to obey those set above you and follow the Law of the Book."

Again, Jack said nothing.

Elder Matthews sighed. "Brother Jack, a sin by one is a sin by all. You are no longer a lonely human lost in a wicked world. Your stubbornness affects us all. Especially your friend Anna."

Jack leaned forward. His hands tightened into fists. He wasn't going to let the elder drag Anna into this. If anyone was going to be punished, it would be him and him alone.

"Anna follows the rules," he said.

"She does, for now. But I wonder how long that will last with your constant attempts to lead her astray."

Jack sat back. He wasn't going to try to argue. It would only make things worse.

Elder Matthews stared at him for a moment as though he had expected a response. Outside, the bell rang. Elder Matthews surrendered and got up. "Come. It is time for prayer. Afterward I think it might be best that you see what happens to those who do not remain true to the Law of the Lord."

Jack didn't like the sound of that. He followed Elder Matthews into the church. Anna looked surprised and then worried at seeing him with Elder Matthews again. He smiled, faking confidence to calm her. It didn't seem to do any good.

Jack took his place between Alfonso and Joseph. The prayers dragged on forever. Jack didn't even try to listen. He sat on the bench, clutching the seat with both hands. Clearly there were worse punishments than the stocks. He tried to imagine what they could be. In a world where there was no discomfort, no pain, no death, what could they possibly do to him? Except separate him from Anna. They could do that. They could lock him in a tiny cave, too small to stand up in. They could roll a stone in front of the door and leave him there, alone in the dark for days or weeks, unable to sleep or starve.

Lost deep in his imagining, Jack nearly missed the moment when Elder Matthews lowered his hands and the congregation fell silent. When the quiet finally reached him, Jack raised his eyes to the front of the room. Elder Matthews was staring at him. Jack held his gaze. He wasn't going to give Matthews the satisfaction of looking frightened.

"Brothers and sisters, our community is strong. To remain so, we must trust in the Law of the Lord. Those who do not follow the Law must be corrected to protect the good of the community. It is time again that we remind ourselves of consequences of our sinful acts, that we might better protect ourselves against the snares of the Evil One."

The congregation stood as though by some signal Jack hadn't seen. He jumped up beside Alfonso.

"What's going on?" Jack asked.

"We're going to the pits."

Jack closed his eyes for an instant, trying to hold back images of dark holes, boiling lava, and swirling mist. He felt the same sense of plummeting inevitability as when Anna had grabbed his hand and jumped off the cliff. Maybe he wasn't really here. Maybe they were still falling, would keep falling forever, and his mind was creating this delusion to fill the time until eternity. He wished it could have found something better. He opened his eyes and followed Alfonso and the others out of the church.

They walked through the streets and past the rows of shacks to the empty space on the edge of town. Here a river of lava moved sluggishly. Now and then it sent up a thick bubble that popped soundlessly. The air seemed to shimmer, made thick with the rising heat.

On this side of the cave, the ceiling sloped drastically. A series of metal hooks were bolted to the stone. A rope was looped through one of them. One end was tied around a rock on the shoreline. The other disappeared into the lava. As Jack and the others watched, one of the heavies picked up the rope and heaved on it. Slowly, something rose out of the lava.

Jack looked around for Anna. She was standing near her roommates. When their eyes met, she began to creep away from them. He sidled toward her, pretending to be jockeying for a better view, trying to move nonchalantly out of Joseph's line of sight.

When they were close enough to speak, Anna whispered, "What *is* that?"

Jack looked up at the thing being pulled toward the ceiling. It was about the size and shape of a dishwasher. As the lava fell away, Jack saw that it was a wire cage—the kind you might kennel a Rottweiler in. There was a person inside, sitting with her arms wrapped around her knees and her head down on top of them. She raised her head, and pawed at her eyes and ears, trying to clear the lava from them.

"Oh my God," Anna said.

Jack imagined being trapped under the lava for days or weeks. It would be utterly silent and darker than anything, darker than the cave, darker than the forest. He would be blind and deaf. The lava would press around him, boiling, thick, cutting off all other sensation. He took Anna's hand.

Elder Matthews spoke to the woman. "Sister Andrea, you have sinned against your community and against your God. You have preached false laws and encouraged discord among the people. But the mercy of God is available even to you. Once again, we come to offer you redemption. Will you repent for your sin?"

Blinking, Sister Andrea looked at the gathered crowd. Her eyes settled on Elder Matthews at the front of the group. She pushed her hair back from her face, sending clumps of lava splattering in all directions. Her expression was serene and a little sad.

"I will not." Her voice carried easily across the crowd. The people muttered. Sister Andrea sat with her hands folded in her lap. "I have done nothing outside the will of God. I will not be bullied into false testimony. Not even by you."

Elder Matthews shook his head sadly. He gestured to the heavies. "Then you must continue to serve your penance for another year."

The cage lowered slowly toward the lava pit.

"People of the Law, listen to me." Andrea's voice was low and calm. "You were all given a path to follow, and you left it of your own accord, but it is still there, waiting. Stop hiding in this pit and go out into the world."

Anna squeezed Jack's hand and then let go. Jack looked around, expecting to see someone watching them, but all eyes were on Andrea. When he turned back, Anna was gone. She was drifting backward through the crowd. Jack followed, carefully. They were going to get out of here today.

Andrea continued. "This is not a test of your faith. It is a test of your character. Faced with the unknown, will you cower behind your man-made laws? Or will you go boldly down the path that God has created for you?" Her hands clutched the bars of her cage.

All around Jack, the people muttered to each other. He was almost to the back of the crowd. He tried not to bump into anyone, while keeping his eyes on Andrea. Her cage had reached the surface of the lava and was now sinking like a boot in a mud pit. "Go," she said, and Jack felt that she was talking directly to him.

Jack looked around. There was no one at his back. He was out of the crush of people. Anna took his hand again. "Ready to go?" she whispered.

"Been ready."

They ran. They ran past piles of trash stacked for processing. They ran past rows of ramshackle houses. They ran past the church and the bell tower. And then Andrea's voice echoed through the cavern. "Run!"

Jack looked over his shoulder. The heavies were hurrying toward him. They did not look happy. "Faster," he told Anna. She let go of his hand and ran ahead of him.

Streets, houses, trash. The sound of the heavies' shoes hitting the ground behind them. Andrea, shouting, her words no longer coherent. Anna was at the ramp now, waiting for him.

"Go," he said.

"I'm sorry."

"No time." He reached her, pushed her forward. "Go."

She bounded up the ramp. Jack looked over his shoulder again. The heavies were still coming, maybe twenty feet back, with a small group of believers behind them. He looked around wildly for something, anything to slow them down, but there was nothing. He gave up and ran.

Chapter Seventeen

The sun was too bright after the darkness of the tunnel. Jack blinked, trying to force his eyes to focus. He heard Anna screech. He knew they were caught. They would be dragged back down into the dark. The heavies would stuff them into cages, hook them to the pulleys, lower them into the pits. They would sink slowly. Hot molten rock would rise around them, pressing in on all sides, blinding, deafening.

He turned, ready to fight. Anna was standing on the rocks above the cave mouth, the groundskeeper next to her.

"Who are you?" she asked.

"That way," the groundskeeper said. He swept her aside and then extended his hand toward Jack. "Come on."

The voices of the heavies echoed up the passage as Jack partly climbed and partly was pulled up the rock face. As soon as Jack's feet touched stone, the groundskeeper took off after Anna. Jack followed.

Anna kept looking over her shoulder. Frightened of what he would see, Jack glanced back too. The townspeople were on the beach, bunched together, some of them with an arm raised to block the sun.

A hand grabbed Jack's arm. He managed not to scream. The groundskeeper tugged him sideways behind a boulder large enough to hide all three of them.

"They probably won't look up," the groundskeeper said. "But just in case, try to stay behind the rocks as much as possible."

"Who—" Anna began, but the groundskeeper shushed her. She glared at Jack, as though it was somehow his fault, but she shushed, which bothered him. He'd somehow hoped that if he could get her out of that cave, she'd go back to normal.

They ducked from boulder to boulder until they reached one below the bowl of the volcano. There was no cover ahead. They'd be out in the open for the few minutes it would take to reach the other side. Jack looked back. The believers had fanned out across the beach. As far as he could tell, no one had spotted them yet.

"When I say go," the groundskeeper said, "go quickly. Stay as low as you can. Don't. Stop."

He peeked around the boulder and seemed satisfied by what he saw. "Ready? Go."

Bent at the waist, Jack stumbled forward. Anna was beside him, also bent and moving awkwardly. The distance stretched into miles. All it would take was one glance, one believer looking up instead of down. With every step he expected to hear someone shout, "There they are!" But the cry never came.

They made it to the downward slope. Jack straightened up, slowed down. They couldn't see him now.

The groundskeeper prodded Jack with a forefinger. "Keep moving. They'll work their way around to this side of the island eventually."

Jack picked up his pace again. It was a struggle to stay on his feet. Scree kept shifting under him. He knew he could have rolled the rest of the way with no fear of breaking a bone or even getting a scratch, but somehow he couldn't convince his mind that falling was okay. He fought to stay upright.

They were headed for a narrow beach, a small oblong of sand with a long, low boulder in the middle of it. As they got closer, Jack realized that the boulder was actually a rowboat lying spine side up.

The groundskeeper went to it and flipped it over. There were oars underneath. "Here, help me get her to the water."

Jack picked up the other end of the boat, and, with Anna carrying the oars behind them, they moved it to the shoreline. Jack climbed in.

Anna hovered on the beach, an oar in each hand. "We can't take your boat."

"Don't you know how to row? It isn't hard."

"I mean, if we take your boat, you'll be stuck here." She tried to offer the oars back, but the groundskeeper shook his head.

"I'm not stuck," he said. "Now get in, before Matthews thinks to look for me. Row with the sun behind you. When you get to the other shore, put the oars in the boat and push her into the current. She'll float back to me."

"Thank you, Mr. . . . ." Anna said.

"I'm just the groundskeeper," he said, and pushed the boat into the shallows.

Anna set the oars in their locks and began to row. Jack turned in his seat and waved. The groundskeeper waved back.

"I hope he doesn't get into trouble because of us," Jack said.

"Do you know who he was?"

"Not really. He's been there a long time, I think. Maybe since the beginning."

"If he runs around helping people escape, I wonder why they don't stick him in a cage like Andrea," Anna said.

"That's exactly what I'm worried about."

They both fell silent. The groundskeeper seemed like he could take care of himself, but Jack hoped the man had a place to hide out until things blew over.

Something clanked against the side of the boat. Jack reached over the side and came up with a rusted tuna can. He threw it back. The townspeople would probably find some use for it.

"They're still looking for us," Anna said.

Jack turned. Anna's rowing had brought them around to the other side of the island. He could see people moving on the beach and climbing the rocks.

"They won't follow us, will they?" Jack said.

"I don't think so. My roommates told me that they're not supposed to go into the water because it's unclean."

"But that's how they got to the island in the first place," Jack said.

"Yeah, well, don't start looking for sense now." Anna sighed. That seemed to be all she had to say on the subject.

Jack, on the other hand, had a lot to say, but he wasn't quite sure how to start. *What the hell were you thinking?* probably wouldn't get him anywhere. He tried a more subtle tack.

"So," he said after a while. "That was . . . different."

"Yup."

He waited. Anna rowed. He tried again. "Maybe I wasn't paying close enough attention, but why were we there, again?"

"The storm brought us there, remember?"

She had to be misunderstanding him on purpose. There was no way she'd changed this much in three days. Jack felt frustration rising. She'd dragged him off the path, made him join a cult, and almost gotten him buried alive in lava, and she couldn't even give him a straight answer as to why.

"No, you brought us there. Why?" There, that was direct enough.

She shook her head as though she wasn't going to answer him, but almost immediately said, "It was nice in a way—"

"Nice?"

"To have rules again, rules that didn't change. It was nice to belong somewhere. You know?"

He semiseriously wondered if they'd switched her for a clone when he wasn't looking. "I'm sorry, do I know you? Since when do you like rules?"

"Rules are good. They keep you grounded."

"And they give you something to break every now and then," Jack said.

Anna smiled. It was a sad smile, but Jack would take what he could get.

"That too," Anna said.

"You're good now, though, right?"

Anna shrugged. "I'm not going back, if that's what you mean. Watching my best friend drown in lava isn't my idea of fun."

"What makes you so sure I'd be the one in the cage?"

"You were in trouble every day."

"Maybe, but only because you were acting like a crazy person."

Her voice rose. "I was—?" She stopped. "You're right. Sorry."

Jack stared at her. Her head was down, so he couldn't read her expression, but he definitely didn't like this. Something was still wrong, and she wasn't going to tell him what it was.

"Will you please tell me what the hell is going on?"

"Going on with what?"

"With you, since the forest—"

"I don't want to talk about—"

"Tell me why. Why did you leave the path? Why have you been acting like a zombie? Why didn't you spit in Matthews's eye when he made you cover your damn head?"

Anna rowed harder. "There had to be more. It was all just sand, and we were all alone. There had to be something else out there. I wanted . . . I wanted there to be more to it."

Jack sat silently, watching Anna row the boat, her hands drawing the oars through the waves, then raising them, dripping, out of the sea, then plunging back down in a steady rhythm.

He said, "The City will be different."

"How do you know?"

He couldn't explain it. "It has to be."

They rowed on. The sea got dirtier and dirtier, until what little they could see of it was a muddy brown. The rest was floating trash. It got in the way of the oars. Every few strokes they caught a trash bag or a length of nylon rope or a knot of fishing line. Jack tried not to look at the water. It made him feel dirty. Instead he looked out over the horizon, searching for signs of land. Finally, he spotted it in the distance.

"Avast, me beauty, land ho. Full speed ahead."

"Give me no orders, you scurvy dog," Anna said. They were the right words—words pre-Haven Anna would have said—but the tone was all wrong, flat and disinterested.

Jack was almost happy to see the mountains of trash looming over the beach. At least it meant they were nearly back where they should be. When they reached the shallows, he jumped out and held the boat steady while Anna disembarked.

She carefully unlocked the oars from their clips and arranged them in the bottom of the boat. Then she turned the boat around, walking beside it with one hand on the front, as though guiding a skittish horse, until the bow faced back the way they had come. She shoved it gently in the right direction, and together they watched as the current caught it and pulled it out to sea.

"It will get back to him, won't it?" Anna said.

"He said it would. It seems like he's probably done this before."

"I've been thinking about it. He must be a monk," Anna said. "The shaved head, the silent but helpful bit. It makes sense."

"Boring."

Anna waded out of the water. "Okay, then who do you think he was?"

Jack shrugged. "Maybe the long-dead ruler of an alien race who lost his army in an egomaniacal war for intergalactic dominance and is now cursed to rescue one thousand souls to save his own."

"There's nothing wrong with saying 'I have no idea,' you know."

Jack laughed. "No, but what I said was far more interesting and showed my cleverness and creativity."

She shoved him gently, but he saw her bite her lip, trying not to laugh. "Come on, we have to find a way back up to the path."

"We could climb?" Jack said. It was not an idea he relished. The cliff was high. It faded into mist far overhead.

"I'd rather not if it's all the same to you," Anna said.

"Do you have another plan?"

"Walk along the cliff face until we find an elevator."

"Why would there be an elevator in the side of a cliff?"

"Why would there be a town full of people living in a cave in the side of a volcano and pretending that they aren't dead while they await the Second Coming?"

"Okay," Jack said. "Let's go find the elevator."

There was no elevator. There was, however, the longest rope ladder Jack had ever seen. It was only about thirty yards down the beach from the place where they had landed.

"Huh. No kidding," Anna said, and pointed. The bottom rung was made out of a broom.

"All-knowing deity slightly lacking in interpersonal skills?" Jack said.

"Amen," Anna said. She put her foot on the broom handle, grabbed a rung, and began to climb. Jack followed.

~

It was a long climb. The air was starting to get hazy when Anna stopped and hooked one arm into the ropes. She swung away from the cliff wall and looked back over the ocean. Jack wasn't afraid of heights, or at least, he hadn't been before the jumping-off-the-cliff incident, but the sight of her swinging so carelessly made him close his eyes.

"Oh wow, look at that." Anna pointed toward the trash mounds.

Jack opened his eyes and turned as carefully as he could. "What am I looking at?"

"The trash is falling out of the sky. It's falling right out of the sky and onto those piles."

"I thought I noticed them shifting when we were here the first time."

"Where does it come from?"

Jack put both hands back on the ladder. "Maybe it's from the living world?"

Anna began to climb again. "Why should our trash end up here? And how is there trash falling from the clouds?"

"You know what?" Jack said. "I have no idea."

Soon the mist closed around him, obscuring everything but the rung in his hand and the one above.

"How are you doing?" he asked, to make sure Anna was still there.

"I'm sorry," Anna answered.

"For what?"

"For making you go to that awful island. I didn't want to be dead . . . I don't want to be dead. It hit me, in the forest, you know? It hit me—I'm dead and we're never going home."

"Anna, in the forest—"

She interrupted him. "I died."

Jack winced. He wished she would stop saying that. "I know. I'm sorry."

"No, I mean in the forest. I died *in* the forest."

Jack was afraid then, afraid that he was losing her. Maybe the River Styx had leached her memory, or maybe this fog was stealing it away. By the time they reached the top, if they ever reached the top, she wouldn't even know his name.

Jack said, "We've been dead for ages. We saw the doctor and we crossed the River Styx and we met Ricky in the factory. Remember?"

"There's nothing wrong with my memory," Anna said, "but I wasn't dead then."

"Of course you were."

"No, I wasn't. I just let you think that so you didn't feel alone."

"But you're here," Jack said.

"When you went to the doctor, did she put a thing on your arm that looked like a blood pressure cuff?" Anna asked. "And then she said something like, oops, looks like you're dead, right?"

"I don't think those were her exact words, but yeah, more or less."

"Yeah, well, she told me I wasn't dead. I was having a near-death experience. She said it was some kind of coping mechanism. Like my body was too beat up to stay in right now so it had sent me off to a hotel for a couple of days until the repairs were done."

"You said what happened in the forest wasn't real. You said I wasn't crazy. Either what happened to you was a nightmare or I'm crazy. It can't go both ways."

"Jack, that's silly. You're not crazy. But I did wake up in the hospital. She said I might, and I did. Nathan was there, and Michael, and then later my mom and dad. But I thought I heard you calling me, and I got out of bed to look for you. I fell down. All the nurses and doctors came in. There was this noise like a—like a heart monitor flatlining. And then I was back in the forest and you were screaming, and I ran . . ."

She had stopped climbing.

She could have left him all alone. She could have left him, but she hadn't. He felt relieved and hated himself for it. He reached up and squeezed her ankle. It was the only part of her he could reach. "I'm sorry," he said. Crazy or not, this time he really had killed her. And since then he'd done nothing but worry that she would leave him. He was an asshole.

She pulled her foot away, up onto the next rung where he couldn't see it. "Why are you sorry? I'm the one who lied to you and then dragged you off to hell via the dump."

He didn't want to talk about it anymore. "Call it even," he said. The mist was clearing. "Looks like we're almost there."

"Nope. We are there."

Jack looked up as Anna pulled herself over the edge of the cliff. She sat with her feet dangling over the side and watched him climb up beside her. He reached out a hand to help her up but pulled it away at the last second. "Promise not to jump this time?" he said.

"I promise. Let's go find this path. I'm all about the path."

Jack took her hand and pulled her to her feet. He couldn't see the path yet, but he could feel it. He struck off across the sand with Anna beside him.

~

The groundskeeper sat cross-legged in the middle of his hidden beach. His hands were on his knees, his face tilted back to catch the rays of the sun. It didn't give off any warmth. He was fairly certain it wasn't even really the sun, but old habits die hard.

It was impossible to access this spot without climbing over the top of the hill or wading knee-deep in the ocean. The cooled rock of the volcano extended partway into the water, creating an effective barrier between him and the rest of the island. So when he heard voices approaching, he didn't bother to open his eyes. The townspeople wouldn't come this way.

He heard Matthews's voice on the other side of the rocks saying, "Go back and check in with the other group. I'll follow in a few moments."

Several people said, "Yes, sir." And "Certainly, Elder." And then there was a moment of silence. The groundskeeper imagined Matthews standing still, waiting for his people to move out of sight. Soon, he would step into the water.

And there it was, water splashing, as if from a foot stepping into the gentle surf. The groundskeeper listened to Matthews walking toward him. The sound changed as Matthews stepped onto the rocky sand. He moved forward a few steps and then stopped. The groundskeeper remained unmoving, eyes still closed.

"You helped them leave," Matthews said.

"Hello, Jedediah."

"You said you wouldn't interfere."

"Yes. I did say that."

Still, the groundskeeper's eyes remained closed. Matthews loomed over him, casting a shadow across his eyelids.

"I am *trying* to save these people," Matthews said. "We were getting somewhere with the girl. She was fitting in well. Her friend was headstrong, but he would have gone along with her in the end. But now, thanks to you, they're both lost."

The groundskeeper smiled. "I'm sure they know where they're going."

The smile made Matthews angry. "I could have you dragged to the pits."

The groundskeeper opened his eyes. "You could do that," he said, his gaze meeting Matthews's for the first time.

Matthews looked away. "It wouldn't teach you anything, though, would it, you stubborn old fool. You'd just go on meddling. Like . . ." He stopped.

"Like Andrea," the groundskeeper said.

"Stubborn. That's what you are, both of you stubborn as a pair of donkeys." He turned and walked away.

"How *is* your better half?"

Matthews's shoulders tensed ever so slightly, but he didn't stop. "God have mercy on you," he muttered.

The groundskeeper watched him step into the ocean and wade around the shoulder of rock. Then he closed his eyes and tilted his head toward the sun.

Chapter Eighteen

This time there was no mistaking the dark smudge in the distance. It wasn't a river or a factory or even a pay phone. It was the path, stretching endlessly in both directions. Jack had to stop himself from running to it.

Jack felt better, much better. The pull of The City was back, and somehow, it seemed stronger than before. It made him feel like everything was going to be okay. He looked at Anna. She didn't look exactly happy, but her face had a little more animation than he had seen in a while. She was looking up the path—staring, really. He followed her gaze.

"Is that The City?" he asked.

"I didn't expect it to be so glittery," Anna said. "Or so close."

"If it's big, it might still be far away."

"Nothing in the afterlife is far away," Anna said. "It's like as soon as it comes into view, you're right on top of it."

As if to prove her point, the thing in the distance seemed to gain substance. It was definitely not a city.

"Looks like a flying saucer," Jack said. "It's all metal and shiny."

"It could be a diner," Anna said. "You know, one of those fifties-style ones."

"Or a flying saucer that serves burgers."

"Jack, I'm fairly certain there are no flying saucers in the afterlife."

"Why?"

Anna opened her mouth and shut it. Jack let himself smile.

It *was* a diner. As they got closer, this was made obvious by the metallic siding and the neon sign on the roof that wrote *Cosmic Diner* in flickering pink against the empty sky.

"It could still be a flying saucer," Jack said, mostly to annoy Anna. She stuck her tongue out at him, which he took as a good sign.

"Look! Geraniums," she said.

The entrance to the building was decorated with a concrete urn full of red geraniums. Anna ran forward to smell them—she loved geraniums—but stopped in the act of bending toward the plants.

"What is it?" Jack asked.

"They're fake."

Jack looked over her shoulder. They were scraps of red silk on plastic stems. A wooden sign stuck in the soil next to them read *Brought to you by the Afterlife Beautification Commission.*

"Seriously," Jack said. "Who's on this committee?"

Anna was trying to look through the tinted window of the diner. "Do you think they have food in there?"

"Who knows?" Jack said. "It might be food. It might be aliens serving memory banquets. It might be a twenty-four-hour dance party. In this place, there's no way to tell."

"There's one way." Anna pushed the door open.

The smell punched Jack in the face—bacon, and chocolate chip cookies. He stopped in the doorway, blinking. The smell triggered memories of home, and his mother frying bacon, and Ella sitting on her little stool in front of the oven watching cookies bake.

Anna looked at him, her eyes wide. "Jack, do you smell geraniums?"

Jack shook his head slowly. "No, but I smell something. Can we smell now?"

"Apparently."

"How? We aren't breathing."

Now Anna shook her head. "It smells like Grandpa's greenhouse."

"That's funny. I thought it smelled like my mother's kitchen on Saturday morning."

They looked around the diner—all chrome and Formica and black and white tiles. There was even a jukebox in the corner. It seemed to be playing Today's Greatest Hits in Unidentifiable Languages. A man in a dirty apron and a hairnet leaned on the breakfast bar. He nodded when Jack met his eye, and then turned toward the grill.

To the left, a line of booths and tables nestled under the plate-glass windows. To the right was a glass case of the kind you find in museum-houses that don't have room for a gift shop. It displayed an eclectic array of items, including a teddy bear wearing a dress, a pair of paint-spattered running shoes, a small hand mirror in a purple sparkly frame, and a toy truck with *The Texas Company* written down the side.

"Welcome to the Cosmic Diner," said the man behind the case. "We're having a special on spa socks today."

"No thanks," Jack said. "We don't have any money."

The man leaned one elbow against the counter. "Then you're in luck. They don't cost anything."

"How can you stay in business if you give things away for free? What's the catch?"

"No catch. Our inventory comes from the factory. The special isn't the price of the socks; what's special is that we have socks today. Super soft. Make your feet feel like they're walking on clouds."

"Right," Anna said. "I bet they're heavenly." She looked at Jack. "What?" she said innocently, but he could tell by the twinkle in her eye that she knew exactly what she was saying. At least she was feeling better.

The man behind the register seemed to have missed the joke. He was staring at them, nonplussed.

"Do you think we could get something to eat?" Jack said.

"Oh sure, have a seat anywhere you like. Sunshine will be right with you."

"Sunshine?" Anna asked.

"The waitress."

Sunshine plodded over to them as they sat down. She was wearing a faded yellow apron over a black eyelet-lace dress, which did not in any way match the decor of the place. The name the man behind the gift case had used was apparently not a joke, because her name tag said *SUNSHINE* in big block letters.

Jack had never seen a woman who looked less like a Sunshine. She had a long face surrounded by a mane of dirty-blond hair, and she was one of those people whose lips seemed too small for their mouths, so that not only their teeth but their gums showed when they smiled. Sunshine's smile clearly said, *I am smiling at you because I've been told I'm supposed to be pleasant to customers. No need to get friendly about it.*

"Would you like to see some menus?" she said.

"Yeah, that would be great," Jack said.

Anna was staring through the window at the fake geraniums. "So no money here, right?" she said.

"That's right, kiddo. First meal's free."

"Does anyone ever get a second meal?" Jack asked.

"Not really. People tend to move on pretty quickly afterward. The pull's a lot stronger this side of the forest. It gets to be too much for them."

"What about you?" Anna asked. "Why do you stay here?"

Sunshine looked at Anna as though she had asked the stupidest question in the world. "Well, I work here, don't I?"

"Fair enough."

Sunshine put a pair of menus on the table. "I'll just get your water, then."

When she was safely behind the counter, Jack said, "Friendly, isn't she?"

Anna ignored this. She was looking at her menu. "Fish-and-chips, pasties, bangers and mash? What is that? It sounds like a criminal charge. The defendant stands accused of one count of burglary and one count of bangers and mash."

"Or a rock band," Jack said. "Now please welcome to the stage Bangers. And. Mash."

On her way back to their table with a glass of water in each hand, Sunshine peeked over Anna's shoulder. "That's a British menu. I guess I'll have to find you an American one."

She thumped the glasses down on the table, slopping water over the rim.

"Don't bother," Anna said. "We'll share." She got up and slipped into Jack's side of the booth. She read his menu out loud. "Grilled cheese and tomato soup, macaroni and cheese, pepperoni pizza, apple pie. That's better. What are you going to have?"

Jack only half heard her question. His attention was taken up by a framed poster that had, until that moment, been blocked by Anna's head. It showed a racially ambiguous girl wearing a pair of mouse ears. Cinderella's castle was in the background and the words *Visit Disneyland* floated over her head. It seemed like the worst advertising placement in the world. Nobody who saw it was in any position to go to Disneyland. Then he squinted at the fine print at the bottom of the poster. The letters resolved themselves into the words *Afterlife Resort*.

"You have got to be kidding," Jack said.

"What?"

He tilted his head toward the poster. Anna read it.

"Oh, my God. No way."

"I dunno. I guess it makes sense. How long ago did Walt Disney die?"

"Yeah, but . . .Wow, just wow."

"Agreed."

Sunshine rolled her eyes at them. "You know what you want?"

"I'm having the grilled cheese and tomato soup," Jack said.

"Of course you are," Anna said. "I think I'll try the apple pie. Is it any good?"

Sunshine wrote their orders in her notepad. "It'll be the best thing you ever tasted," she said.

"I don't know, my mom makes a pretty awesome apple pie," Anna said. "She makes her own crust and everything."

"It'll taste like that. No worries."

Anna opened her mouth to object, then closed it. Jack could practically see the thoughts forming behind her eyes. Sunshine waited. When Anna finally spoke, she said, "There isn't any pie, is there, it's just, like, the memory of pie or something."

Sunshine's grin was only slightly cruel. "Best not to think about it," she said.

When she had gone away again, Anna leaned her head on Jack's shoulder. Jack froze, afraid to twitch and make her feel like she had to move. He looked down at her out of the corner of his eye. He couldn't see her face, only the part in her hair and her fingers drumming on the edge of the table. Something was obviously on her mind.

"Jack?" she said finally.

"Yes?"

"Thank you."

"For what?"

"Putting up with me."

"You are entirely welcome."

She was about to say something else, he could see it in the rhythm of her fingers, but before she could, Sunshine came back with the food, interrupting what might have been a touching moment. "Here you go, kids."

Anna sat up. Jack looked out the window. He didn't care about the food. He wanted to know what Anna was going to say. Oblivious to Jack's mood, Sunshine set their plates on the table. Anna switched seats again, so that she was sitting across from him.

"Okay," she said. "Let's see about this pie."

Jack bit into his grilled cheese and instantly stopped being angry. Nothing could be bad in a world where food this good existed. He looked at the inconvenient waitress. "Hot sauce?"

"Right here." She pulled a bottle of Tabasco out of her apron pocket.

"Awesome," Jack said. "How's the pie?"

Anna shielded her mouth with her hand. "Best imaginary food I've ever eaten."

It was good. The best. But by the time he'd started in on the second half of his sandwich, Jack was getting restless. He could have sworn the pull was getting stronger with every bite. Anna seemed to feel it too. She was fidgeting while she chewed, staring out the window over the sand.

Anna put her fork down. Jack found himself on his feet before he could think about it. The last bit of sandwich was still in his hand.

"Ready to go?" he asked.

Anna nodded.

Jack bolted the sandwich and took off toward the door. Sunshine twiddled her fingers at them as they passed. Her smile seemed to say, *I told you so.*

Chapter Nineteen

Jack felt better once they were on the road again. In fact, he felt great, better than he had since the accident. They were back on the right path. Anna seemed to have gotten over her initial shock at being dead. The City felt like it was within reach. He wondered what they would find there. Would it be heaven, all light and harps, or a shadowy netherworld like the Egyptian city of the dead? Nobody seemed to know, really *know*, anything about it. Jack knew he should be worried, but at the moment he felt too good to care. It occurred to him to wonder if Sunshine had drugged his hot sauce.

"I feel great," he said.

"Me too, isn't that weird?" Anna was smiling.

"It must be The City. We're getting closer."

"How can you tell?"

Jack shrugged. "Just a feeling."

They walked for a long time, not saying much of anything to each other. Jack was happy to be there with her, walking, moving forward. The distance didn't seem to matter. Anna hummed to herself.

~

Eventually The City came into view. At first it looked like a huge cloud hanging low on the horizon. A little closer and they were able to make out a tower splitting the sky. Closer still and they could see the individual buildings that made up the skyline.

The City seemed to generate its own light, which was reflected from the windows and overflowed the brick wall that surrounded it. It was beautiful, but the tower drew Jack's attention. His eyes followed it up and up into the empty sky. He couldn't see the top.

If Jack had expected pearly gates or a portal of gold, he would have been disappointed, but he'd been in the hereafter long enough not to be surprised that the gate to The City was a simple construct of wood and iron. It was maybe twelve feet tall and wide enough to drive a truck through. In the center of the gate, at about head height, was a wrought-iron knocker in the shape of a scarab beetle. Its head was downward, so it seemed to be hanging from its back legs.

"Should we knock?" Jack said.

"Did you want to spend a little longer enjoying the scenery?" Anna asked.

As Jack reach to lift the knocker, he half expected it to come to life and bite him, or crawl up his arm, or morph into Marley and spout dire warnings. It didn't. It was just cast iron, cold to the touch and heavier than he expected. When it fell back against the door, it rang like a bell.

The gate swung inward. Jack looked into an open square. A collection of low buildings cut the small courtyard off from the rest of The City. About thirty people stood in a queue that doubled back on itself three or four times in front of a concrete building.

"Welcome to The City." Until the man spoke, Jack hadn't noticed him standing next to the open gate. "Please move along—there are others waiting to enter."

"No there aren't," Jack said.

"The gate's already open," Anna said.

"Exactly."

Jack and Anna crossed into the courtyard. The gate shut behind them, then almost instantly opened again to admit another traveler. Where had she come from? Jack and Anna joined the back of the line. A man in a leather jacket turned to look at them, smiled at Anna, and then turned away.

A tone echoed over invisible loudspeakers, followed by a recorded voice: "Please be sure to complete your customs form before you reach the customs official. You must declare all possessions. Please remove your shoes when crossing the security checkpoint. Thank you." The tone sounded a second time, and the voice went silent.

Jack and Anna spoke at the same time.

"Seriously?"

"Customs form?"

The man in the leather jacket turned around again and pointed at a glass-topped desk standing against the wall of the building. "The forms are over there."

"Thanks," Anna said.

He stuffed his hands back into his pockets. His eyes slipped down to his toes. "No problem," he mumbled.

As they left the line, Jack whispered, "That dead guy checked you out."

"What is this, *Twilight*? You're crazy."

Jack followed Anna over to the desk. It was the kind of thing that would have fit right in at a bank—fake wood with a sheet of glass on top to keep it from getting scratched. Notices were pressed between the glass and the tabletop. They said pretty much exactly what the recording had already told them. There was also a form. The word *sample* was stamped across it in red ink. It read:

Name (Last, First Middle): Sample, John Joseph

Age: 33

Date of birth: 3/3/1303

Date of death: 3/3/1336

Reason for visit: Poison

Bags: 0

Last words: "Does this mutton taste funny to you?"

Previous Address: 333 Livingworld Lane, Livingworld, London, England

"Mutton?" Jack said as he drew a form from the pile. "What kind of last words are those?"

"Better than yours," Anna said.

Jack paused in the act of searching for a pen. "Wait, what were mine? I don't even remember."

"I believe they were something along the lines of 'Oh, shit, oh shit, oh shit.'"

"We were about to crash into a semi," he said as a kind of excuse. "Let's fill out the stupid forms and get back in line." He plucked a pen out of its holder. It was chained to the table. Jack tugged at it. "Who's going to steal a pen in the afterlife?"

"Someone who needs a pen," Anna said. "Half the time people don't mean to steal pens anyway. They just sort of wander away with them." She snatched the pen out of his hand and began to write.

"I can see that interview with God. Well, Joe, we were going to send you to heaven, but then you stole a pen from the customs desk and, well, turns out you've been rerouted."

Anna paused over her customs form. "You know, the doctor told me it doesn't actually work that way."

"Yeah, we had that talk. I meant to ask how it does work, but I sort of forgot. I wasn't exactly thinking clearly at the time."

"One way to find out." Anna stuck her pen back in its holder. "You done?"

"Hold on." Jack scribbled on his form. "What's your hurry? These lines always take an eternity."

"Yeah, and here that's a literal possibility. I'd like to get this over with as soon as possible, thanks."

"Why?"

She glanced up at the tower and then back at her form. "I hate security checkpoints. They always make me feel like I've done something wrong."

"Have you?"

"No! That's the worst part. I'm, like, a model traveler."

"So what are you worried about?"

She shrugged, folded the form in half, and shoved it, and her hands, into the pocket of her shorts.

They headed back toward the end of the line. More people had come through the gate by this time, so the man in the leather jacket was no longer directly in front of them. They queued up behind a one-legged man in a wheelchair.

Anna looked at Jack, darted her eyes toward the wheelchair, and then looked back at Jack. He could almost hear the words she couldn't say out loud, which were more or less *How unfair is it that this man is still in a wheelchair even in the afterlife? Shouldn't his right leg have grown back or magically reappeared or something? Is he really going to spend all eternity in a wheelchair because that's how he died? That sucks. Where's the justice?*

Jack shook his head and shrugged. *I know*, the shrug said. *What can we do?*

Person by person, the line inched forward. The tone sounded again, followed by a different recorded message. "Persons traveling together should approach the customs agent as a group. Otherwise, please wait behind the red line until the traveler in front of you has been processed. Thank you."

They heard both recordings three or four times before they reached the red line. A customs agent sat on a tall office chair inside a bar-height cubicle. A plate-glass wall separated him from the travelers. He spoke to the man in the wheelchair through a small open window in the side of the cubicle. After a brief conversation Jack couldn't hear, he took the man's form, stamped it, and waved him into the building.

"Next," he said in a bored voice.

Jack approached the window, with Anna behind him.

"Traveling together?" the man asked.

"Yes."

Anna was toying with her form, folding and unfolding it.

"Forms, please," the man said. Jack tugged Anna's form away from her and handed it to the man along with his own.

Inside the box, the man held their forms side by side, comparing them. "You died in the same car accident."

"Yes, sir," Anna said.

"Who was driving?"

"Why does everyone ask that?" Jack said. "I was."

The man looked at Anna with a severe tilt to his eyebrows. "It says here your last words were something about wine. Were you drinking in the vehicle?"

"No, sir, nothing like that, I was singing a song. The lyrics go . . ."

He waved a hand at her. "Yes, yes. Approved." He stamped their forms one after the other, slid them back through the window, and waved Jack and Anna forward. As they passed into the darkness of the gray building, they heard him say, "Next."

Chapter Twenty

Fluorescent lights flickered overhead. The floor was linoleum, and that, coupled with the concrete walls, turned the whole place into an echo chamber. The voices of the travelers cascaded back on each other, building to the dull roar of a conch shell held against your ear. The line switched back on itself maybe twelve or thirteen times and spanned the entire width of the room.

Anna plopped her head down on Jack's shoulder. "We are in hell."

Jack patted her head as though she were a sad puppy. "Not hell. Purgatory, maybe."

"Or limbo, except that isn't a thing anymore," Anna said.

"What isn't a thing?"

Anna straightened. "Limbo. The Catholics got together and decided they didn't really believe in it anymore, so they voted it off the island."

"Can they do that?" Jack asked.

"It's their thing. I don't see why not."

"So where do all the unbaptized heathen babies go then?"

"I don't know, maybe they get recycled."

Jack made a face. "Gross."

"What do you mean, gross? People donate organs. Couldn't God move some souls around if nobody was using them?"

"You're thinking of reincarnation," Jack said. "I'm pretty sure that's not allowed unless you're a Hindu or a Buddhist . . ."

"I think Jews can believe whatever they want about the afterlife," Anna said.

Jack talked over her. He was on a roll. ". . . or one of those crazy people who sells crystals at the farmers market. There's one back home who thinks she was Empress Wu Zetian in a former life."

"The lady with the henna tattoos all up and down her arms? She always wears skirts that look like they're knotted together out of carpet remnants and silk hankies?"

Jack nodded. "That's the one."

"Have you ever noticed how nobody was ever Joe Schmo from Idaho in their former life? They're always some important historical figure like Cleopatra or Napoleon. Why is nobody ever the maid who dumped out King Charlemagne's chamber pot?"

"Maybe they suppress those lives or forget them because they're boring," Jack said.

"I remember when I thought life was boring." Anna sighed. "All that time I spent whining about being bored, when I could have been learning to surf."

Jack shook his head. "We lived in Maine."

"Learning to snowboard, then," Anna said.

"You hate the cold," Jack said, "and sports."

"Missing the point you are, young Padawan."

"No really, I know what you mean."

"Seventeen years," Anna said, "and how much of it did I waste being bored, or feeling sorry for myself, or sitting in front of the television watching terrible reality shows."

"I know." He nudged his shoulder against hers.

She smiled.

They fell silent for a while. Jack tried not to think about all the things he had meant to do, all the adventures he'd meant to have, all the random skills he had meant to learn before he died. Like juggling. He had wanted to learn how to juggle, not for any good reason, but because it was one of those things that would instantly impress someone. Boring people don't juggle, interesting people do. Jack had meant to be an interesting person before he died.

He tried to distract himself by looking around at the people. Some of them looked interesting. Aside from the guy with the wheelchair, there was a woman in a purple nightgown with the words *we're all mad here* printed across the front. There was a girl dressed entirely in black with black dyed hair, black nails, and heavy eye makeup. There was a guy wearing American flag swim trunks. Jack wondered where they all came from, how they had died. The line crept on.

"Is it rude to ask a complete stranger what killed them?" he whispered.

"Possibly, but at this point, who the hell cares," Anna said. "Who do you want to ask?"

"Nobody, really, I just wondered."

Anna rolled her eyes. "Wuss." She turned to the woman standing behind them, who looked like somebody's great-grandmother. She was short and plump, with curly white hair and her glasses on a string around her neck. All she was missing was a ruffled pink apron and she could have been a guest star on *Leave It to Beaver*.

"Excuse me, ma'am."

"Well of course, miss."

If she hadn't looked like such a sweet old lady, Jack might have thought her tone was mocking.

Anna forged ahead. "I was wondering if I could ask you how you died, if that's not too rude a question."

"Rude? Honey, you don't know the first thing about rude. Rude is when a sailor grabs your ass and calls you Kitty," the nice old lady said.

Anna seemed to have forgotten how to close her mouth. Jack stared. The woman grinned. Her false teeth shone.

"But to answer your question," the grandmother continued, "the story of my death is a boring one. My body was old. When you get old, things start to shut down. My brain still worked, but the rest of me? Junk. One day the ticker just shit the bed. If you want to hear a good story, let me tell you about the time I almost went to Europe. I was twelve years old and my mother was going to Europe to visit her family that lived in Poland. She was going to take me with her, but do you know what happened?"

"No, what happened?"

"Hitler invaded Poland."

There was a pause, during which Jack and Anna remained silent, letting this sink in. Finally Anna said, "That jerk."

"I know. He ruined my vacation. I never did get to go to Europe."

"I always knew I hated Hitler," Anna said. "Now I know why."

The old lady cackled. They were reaching the front of the line, which gave Anna an excuse to turn around. Jack turned too, and was careful not to catch Anna's eye. He knew that if they looked at each other, they would both start laughing. The last thing he wanted to do was laugh at this brazen old woman. Encourage an old person like her and you could end up spending the next three hours listening to dirty stories about the assisted living facility.

The line was moving pretty quickly. The man in the wheelchair had already reached the security checkpoint. There were four stations ranged along the Plexiglas wall that divided the room. Two guards stood at each checkpoint, one inside and one outside the divider. A short conveyer belt lay between them. Jack tried to imagine what kind of contraband they could be looking for. Did people try to sneak into The City with forbidden cheeses hidden in their shoes?

The guard asked the man in the wheelchair a question Jack couldn't hear over the general noise in the room. The man in the wheelchair shook his head. The guard insisted. Slowly the man bent down and removed his sneaker from his foot. Jack found himself wondering if he had to buy shoes in pairs or if there were stores that would sell you only one shoe if you had only one leg.

The guard motioned the man forward. Balancing carefully, the man stood, holding his shoe in his left hand. The guard offered his shoulder, but the man shook his head. He hopped heavily over to the conveyor belt and put his shoe on it. Steadying himself against the metal frame, he watched as the shoe was pulled into the scanner and disappeared.

Then, at a wave from the far guard, he hopped toward the metal detector. The guard on Jack's side of the checkpoint folded up the wheelchair and set it on the belt. *What's he supposed to do now?* Jack thought. The man hopped through the checkpoint. No alarms, no flashing lights. Nothing to distract Jack from the fact that a man who had passed into a metal detector with one leg had stepped out with two. He tentatively set his new foot on the ground.

Anna tugged at Jack's arm. "Did you see that? The guy in the wheelchair. He had one leg, and now he has two."

"Did you see what happened?" Jack asked.

"I don't know. I was watching the whole time. I saw it, but nothing happened. You know?"

"I know, I saw."

The man paused for a moment. He said something to the guard. The guard pointed to a door on the other side of the room. A green exit sign glowed above it. The man walked a few steps toward the door. Suddenly, the reality of the situation seemed to hit him. He shouted, "Hoo-rah!" and broke into a run. He burst through the door and disappeared.

Jack realized he was grinning madly. Anna was laughing. The guard waved at them. It was their turn now.

"One at a time," the guard said, holding up a hand to block Jack's progress.

"We're together," Jack said.

The guard looked at his partner, who shrugged. He dropped his arm. Jack bent to take off his shoes.

"Any baggage, money, or produce to declare?" the guard asked.

"Produce?" Jack said.

Anna said, "No, sir."

"Move along then."

Jack put his sandals down on the conveyor belt and stepped through the checkpoint. Anna hung behind, watching their shoes pass through the scanner. The belt rolled, carrying two pairs of sandals slowly toward the big metal box that Jack assumed housed an X-ray machine. Their sandals went into the box. Jack and Anna waited. They didn't come out the other side. They waited a bit longer.

"I said move along, there," the guard said. It was not his happy voice.

Anna moved along. The metal detector beeped, red lights flashed.

"Step back, please," the guard closest to Jack said.

Anna backed up and looked at Jack. He raised his eyebrows at her.

The guard stepped through the checkpoint and approached Anna. "Are you wearing or carrying anything from the world before other than your clothes?"

"No, sir."

The guard sighed. "Empty your pockets, please."

"Why?"

"You are entering The City. Nothing from the outside can pass the checkpoint." He said the words like he'd said them a million times, completely disinterested.

She stuck her hands in her back pockets first. "I'm from the outside," she said.

"No you're not. Nobody is, really," the guard said.

"Okay, fine," Anna said. "What about my clothes? They're definitely from the outside."

"Your clothes don't really exist. They're a construct to keep you from feeling embarrassed."

Anna crossed her arms over her chest. "So I'm actually naked right now?"

"Everyone is naked"—the guard grinned—"underneath their clothes." This comment was apparently meant to be humorous.

"Then what about my shoes? If my shoes are a construct, then why did you take them?"

"It's more of a symbolism thing. You're holding up the line, you know."

The guards retreated to their stations.

"But, I don't understand," Anna said to the guard as she stepped through the checkpoint. The alarms went off again. Anna jumped backward. Jack stepped forward. The guard closest to him held out an arm to stop him.

"I did tell you to empty your pockets," the first guard said.

"They're empty." Anna turned them inside out. "See."

The guard's eyebrows huddled in confusion. He unclipped a security wand from his waist and waved it over Anna. It beeped. He looked down at it, shook it, tried it again. Beep. He motioned the other guard over. They held a whispered conversation.

Anna watched them, biting her lip.

Both guards approached Anna. "I'm sorry, miss, but only the dead can pass through this checkpoint."

"I am dead. I died. I remember dying."

The guard shook his head. "You're in a vegetative state."

"I'm dead." She looked at Jack through the layer of Plexiglas that divided the screened from the unscreened. Or, the dead from the undead.

"Look," the guard said. He waved the scanner over his own chest. It was silent. He did the same to Anna. It beeped.

"See. You're not dead, but if you cross this checkpoint, you will die. Irrevocably."

"But my friend."

"Is dead." His tone softened. "You aren't, you still have a chance."

"You have to let me through. Where else can I go?"

"There are a lot of places. Have you been to the Disney Afterlife Resort?"

"I'm staying with Jack."

Jack knew how to solve this problem. He walked back through the scanner. At least, he tried to. The air seemed to solidify in front of him. It was like walking into a sliding-glass door that you thought was open.

The guard closest to him made a sound halfway between a laugh and a sigh. "Nice try. Once you cross the security checkpoint, you have to keep moving. There is no turning back."

Anna hadn't even smiled when Jack bounced backward. She was thinking. "Wait, you said if I cross the checkpoint, I'll die. So I can cross the checkpoint?"

"Anna, don't be crazy. That would be suicide," Jack said. He thumped his fist against the invisible door. It was perfectly solid.

"If my parents decide to shut off my life support machines, would you call that murder?"

"What? I . . . Some people would."

"Would you?"

"I don't know."

"Fine, then if a man is being kept alive by dialysis, and he chooses to end treatment, would you call that suicide?"

"It depends," Jack said. "How old is he? Is he suffering? Does he have other complications? You don't know all the facts. You can't make this decision without all the facts."

Anna turned to the guard. "Who has the facts?"

The guard scratched the back of his head. "I can refer you to the supervisor."

"Do that, then. Please."

Anna's guard looked at Jack's guard. He nodded.

Anna's guard holstered his life detector. "You might not like what she has to say."

"I have to know," Anna said.

After a crowded series of moments during which other guards were called, and the situation was explained, and responsibility for the checkpoint was turned over to the new arrivals, Anna's guard led her to a window set in the concrete wall of the building. It looked like a teller's window. Jack started to follow. His guard moved to block the way. "Keep moving, please. Your shoes will not be returned to you. That way to the exit."

"That's not happening," Jack said. He sidestepped the guard.

"Sir, I really must insist."

Jack sped up, trying to keep Anna and her guard in view. "Insist, then." He saw Anna stop in front of the window while her guard talked to someone hidden by the glare on the window glass. The guard grabbed Jack's arm. Jack half turned, keeping one eye on Anna while he talked.

"Do you see that girl? She was my best friend and I killed her." He fought to keep his voice level. "She is my responsibility, and there is no power in this life or the last that is going to keep me away from her right now. Do you understand?"

The guard dropped his arm and stared into Jack's face. "Yes," he said finally.

Jack left the guard nodding to himself and got as close as he could to the window. The glass between him and Anna muffled the sound, but he could see a woman inside the teller's window. She was leafing through a file and talking to Anna. Anna was nodding. She asked a question. The woman replied. Anna looked at Jack and smiled. He smiled back, pointed to his ear, and shook his head. Anna gave him a thumbs-up sign.

Anna turned back to the supervisor. She motioned toward Jack and said something. The woman shook her head, replied. Anna nodded. The supervisor turned away with the file in her hand.

Jack trailed Anna to the nearest checkpoint. "What did she say?" he asked as soon as he thought Anna could hear him.

"She said that there is no way of knowing when or if I'll wake up, but that my body is in a really bad condition. My leg is broken. One of my lungs has collapsed. I have internal bleeding that the doctors haven't noticed yet. And my brain is damaged, probably irrevocably."

"But you could still wake up. You could still live."

"Listen . . ." She bit her lip. "I could stay on this side, not dead, not alive, just waiting for something that might never—that probably will never happen . . . or I could take one step."

"And die."

"We all have to die sometime."

"But you don't have to die today."

She closed her eyes. "Jack, if I don't do this, I might as well go back and live with the crazies under the volcano."

Jack didn't see how that followed. He tried to say so, but she continued.

"In a way, this is my life now. This is the world I have to work with, and if I refuse to move forward because I'm afraid to lose something I don't have anymore . . . You can't spend your life so trapped by the past that you never reach the future."

Every guard within earshot was nodding.

"We keep thinking of our lives before as the real world, but that's not right. This is real now. This is what we have to work with, and I refuse to waste it." She stepped through the checkpoint. The alarms were silent.

For half an instant, Anna looked as though she had plunged headfirst into an icy ocean. But the expression broke almost before Jack was certain he saw it. She smiled and held out her hand. Jack took it. Together they walked toward the door. Just before they reached it, he realized she was humming, almost too softly to hear. It sounded like, "We're off to see the wizard . . ."

~

Michael was on his way to work when his cell phone rang. He glanced at it propped on the dashboard beside his tachometer. Dad. That couldn't be good. Dad was at the hospital with Anna. Michael flipped his blinker, inspected the rearview mirror—empty road, trees, and a small fenced cemetery—and pulled his car to a stop on the soft shoulder.

The phone was still ringing. Michael thumbed the switch to turn on his hazards. Only then did he pick up the phone. He prodded the answer button, lifted the phone to his ear.

"Michael." Dad's tone told him everything. Michael didn't want to hear the words, but Dad said them anyway. "She's gone."

It wasn't as bad as he'd thought it would be. The words didn't carry the weight he had expected. They were just words—sounds broadcast into his ear—empty, insubstantial.

"Okay. I'm coming," Michael said. "I'll be there as soon as I can." Even his own voice seemed vacant, void of inflection, dead.

"Drive safely," Dad said, his voice finally breaking

"Yes," was all Michael could manage to say. He touched the End button with his thumb. Then he leaned across the front seat, opened the glove compartment, and stuck the phone inside; he didn't want any distractions. He sat up and rested his hands on the wheel. Outside, the apple trees shivered in a passing breeze. He turned off the hazards and turned on his blinker. Once again, he looked into the rearview mirror—still no traffic. He pulled into the lane and drove, five miles an hour under the speed limit, toward town.

He'd already passed the doughnut shop before he realized that he hadn't called to tell them he wouldn't be at work today. He thought about turning around, running inside, telling his manager what was going on. He tried to imagine what words he would use. *I'm going to miss my shift. Dad called. Anna is* . . . No. *Sorry, I can't work today, my sister* . . . He kept driving. He'd call them later, from the hospital or wherever.

It occurred to him that with all this thinking, he'd missed the turn that would have taken him down the back roads toward Bangor. Now he was headed toward the highway. He could turn around, but traffic had picked up now that he was in town, and it seemed easiest to keep going. He hadn't been on the highway since the accident. People drove so fast on the highway.

He held his breath as he turned onto the ramp. Nothing cataclysmic happened. The tires rolled along the road, bringing him closer and closer to the hospital and his parents and his sister, who wasn't there anymore. He was surprised at how easy it all was. He had expected to break down when he heard the news. For the last few weeks he had been playing scenarios in his head, imagining where he would be, what he would do if they called and told him she'd woken up, or if they called and said she hadn't.

Sometimes he'd thought he would break down weeping, wailing aloud. Sometimes he'd thought he might rage and throw things, tearing pictures off the walls, defenestrating knickknacks.

But now, this numbness caught him by surprise. He wondered if something was wrong with him. He should feel something, shouldn't he? What kind of heartless bastard was he, who couldn't even feel sorrow at the death of his own sister? That was sick, right?

He wondered if he would see her before they took her away. Would they leave her in her bed in the children's ward, with its primary-colored walls and framed crayon drawings? Or would they bring her down to the morgue and lay her on a metal table under a white sheet? Would she still look like her?

He had seen a dead body only once before, when a girl in his class had died in a snowmobile accident and he'd gone to the wake. She'd looked so healthy and alive that he and his friends had gotten together after the others had left and touched the back of her hand, to convince themselves that it was cold.

That was after the funeral people had prepared her, though. At this point, Anna wouldn't have the benefit of their makeup magic. She would be herself, but empty. Probably as pale as she had been these last few weeks, with dark circles around her eyes and bruises covering huge patches of her body. He wondered how long it would take to convince himself that she was dead.

He was approaching the Carmel Road exit. A car had gone off the road there a few months ago, missing the exit in the dark. Without meaning to, Michael slowed even more. Someone had put a cross in the grass on the shoulder. It was made of metal pipes bound together by wire. He wondered if anyone had marked the spot where Anna . . .

Michael's vision blurred. His heart pounded. He pulled the car into the breakdown lane without signaling, without really realizing what he was doing. He sat there and sobbed until he couldn't breathe. And then he opened his door and threw up onto the asphalt, until his stomach was empty and his hands trembled.

Chapter Twenty-One

Outside, Jack couldn't help but look up at the tower in the center of The City. It broke the empty whiteness of the sky, easily taller than any three of The City's other skyscrapers, so tall that he couldn't see the top. It gave him a sense of reverse vertigo—not as though he were about to fall, but as though the relentless pull of gravity was a huge weight about to crush him.

He lowered his eyes to the wide street on which they stood. There were no cars, no buses. Now that he was paying attention, he realized he couldn't see or hear traffic of any kind. The City was also unnaturally clean. There was no litter on the ground, no gum stuck to the sidewalk, no dirt at all.

Anna pulled his hand to get him moving again. "Are you going to stand there forever?"

He stared at her, as though seeing her for the first time. She was the same Anna he'd always known, smiling, pretty. Her eyes radiated contentment, as though nothing out of the ordinary had happened, as though she hadn't just made her final choice. It was insane, except that it wasn't. All her arguments made sense. The thing was, he felt guilty for being so happy that she was here with him and not riding the Tower of Terror at Afterlife Disney. He squeezed her hand and allowed himself to be dragged to a booth set up near the doorway.

It looked like the kind of thing you bought tickets out of at the county fair. A woman with a dark, elbow-length braid leaned forward out of the window. Her skin was the color of sweet coffee. When she saw them coming over, she smiled, showing a row of straight white teeth. Jack liked her instantly.

"Hello," the woman said. "My name is Dahlia. Welcome to The City."

"What's this city called?" Jack asked.

"The City."

"It must have a name."

"It is always called The City. It has other titles, I guess: the New Jerusalem, Gan Eden, Jannah, the Pure Land."

The exit door opened, and all three of them turned to look at the man coming out. He was wearing a suit, and his socks had a hole in the toe. He didn't even pause, but kept walking straight up the road like a traveler headed for his gate at the airport.

"But we usually call it The City," Dahlia concluded.

Next to the information booth, a map of The City was printed on a metal sign. It looked, at least on the map, like it was perfectly circular. Six gates were evenly spaced around the outer edge. They were labeled *Gate of Africa, Gate of Asia,* and so on. Next to the one marked *Gate of America, North,* there was a red dot labeled *You Are Here.* A road led from each gate to the center of town, dividing The City into six wedge-shaped neighborhoods. Other roads rippled out from the center in concentric circles. In the center of the map was a smaller circle labeled *The Tower.*

Jack and Anna both reached to touch it at the same time. Jack raised his eyes to the real thing. Looking at it, he felt the pull intensify. This is what had been leading them forward all this time. People might call The City the end, but the tower was the destination. He knew that like he knew which direction was up and how to wiggle his fingers.

"We're almost there," he said.

Dahlia said, "The tower is the iconic center of The City. More than a hundred and fifty-five thousand people flock to The City each day to visit it. It is the tallest structure in the hereafter and is clearly visible from anywhere in The City. The tower is always open to visitors. Admission is free."

She sounded like an audio tour recording.

"How about The City itself?" Anna said. "Can you tell us about that?"

"The City is the largest population center in the hereafter. About a hundred and forty-four thousand people work within its walls. It has no restaurants, no shops, six museums, six libraries—"

"So Professor Haggarty was right," Jack said.

Dahlia didn't even pause. "— and three public parks. People of all colors, creeds and nationalities pass through the six gates of The City at a rate of about fifty-six million per year."

"Wow, um, thanks," Anna said. "That was . . . informative. I guess we'll go look around then."

"But I still have the spiel about the parks I could do."

"Actually, wait: could you tell us how to get to the library?"

"Why do you want to go to the library?" Jack asked.

"Is that a trick question?" Anna asked. "It's a library. In the afterlife. They must have every book ever written. Besides, there's something I want to look up. So how do we get there?"

"There's one fairly close. This is Americas Avenue." Dahlia leaned out of her window to point the direction. "Walk straight up this street and take your first right. You'll cross Main Street. Keep going until you hit Canadian Boulevard. Take a left there. The library will be up the street a bit on your right. You can't miss it. It's the one with the columns in the front."

"So it's right, left, right. Right?" said Jack.

"Don't worry," Anna said. "I've got it. You have no sense of direction anyway."

"I do too. I can't read a map in a moving car, that's all."

"Which explains why we ended up in New Hampshire when we were trying to get to a concert in Portland."

"That was not my fault. I get carsick. You'd think you would have noticed all the signs that said *Portland this exit*."

"Uh-huh. Thanks, Dahlia. You've been a big help."

~

Jack knew that every city has a few empty storefronts. They usually have wires hanging from the ceiling and *For Rent* signs in the windows. Or the windows are boarded up entirely and someone has spray painted *No Trespassing* on the plywood. Either scenario would have been much less creepy than what he saw now—empty storefronts, not abandoned or dilapidated, just empty. Through the plate-glass windows he could see gleaming paint and immaculate floors, but no merchandise, no signs, no carts or cash registers. It was as though someone was about to move in at any minute. Or as if something had spirited away all the people and anything else that wasn't bolted down.

Anna, who had been leaning against a window with her hands shading her eyes so she could see inside, backed away and said, "This is creepy. What's-her-face, Dahlia, said there were tens of thousands of people working here. Where are they?"

"It's like the Twilight Zone," Jack said.

"Oh, the one with the man who finds the diner with the coffee still brewing, and there's this mannequin he thinks is a woman, but then she falls out of the car and he gets stuck in the phone booth, but it turns out he's part of a government experiment to see how astronauts handle solitude. I love that episode."

Jack smiled at her. "It's a good thing you don't have to breathe."

"Don't pick on me."

"I would never."

"Lies. Hey, look at this." Anna ran forward.

Jack ambled up behind her. She seemed to be happy with her decision. He should stop beating himself up about it. He should, but he knew he probably wouldn't.

Anna stopped in front of a storefront. This one was different from every other store on the block. The plate-glass window was framed by expensive-looking velvet curtains held back by gold ropes. Between the curtains, a crystal ball the size of Anna's head stood on a pedestal. Gold writing on the window said *Madame Bonaparte* and *Medium* in curly letters.

"A medium in the afterlife?" Anna said. "That has to be a fairly simple job. I will allow you to speak with the soul of your dearly departed. Now, what's his phone number?"

Jack held out his hand, palm up. "This line is your life line," he said. "Observe how it ends suddenly. This means that you are dead."

"I see that you have completed a long journey."

"The spirits are restless," Jack said, pressing his hands to his temples. He looked up. "Hey, folks in the corner, if you could quiet down, please. I'm trying to communicate with this dead guy here."

"So you want to go in?" Anna said.

"Oh, yes."

They pushed open the door. A series of bells tinkled overhead. The room was surprisingly bright. The walls and ceiling were painted blue with fluffy white clouds. A carpet woven in shades of green covered the floor. Overhead a light shone in a yellow globe. It wasn't quite the great outdoors, but it was oddly comforting. Anna spread her arms and tilted her face toward the light.

A young man came into the room through a curtain at the back, moving quietly on bare feet. "Welcome to Madame Bonaparte's. Madame is with a client right now, but if you care to wait, she will be happy to contact your loved ones for you."

"How does this work exactly?" Anna asked.

"Using her special abilities, Madame Bonaparte will attempt to contact your loved ones on the other side."

"Aren't we already on the other side?" Anna said.

He smiled, and Jack thought if you replaced the black T-shirt and jeans with a yellow robe, he'd look exactly like a Buddhist monk.

"It's all a matter of perspective," the monk said. "Until you crossed over, this was the other side. But now that you're here . . ."

"Wait," Jack said. "Are you saying I can talk to my family?"

"Perhaps, if any in your family are psychically inclined, or if they choose to consult a medium. I'll just need you to sign a couple of waivers." He ducked through the curtain to the back room.

As soon as he was gone, Anna said, "I don't want to do this."

"Why not?"

"It seems creepy. And I don't have anything to say to anyone."

"There's no one you want to say goodbye too?"

"I'm dead. It's over. I just now got around to accepting the fact." Anna crossed her arms over her chest. "Creeping out the family isn't going to help anything."

Jack could see her point, but— "I still want to," he said.

"I'll come with you. I don't mind. But I don't want to talk to anyone."

The young man came back with a pile of paperwork and a couple of pens.

"This is a standard legal release authorizing us to use your spiritual signature to contact friends and family members on your behalf." He flipped to the second page. "This states that you understand that the process is not foolproof and we cannot guarantee contact with any particular family member or any other person, living or dead. Finally, this page says that you will not hold us responsible for any disputes, confusion, or lawsuits arising from said communication."

"Lawsuits?"

"Just covering all eventualities."

Jack signed the papers. Anna said, "I'll just watch, if that's okay," and handed the packet back unsigned.

"Very well." The man produced another form. "Then could you please sign this observer's agreement stating that any and all interactions as well as the communications, ideas, and products therein are the sole legal property of Madame and may not be reproduced in any way."

"Seriously?" The lawyer-Buddhist gave her a stern look and thrust a clipboard toward her. She signed.

A woman came out from behind the curtain. Her shoulders were slumped, and she looked shaken.

The man seemed not to notice her distress. "Thank you for visiting Madame Bonaparte's," he said. "Please come again."

The woman pushed through the door and was gone.

"Madame will see you now."

The man held the curtains back to let them pass. A fat woman sat in a chair next to a round table. The table was covered by a multicolored cloth woven in gold and silver, topped with a crystal ball in a cast-iron stand. A chandelier hung from the ceiling. A couple of chins and some shimmery earrings hung from Madame.

She welcomed them with a voice like an old-timey preacher and asked them to sit. Jack took the chair across the table. Anna chose one of the wooden stools lined up against the wall. Jack could just see her out of the corner of his eye.

"Join us, my dear," Madame said, waving one bracelet-laden arm at Anna.

"That's all right, I'm just going to watch, thanks." Anna crossed her legs, leaned back against the wall, folded her arms over her chest.

Madame took the hint. She turned her attention back to Jack. "Now, young man, you are reaching the end of a long journey, and you would like to reassure your family that you are well."

"Yes."

"Please extend your hand. I need to get in tune with your spiritual energy."

Jack put out his hand, palm up. Madame enveloped it in both of hers.

The room was silent for a few moments, and then a rumbling hum filled the air. Jack was beginning to have second thoughts. He glanced at Anna. She was watching Madame, who was swaying ever so subtly from side to side with her eyes closed.

Suddenly, Madame's eyes popped open and looked directly into Jack's. Jack twitched, but held her gaze. Madame put her hands on the crystal ball. "We would like to contact the family of Jack Pratt," she told the crystal. "Is there one who is open to messages from the spirit world?"

The crystal ball made a noise almost exactly like a dial tone.

Anna said, "Seriously?"

Madame shot her a dirty look and Anna shut up.

The crystal was dialing, no doubt about it. Jack could hear the unmistakable tones of phone buttons being pressed. It went on for a long time, maybe fifteen or sixteen numbers; he lost count. There was a pause, a ringing noise. Then a girl's voice said, "Hello? Is anybody there?" She sounded only half awake, and a bit frightened.

"Ella?" Jack leaned over the crystal. He couldn't see anything in the opaque glass, but that was definitely his sister's voice.

Ella squealed. Her next words were muffled, as though she had a blanket over her head. "Is that you, Jack?"

"Ella," Jack said.

"I can't see you."

"I can't see you either."

When she spoke again, her voice sounded clearer. Jack could picture her sitting up in bed, probably wearing her favorite blue nightgown. Her white-blond hair would be loose around her face. She would be surrounded by dolls and stuffed animals—her friends, she called them.

"Jack, Mom and Daddy say you're dead. I went to your wake, but you were sleeping the whole time. Mom cried and cried."

Jack laughed because he couldn't remember how to cry. Anna came over and put a hand on his shoulder. He leaned against her.

"Sorry, Ella Bella. I didn't mean to die."

"Are you going to haunt me now?"

"No, of course not."

"Oh." She sounded disappointed. "That would have been cool."

"You think so?"

"All the kids at school would be so jealous. They won't believe it when I tell them you talked to me. It's like Casper."

Jack imagined Ella telling her friends about this encounter. They would tell their parents, or a teacher would overhear. The adults would nod solemnly to each other. There would be whispered conversations. Her parents would be called. They would put her in counseling, tell her she was crazy. They would say it over and over until she believed it, until she couldn't trust her own senses, until she didn't know what was real anymore. And then she would *be* crazy. One day she would snap, and do something completely insane, and the adults would all stand around congratulating themselves on catching it early.

Jack sat up straight. "No!" he said, too loudly. He struggled to control his voice. "You shouldn't tell anyone about this, Ella. They might not understand. Tell Mom and Dad that—tell them you had a dream about me and I was okay and happy."

"But it's not a dream, right?"

"No, it's not a dream. It's really me. Anna is here. We've been going on an adventure, but it's almost over now."

"Have fun. Ooh, Jack, is Octavius dead too?"

"Octavius?" Right—the octopus she'd given him before he left the house that morning. He felt in his pockets. It was gone. He remembered putting it on the dashboard of the car. Probably it hadn't survived the fire.

"Yes, he found a bunch of friends here." He probably had too. Most likely Octavius was somewhere in the factory mixed up with all the other toys and blankies and much-loved things.

"What about Optimus Prime?"

Jack looked at Anna out of the corner of his eye. She raised her eyebrows at him.

"I'm losing the connection," Madame whispered.

"He's here too. He's with Octavius. I have to go now. I love you, Ella Bella."

His only answer was a dial tone.

Jack turned toward Anna, not really seeing her. But he felt her standing next to him. She put her arm around him. He hugged her waist and pressed his face against her side. He wanted so badly to cry. Somehow it would hurt less if he could let it out. Or maybe not. Maybe you couldn't cry in the afterlife because once you started, you'd never be able to stop. Anna smoothed her fingers through his hair.

Finally, Jack pulled away. He wanted to yell at Madame, to take out all his anger and pain on the fat sack of crap that had made it possible. Why did she do this to people? What was the point? But when he looked at her, she was leaning back in her chair with her eyes shut, her mouth a thin hard line, her shoulders slumped. She looked exhausted.

The young man stuck his head into the room. "Madame, you have another guest."

"Thank you, Ethan. I'll take them as soon as I'm done here."

Ethan went away.

"Why do you do it?" Anna asked.

Madame's thick fingers twitched. She spoke in a heavy voice without opening her eyes. "Back in the world, I made my living by promising to connect the dead to their relatives and friends who had crossed over. I didn't have any real talent, but I wanted to." She opened her eyes, looked into Anna or through her. "I wanted to be special. I wanted to have a gift. I didn't really mean to lie to anyone. They all seemed happy with vague assurances that their loved ones were happy. Everyone was happy."

"Can we go now?" Jack stood and strode toward the front room. He paused when he realized Anna wasn't moving.

She looked around the small room. Her eyes drifted over the crystal ball, the table, Madame slumped in her chair. "Is it a punishment, then?" Anna asked.

Madame shook her head slowly. "Not a punishment, a penance. You passed through the forest?"

Anna nodded.

"Then you understand." Madam's eyes shut again.

Jack pulled back the curtain, and Anna followed him out of the room.

~

Outside, Anna took Jack's hand. He squeezed her fingers, holding on to the last bit of normal left in his world.

"Hey," Anna said. "Why don't we walk through the park?"

Jack shrugged and followed her under a wrought-iron arch into the park. He noticed that there was gravel underfoot, but didn't bother to look around at the scenery. His mind was in another world. He wondered what Ella thought of their exchange. Would she believe it was a dream? Would she pass his message on to Mom and Dad, and if she did, how would they explain it to themselves? He had heard stories of people who, after the death of someone they loved, saw that person in dreams, or had some strange experience where a picture fell off of a shelf or a light bulb shorted out at a meaningful moment. He had always attributed such things to overactive imagination exacerbated by grief and restless sleep. Now he wasn't so sure.

Anna must have been thinking along the same lines, because she said, "Do you remember our neighbor Mrs. Sealy?"

"The one who owned your house before your parents? She died a couple of years ago, didn't she?"

"Yeah. Well, one day she came to the house to see the work my parents had done. There were hollyhocks growing in the front garden that had been there since she owned the place. She said, 'Did you replant those hollyhocks?' and Mom said, 'No, why?' and she said, 'Because I swear they used to be pink.' Mom was certain they had never been pink. She had pictures of the house that showed white hollyhocks. Mrs. Sealy died a few months after that, and do you know what happened the next spring?"

"Let me guess: the hollyhocks came up pink."

"The hollyhocks came up pink," Anna said. "I wonder if Madame had a hand in that." Then she added, "This place could use some real flowers."

Jack finally spared a bit of his attention for the perfectly manicured, and apparently plastic, flowers, grass, and trees of the park.

"It does look like the Afterlife Beautification Commission's been here." Jack nodded to a round garden of fake flowers, all perfectly spaced in their raised bed.

"The grass isn't real either," Anna said, bouncing on her toes. "It's like that stuff they use on football fields."

Jack noticed a couple of people walking toward them along the path. "At least there are people," he said.

Anna looked up, ran forward a few steps, and stopped with one hand shading her eyes as though there was a sun to glare in them. She looked back at Jack. "I don't believe it. It's Ricky."

"It can't be," Jack said. "What are the odds?"

But Anna was already waving one arm over her head, in unconscious imitation of Ricky as they had first seen him. The shorter of the two figures waved back. It *was* Ricky. Anna ran toward him. Jack followed behind at a slightly more sedate jog.

Chapter Twenty-Two

Ricky picked Anna up in a bear hug. Anna laughed as he spun her around in a circle and then set her gently on her feet. Jack felt a twinge of jealousy. He told himself he was being ridiculous. Of course Anna liked Ricky—he was a likable guy. And girls loved that tortured soul, dark past stuff. But Anna had had the chance to stay with Ricky and hadn't taken it. She'd gone with Jack.

That should have made him feel better, but it didn't. Guilt replaced jealousy. If she'd stayed with Ricky, she wouldn't have gone through the checkpoint. She might still be alive. Alive and brain damaged, maybe, but alive. He guessed it was her choice to make, but she shouldn't have had to make it.

Ricky grabbed Jack's hand and shook it. "Good to see you again," he said.

Jack realized he was being an awkward jerk. He pulled himself together. "Is this your dad?" he asked, turning to the older man who had been standing outside the commotion of their greeting.

"No, this is my grandfather. Papa, these are the people I was telling you about."

The older man smiled. He was probably in his seventies, and it was easy to see where Ricky got his curly hair and easy smile. When Jack shook the old man's hand, the skin was covered in calluses that chafed against Jack's palm.

Anna took Ricky's arm and lowered her voice. "I thought you were going to wait for your dad."

"I was, but Papa found me first."

Ricky looked at Papa, who was watching a pair of college-age men kick a soccer ball back and forth. Where had the ball come from?

"My dad is okay. Like, really okay. He started a scholarship in my name." Ricky was grinning like a proud father. "He volunteers with a suicide prevention organization. He even went before the state legislature to help pass a law about training teachers to spot signs of suicide. Papa told me all about it. And he got married again."

Concern crumpled Anna's forehead. "Doesn't that make you a little bit sad? I mean, he moved on."

"Sad? How could I be sad? I did this incredibly stupid, awful thing, and he turned around and did good with it. If he was just sitting in the dark mourning me, that would be . . ." He shook his head. "Papa says Dad visits my grave almost every day. He carries his work papers in my backpack. I'm always with him—I don't have to wait for him."

Jack imagined Ella carrying his backpack to school. It would be far too big for a first grader's books, but she would insist, and his mother would give in, because Ella was stubborn. And it wasn't as though she was hurting anyone. Every now and then someone would notice that the initials embroidered on the front weren't hers, and someone would ask her about them. "They're my brother's," she would say. "He died." The other children would nod. Any nearby adults would wince. But he would be remembered in that small way.

He tuned back in to Ricky and Anna's conversation. Ricky was saying, "The forest wasn't so bad, actually. I had these . . . visions, I guess you'd call them, of my funeral. People were mad at me and . . . Papa had told me all about it already, so I knew what really happened and who was there and everything. It wasn't real."

Jack envied Ricky's confidence.

"Brownies," Papa said, looking at Jack.

"What?" Jack wondered if the old man had dementia. Ricky hadn't mentioned what he'd died of.

"I'm guessing that's what you smelled at the diner. Brownies. But you ordered peanut butter and jelly."

"Almost. Chocolate chip cookies, and I ordered grilled cheese and tomato soup." Jack thought that this must be the afterlife equivalent of talking about the weather. He fidgeted. Small talk wasn't really his thing. "What about you?"

"Motor oil and chocolate ice cream."

"Oh, were you a mechanic?"

"A contractor, but I liked cars." He sighed. "I miss my El Camino. It could have gotten us here in a third of the time and with half the strangeness. What kind of car did you drive?"

"Me, an oh-three Chevy Malibu."

Papa raised his eyebrows. "What kind of car is that for a young man?"

"I wasn't much of a car guy," Jack said, fidgeting, "and it was cheap."

"There are some things a man shouldn't skimp on," Papa said.

"You're probably right." Jack thought that if he'd had a nicer car with better brakes or a stronger frame, he and Anna might not be here today.

"Jack and I are going to the library," Anna said. "Do you and your grandfather want to come?"

Ricky shook his head. "Papa and I still have a lot of catching up to do. But you should keep a lookout for Professor Haggarty."

"You've seen him?"

"Not since we left the factory, but I'm sure he's around. He'll probably spend the next hundred years comparing the index pages of every book in the library." Ricky rolled his eyes.

"If I see him, I'll tell him you said hello."

After they'd said their goodbyes, Anna struck out across the park. Jack, trailing behind her, asked, "Why are we going to the library?"

"I told you already."

"I didn't believe you. You have a reason."

"There's something I want to look up."

"Seriously?"

She looked at him, eyebrows raised.

"To the library, then," Jack said.

She strode down the street. Jack followed her. He assumed she was following Dahlia's directions. He looked at his feet as they walked, avoiding the sight of the empty storefronts.

They didn't have to walk far. The library was around the corner. When they saw it, Anna said, "Holy Greek Revival, Batman."

The building was practically made of columns. Three stories tall, they lined the front of the building, which wrapped around three sides of a square courtyard. A statue of a woman wearing a draped toga-dress and holding a pitcher of water stood in the center of a square reflecting pool. They crunched along the gravel walk and climbed the stone steps.

"I wonder how old this building is," Jack said.

"That's sort of a trick question around here, isn't it? I mean, time doesn't necessarily exist in the traditional sense. This building could, in fact, only exist when someone is looking for it and cease to exist as soon as our backs are turned."

"Remember when you told me it was okay to say 'I don't know'?"

The wooden door swung open at a touch. Anna stopped. "Whoa!"

Jack prodded her in the back. "What whoa?"

"It's bigger on the inside."

Jack looked around. "Whoa!"

"That's what I said."

His eyes swept upward, high into the stacks of books. No ceiling. The books just seemed to run together and then to arch overhead somewhere way up there. Jack imagined that if, somehow, they could reach the top, there would be a single book at the apex acting as a sort of keystone. If he removed it, the whole stack would come tumbling down in an endless bookslide.

"Jack, do you smell that?" It smelled like ink and used-book store.

"I guess even death can't take that musty smell out of an old book."

"Thank God." Anna sighed.

They approached an ancient mahogany desk where a real-life stereotype of a librarian stood, reading a book.

"Excuse me," Anna said. "I'm looking for a book."

The librarian read the rest of her sentence. Marked the page with her finger. Closed the book. Looking over her glasses at Anna, she sighed. "Everyone is. What book?"

"A biography."

"That wing is biography. They are organized alphabetically, with anonymous on the first floor and everyone else *A* to *Z* on the floors above. Please keep in mind that this is the North America branch and we stock biographies only from that geographical area."

Anna tilted her head back, taking in the seemingly endless stacks. "How do we get up there?"

"Take the staircase in the corner."

"Thanks," Anna said, but the woman had already reopened her book and didn't answer.

Jack followed Anna into the next wing. They passed tall bookcases crammed full of books and reshelve carts overflowing with books and people sitting at study tables piled high with books. Toward the back of the room they found shelves divided into triangular sections filled with scrolls made of animal skin. Jack touched one, tentatively, as they passed. Finally they reached a spiral staircase in the corner of the room. Steps, hardly wide enough to hold a person, wound tightly around a center post. As they climbed, Jack asked, "Whose biography are you looking for?"

"Yours."

"I'm pretty sure nobody has written a biography about me."

"Back at the checkpoint, when I talked to the supervisor, she said that everyone has a biography in one of the libraries. She said they keep records throughout your life and that after you cross the checkpoint, the books are moved here."

"So they've got my whole life in a book somewhere? Even the part when we died?"

"You didn't kill me, Jack. Not on purpose. I'll prove it to you."

At the top of the stairs, they stopped. They were on a narrow catwalk along a shelf of books. The stairs didn't go any farther. Far off in the distance, in the next corner of the room, they thought they could see another spiral staircase spinning up to the next floor.

"This is going to take a while," Jack said.

"I don't mind. I could stay here forever. I could read and read and never get tired or have to stop to make lunch or go to school or anything."

"That's a *Twilight Zone* episode too, with the guy who just wants to be alone to read and then the world ends."

"Oh right, and he breaks his glasses."

They passed a library ladder on a track. Jack pushed it experimentally. It rolled a few feet and stopped.

"Anna, climb onto this ladder. I've always wanted to do this."

"I always wanted a library with a ladder," Anna said. She climbed up a couple of steps and held on.

Jack jogged forward, pushing the ladder ahead of him until he was running full tilt. Then he jumped onto the rolling ladder beside her. They zipped sideways. Book spines blurred into a continuous mass of brown before their eyes. Anna whooped, then clapped her hand over her mouth—they *were* in a library.

By the time the ladder lost momentum, they were only a few feet from the next staircase.

"That was awesome," Anna whispered. "Let's do it again."

~

It didn't seem to take all that long to reach the *P*s, though when they looked down, the floor below appeared to be only about the size of a facecloth.

Jack took Anna's arm. She looked a question at him. "No jumping," he said.

She laughed. "No jumping. I promise." She trailed her fingers along the rows of books. Big books and small books. Some bound in leather and some bound in paper and some that were only bundles of paper, bound by nothing but the books on either side. Jack wondered how it was decided, the form of your book. Who chose the color of your cover? Was it a matter of wealth, status, importance? There was no way to know, except by reading. And a star could form and burn and explode and die and consume whole galaxies before he had gotten through a third of what was here.

Jack pulled a book from a shelf and opened it to a random page. A line of dialogue caught his eye.

"No. No." I can hear my own breath echoing back through the phone. I'm gasping.

"Calm down," my mother says. "Calm down."

I'm glad she can't see me. At the words He's dead, *I'd backed myself against the wall, pressing into it, as though trying to blend with the yellow paint. My stomach is a dense stone. I try to calm my breathing.*

"I need you to stay with your brother until I get there. Don't say anything to him."

I wouldn't say anything. Why would I? How could I? I remember how he sobbed when his puppy died. I had never heard him cry like that. And this . . . a thousand times worse.

"Jack, I found it," Anna said.

Jack snapped the book shut. He replaced it gently on the shelf. Suddenly the library felt like an echoing tomb, with the ghosts of generations haunting its cramped shelves. He hurried toward Anna.

She held the book out to him. He hesitated. "Can't *you* read it?"

"Jack, this is your life, everything that's ever happened to you, everything you've ever done. It would be like reading your diary."

"We were journal partners in English class."

"Not the same thing."

"Right, you're right." He took the book and flipped to the last page. "Huh, it goes all the way to the checkpoint." He flipped back a couple of pages. "Here's the ocean." And a couple more. "And the forest." He raced past that section, not eager to relive the realization of his guilt. "Here it is. 'I drive the Chevy east on Route 1A.' Take it." He handed the book to Anna. "You can read this part. You were there."

"Are you sure?"

"Certain. Please." He sat down with his back to the railing.

Anna sat down facing him with her back against the bookshelves. It was like watching her support herself on a pile of corpses. Jack looked away.

"'I drive the Chevy east on Route 1,'" Anna read. "'Anna laughs. I glance at her. Her hair streams around her face. With her head tilted back, her eyes look as gray as a cloud-covered lake. "What's funny?" I shout over the wind and the radio.

"'"I'm just happy, that's all," she answers.'"

Jack leaned his head back and closed his eyes, but instantly opened them again. He could picture it happening, just the way Uncle Steve had shown him. He didn't want to. He also didn't want to look at Anna's face. He looked at the spines of the books above her head.

Anna continued, "'I'm smiling for no reason. Anna hands me the yellow half of the worm and leans forward to turn up the radio. I glance at the half worm, shrug, and pop it into my mouth. Anna laughs again.'"

Jack felt himself tense.

"'I grin at her and press the gas pedal. The speedometer needle slips past ninety. As we round a sharp curve, Anna offers me the blue half of a blue-and-orange gummy worm. I lift one hand off the wheel to take it from her.'"

Jack opened his mouth, ready to tell her to stop, forget the whole thing. But he didn't. He made himself sit still and hear the rest. He felt sick.

"'Anna screams.

""'Oh shit," I say. "Oh shit, oh shit." I scramble to get both hands on the wheel, slam my foot down on the brake pedal.

"'It makes no difference. The hood crumples as we hit an eighteen-wheeler that has jackknifed across both lanes of the highway. The windshield shatters. I look at Anna. She's ducked low in the seat, her hands clamped over her ears. Her head collides with her knees, hard. I try to reach for her, but pain hits me. Darkness.'"

Anna stopped. Her voice had started to shake toward the end. Jack leaned forward, looking at the floor, his hands covering his nose and mouth.

"I didn't do it on purpose." His voice was muffled by his fingers. "I didn't do it on purpose."

"I knew you didn't. You're as sane as I am. More so, probably."

Jack sat there, frozen.

"Are there any other parts you want to read?"

He shook his head. He heard Anna get up and slide the book back into place. Silence for a moment. Then she was standing in front of him, one hand extended to help him up. "Come on, Jack, time to go."

"Go where."

"Where do you think, genius?"

"Don't you want to find your book?"

"I know everything I need to know about my life. I lived it."

He took her hand and let her pull him to his feet. He held on to her hand a moment longer. "Thank you," he said.

"For what?"

"Putting up with me."

She smiled, and in this light her eyes were the deep green of undisturbed waters. "You are entirely welcome."

Chapter Twenty-Three

The tower was made of dark glass that reflected distorted views of the buildings and streets. They walked all the way around it once. Six opaque glass doors faced each of the six main streets of The City. Even when Jack leaned against one and curled his hands around the side of his face to block the glare, he could see nothing but darkness on the other side.

"Maybe it's closed," he said.

"I don't think it can be," Anna said. She wrapped her hand around a polished black door handle. "Ready?"

"I guess so."

Anna paused and bit her lip. "We could come back tomorrow," she said.

"There's no such thing as tomorrow."

"Right."

She pulled. The door opened. They stepped into a narrow atrium. The space between the outer wall and the inner was only about the width of an average hallway. Directly in front of them a pair of heavy wooden doors was set in a wall of rough-hewn stone blocks.

"It looks like somebody built a skyscraper around an old watchtower," Anna said.

Jack laid his hand on one of the doors. Each one seemed to be made out of a single continuous piece of wood, though he couldn't imagine any tree large enough to carve them from. He pushed experimentally. They swung open silently.

They couldn't turn back now. Curiosity alone would have been enough to draw Jack forward, but the pull was stronger here, too. So strong that he had to concentrate to keep his feet from moving forward all on their own. Together, he and Anna entered the inner tower.

It was bigger than it should have been. A lot bigger. Fifty feet ahead, a blinding pillar of illumination reached from the black and white tile floor toward the unseen ceiling. Jack felt unreasonably happy. It had something to do with the light. He heard Anna start to giggle softly.

"Go into the light," Anna said.

"Isn't it, don't go into the light?"

They had started walking. Jack wasn't sure quite when. His feet seemed to have moved all on their own, taking advantage of his inattention to bring him closer to the light.

Jack realized he and Anna weren't alone. Six figures were standing in a circle with their backs to the light. Each faced one of the six doors of the building. They were tall, taller than any man he had ever seen outside of a basketball game. It was impossible to tell if they were male or female. They all had the same ragged white hair framing soft faces. The longer he stared, the more he thought that the sense of sameness about them was stronger than the identical haircuts and the matching white uniforms. They all had the same face. Hextuplets. Was that the right word?

The one closest to Jack and Anna lifted its gaze to look at them. Its eyes spilled golden light, like the light of the pillar. Looking into them, Jack felt both mesmerized and hyper-alert. Beside him, Anna rubbed her cheek against her shoulder as if trying to stop her ear from ringing.

"Welcome, Anna Evelyn Poplin. Welcome, Jack Xavier Pratt."

When the angel—it had to be an angel—spoke, all six spoke together, one voice in surround sound. Anna moved closer to Jack.

"Step forward," the angels said.

Jack took Anna's hand, and together they moved a few steps toward the light, then stopped, uncertain under the spotlight of the angel's eyes.

"Who are you?" Anna asked. Her voice was too loud.

"We are the guardian," the angels said. "We guard the light that is the Ultimate. Like all who have been and all who will be, you have reached the end of your journey."

Jack looked past the angel at the light. He could feel it trying to drag him forward. He wondered if this was how a moth felt before it flew into a campfire and fried itself to death. More than anything he had ever wanted in his life, he wanted to throw himself into that pillar of light. He wandered a step forward, but Anna's hand in his held him back.

"This is it, isn't it?" Anna said.

The angels answered, "Yes."

Anna turned to Jack and took his other hand in hers.

"Jack, when I was in the forest, I realized something I wanted to tell you." She looked into his face, and then her eyes slipped down to his chest, where they settled like restless butterflies, ready to flit away at any moment.

"I'm sorry," she said.

He looked down at her dark hair. "For what?" His voice was soft.

"For the note I ripped up and put in your desk the first time you asked me out, and for all the times I pushed you away, for breaking up with you and for not understanding why you were so upset. For our whole relationship, really."

He freed one of his hands to ruffle and then smooth her hair.

"I'm not," he said.

"What do you mean?" Anna looked up at him, her eyes narrowed in confusion.

"I'm not sorry about any of it."

Anna dropped her gaze again. "I was mean to you. For years I was mean to you. I have no idea why you stayed my friend all this time."

"Because I love you, genius," he said.

Anna looked into his eyes and then away. "I love you, too," she said.

He knew. He had always known. But hearing the words somehow made it more true. He surged forward and kissed her cheek. Then fell back, embarrassed.

She smiled. Let go of his hands. Stepped away. Jack reached for her, but she stopped him with a hand on his arm. "Ladies first," she said.

He let her walk toward the light.

"What do I do?" she asked the angels.

"Walk into the light," they said.

Anna laughed, a dry, humorless laugh. "Told you so," she said to Jack.

"You're sure we can't go together?" Jack said. "We've been together this whole time."

"Good friends are a blessing and a comfort on the journey," the angels recited, "but each must take the final step alone."

Anna chewed on her bottom lip and looked over her shoulder at Jack. She stepped into the light.

Nothing happened for an instant, and then the light flared, like an explosion in the heart of a star. Reflexively, Jack threw his arm up to shade his eyes. Anna's laugh echoed clear and joyful around the room. Light flashed over him. He felt a touch, like a hand on his cheek, and then it was over. The light retreated. Jack was alone with the angels.

Jack felt like someone had cut his soul in half. He staggered. It was painful, yes, but it was more than that. At times he had felt abandoned, unloved, misunderstood, but he had never felt so utterly, irrevocably alone.

The angel smiled at him. Jack thought perhaps it understood. "Can I ask you a question?" he said to it.

"You may ask. We may not be able to answer."

"Where did she go?"

"Where all humans go when they reach the end of their journey."

"And where is that?"

"There's only one way to find out."

Jack approached the light as Anna had done and stopped. It took all his will to stop. This was the force that had led them across the desert. This had been their goal all along. This was the end. He stared into the light, unblinking. "Will I ever see her again?"

The angels were silent.

Jack squared his shoulders and stepped into the light. It flared, filling the room. Jack's voice could be heard whooping like a kid on a roller coaster. The light receded. The room fell silent.

The angels smiled.

Chapter Twenty-Four

The golden light faded slowly. Anna could almost feel her brain re-forming itself molecule by molecule out of the pillar of light. She was surprised. She had expected, well, she wasn't sure what exactly, maybe for her soul to explode into a billion tiny fragments that soared over the earth and fell, like invisible snow over the world she had once known, something grand and poetic and above all final.

But here she was, stepping out of an elevator into a vaulted hallway. Tall marble pillars lined both walls and supported an arched ceiling ribbed in heavy, dark wood. The floor was tiled in a pattern of black and white squares that matched the one downstairs and made Anna go slightly cross-eyed. At the far end of the hall a pair of brass doorknobs gleamed on heavy oak doors.

"I thought it was over," she said out loud.

"So did I."

Anna spun, and there was Jack, standing in front of the elevator doors, blinking like an owl woken before moonrise.

"Jack!" She threw her arms around him. "I thought I'd never see you again."

He hugged her. "Surprise!"

Anna released him. "Where are we?"

"Um, a big hall."

"Thanks, that's a huge help." They grinned at each other.

Something squeaked, making them both turn. As they watched, one of the huge doors at the end of the hall opened slightly and a man slipped through the crack. He had a pair of glasses on his nose and a clipboard in his hand. The door boomed shut behind him.

Jack and Anna waited as he skittered down the hall to meet them. His shoes made rapid clicking noises on the polished stone.

"Jack Pratt and Anna Poplin."

"Yes?" they said together.

"The judge will see you now."

"Judge?" Anna said. The man was already skittering away. "Wait."

They followed him up the hall. Once he had opened the oak door, he paused and waited for them to catch up.

"What judge?" Anna asked.

The man prodded her spine to push her forward. "Right this way, please," he said. "The time for judgment has come. Be not afraid."

Who talks like that?

Behind her, Jack muttered, "I do *not* like the sound of that. That sounded an awful lot like 'This won't hurt a bit.'"

They stepped into a courtroom. The room was all polished wood, and brass fixtures, and frosted glass like you'd expect to see in any old city courthouse. But the viewing gallery was packed with men and women dressed as though they were waiting to take their place in a documentary about ancient Egypt. Anna noticed a lot of linen, and beads, and beaten gold. One woman wore a headdress tall enough to block the view for the man sitting behind her. He was reduced to leaning heavily on his neighbor so he could catch a glimpse of Jack and Anna. His neighbor, none too pleased, tried to push him away.

Aside from this minor drama, the costumed audience was silent and still. All eyes were on Jack and Anna. A sudden attack of stage fright made Anna freeze in place, but the clerk was still prodding her toward the front of the room where the judge sat in a huge stone chair. It had to be an illusion. The size of the chair, the size of the man, were unbelievable. If he stood, he would almost certainly graze his powdered wig on the ceiling.

But it was no trick. If anything, he seemed to grow larger the closer they got. And that wasn't the worst thing. The worst thing was the mask that covered his face. It had the long, sharp, black muzzle of a dog that would happily bite the hand that fed it and anything else it could sink its teeth into.

"Anubis," Anna whispered.

Behind her, Jack's muttered commentary continued, "And you know what? I don't like the look of it either. There is exactly nothing about this situation that I like."

Anna shushed him.

Anubis banged his gavel. "Order," he said. "This court is now in session."

Maybe she imagined it, but Anna thought she heard the edge of a growl in his voice.

"Clerk, present the accused."

"Wait," Anna said, her voice louder than she had meant it to be. "What are we accused of?"

The clerk looked over his glasses at Anna. "Would you like to be judged separately or together?"

"Judged for what?"

"You are keeping the court waiting, young lady, quickly now. Separately or together?" Jack and Anna answered, "Together."

The clerk cleared his throat and stepped forward. He read from the clipboard, "Jack Xavier Pratt and Anna Evelyn Poplin, you stand accused of numerous charges of casual cruelty, unfairness, self-absorption, laziness, lying, and general humanity perpetrated during your combined thirty-four years on Earth."

"How do they plead?" Anubis said.

"The defendants plead guilty on all counts," the clerk said.

"Wait, what?" Jack said.

Anna said, "Where's our lawyer? This is a court of law, right? What about due process?"

The clerk rolled his eyes. "Americans," he muttered. Raising his voice he said, "Do you deny that you lived on Earth as human beings for the last seventeen years?"

"Of course we did—we *are* human beings. It's not like we had a choice in the matter." Whispers rippled through the assembly.

"And do you deny that while living as humans, you had free will and a basic knowledge of right and wrong?"

"Well, no, I guess not."

"There, see?" said a shrill-voiced woman in the crowd. Several others muttered, "Guilty, guilty," just loudly enough to cause echoes.

Anna's stomach filled with dread. This wasn't what she'd expected. If she *was* going to be judged, it should be God doing the judging. He would weigh the good things she had done against the bad. Maybe he'd take into account the things she should have done but hadn't. Or the things she hadn't done but could have. But this wasn't fair. How could she defend herself when the only accusation against her was her humanity?

Anubis banged his gavel on the arm of his chair. "Then the time for judgment has come. Bring in the Feather."

Jack grabbed the clerk's arm and whispered, "What is going on here?"

The clerk pulled his arm out of Jack's grip and straightened his sleeve. "There was a time," he said in a stiff voice, "when people expected their souls to be weighed against the Feather of Truth." His tone said that it had been a much better time and he would be happy to go back to it if only he could build a time machine and also find some way of smuggling indoor plumbing and a year's supply of clipboards along with him.

"But, but, that's a myth," Jack said. "An Egyptian myth."

Anna interrupted. "Hey, genius, are you arguing with Anubis?"

Jack looked at the dog-headed man and his jaw went slack. "You have got to be kidding," he said. "We're not even Egyptian."

The clerk was muttering to himself. "Really. What are they teaching humanity these days? About time for another flood, if you ask me. Wash them all out. Start fresh. But no, no, promises were made, promises must be . . ."

His muttering died away as the door behind the bench opened. A pair of shirtless men navigated through the doorway, balancing the front poles of a litter on their shoulders. Linen curtains shielded whatever was inside from the eyes of the assembly. Two more men bore the weight of the back. All four looked familiar.

"They look like the angels," Anna whispered to Jack.

The clerk overheard her and snorted.

Grunting with effort, the angels set the litter down. How heavy did something have to be for even angels to struggle with it? Some of Anna's fear receded. Even weighed together, she and Jack would have to be lighter than that.

As soon as the litter touched the ground, the curtains were flung aside, revealing an obscenely fat woman dressed in a linen shift. Her face was round and beautiful and distant like the face of the moon. Her eyes were two flecks of light buried in rolls of flesh.

She stood. Anubis was a giant, but this woman made him look like a scrawny teenager. Anna could almost imagine that the ground shook as the woman stepped out onto the stone floor. The angels lifted the litter and carried it away.

Anubis stood. "Welcome, Maat, Feather of Justice," he said.

The assembly echoed him. Maat nodded to Anubis and then lumbered over to Jack and Anna. Her enormous right hand cupped Anna's cheek. The left did the same to Jack.

Maat stood for a moment. Eyes closed. Finally she dropped her hands, causing fat to ripple all over her body. Watching her turn was like watching the moon turn away from the earth. She nodded.

Anna looked at Jack. He seemed confused but relieved. Maat must weigh four hundred pounds. There was no way they wouldn't be lighter than the feather. Anna thought it must all be for show. A kind of end-of-life ceremony, like last rites or putting coins on the eyes of the dead. She started to tell Jack this, but Anubis interrupted.

"Bring in the Scale of Justice," he said.

The angels returned, or else a new set came—it was impossible to tell—carrying an enormous balance scale. All four angels could have stood on one platform of the scale with room to spare. When they set it down, it balanced perfectly.

Two of the angels pulled one side down and dropped to one knee to hold it flat against the ground.

"The accused will now step on the scale," Anubis said.

Anna was past arguing. She and Jack stepped onto the scale. The angels let go. The scale didn't budge.

The angels went to the other side of the scale and pushed it slowly to the ground. Jack took Anna's hand as they were both lifted into the air. Maat migrated to the other side of the scale and rotated to face the court. She stepped on.

The angels let go. The scale seesawed. Jack and Anna bobbed up and down. Once, twice. Anna clutched Jack's hand. Finally, the scales settled.

"Jack and Anna," Anubis said, "your hearts are heavier than the Feather."

Anna heard the words, but they might as well have been in ancient Egyptian. She stared openmouthed at the Feather, who was somehow above them. This wasn't how judgment was supposed to work. This wasn't even how gravity worked. The court had gone silent, watching.

Anubis spoke into the silence. "Are there any mitigating circumstances you would like to bring to the attention of the court?"

Jack looked up at the grinning dog mask. "Judge us separately." He stepped off of the scale. The court erupted. Anna's side of the scale sank a bit lower, which shouldn't have been possible. None of this should have been possible.

"Jack, it won't matter," Anna said. "Haven't you learned anything? We have to do this together." She felt ready to cry. "It only works if we're together."

"We stepped into the light alone," Jack said.

Anubis banged his gavel, calling for order.

"One at a time," Anna said. "That's not the same as alone."

Jack shrugged. "So they'll judge us one at a time. It's my fault you're—"

A noise, louder than the rest, cut Jack off midsentence. This time there was no mistaking it—Anubis growled.

The spectators sank into their chairs, like small children warned away from a toy by a dog. Anubis looked around the room, reinforcing their silence. "Now," he said, turning to Jack, "tell me, boy-child, why you should be judged separately from your mate."

Jack cleared his throat. "Well, um, Your Honor, Anna is my best friend, and she—she's a good person. I know she is. She's good to people. She worries about their feelings and helps them whenever she can. I think without me, she would easily weigh less than the Feather."

Anubis leaned forward. "She's good to people." He repeated slowly, "A good person. Do you think that is enough?"

"I can't really say. I didn't make the rules and, to be honest, I don't think I've understood a single thing that has happened since we came to the afterlife, and that makes me realize there's a good chunk of my real life that I didn't understand either. But if good isn't good enough to make a difference, well, it should be."

For once, the court was silent. Anna shook her head. "You're as good as I am. You must know that."

"Maybe, maybe not, but I'm not going to hold you back this time."

"You're not going to hold me back. Did it ever occur to you that it might be me holding you back? Maybe I'm the bad one. I yell at my little brother. I leave my room a mess. I never finished the damned scholarship applications. Maybe it's my soul weighing us down."

"Anna, if the worst thing you've done in your life is not finish your scholarship applications, then someone should hand you a halo right now."

Somebody chuckled at this and was quickly shushed by his neighbors, but not quickly enough to spare him a glare from Anubis.

The masked judge turned his black eyes back to Anna. She could feel them watching her.

"Of course it isn't. The point is"—she paused, bit her lip, then continued—"you don't know what's weighing us down. So don't go all hero-martyr on me."

Jack shook his head, smiled. "Together then." He held out his hand. She took it and helped him climb up onto the scale. He didn't have to climb high.

A whisper darted around the courtroom. Jack and Anna waited for their sentence. All eyes were watching Maat. Her huge mouth was opening, slowly. She was about to speak.

"Your Honor," she said, her voice like the sound of mountains growing. "These children have walked together, helping those who sought help and running from those who through malice or ignorance would cause only harm. They saved a man's life. They were good friends to each other, good siblings to their brothers and sister, good children to their parents." Her eyes twinkled as she added, "Though at times they were headstrong." Anna bit her lip and looked away. Maat continued, "In these final moments they have learned the paramount lesson. I am the voice of justice and order." She thumped her chest with one massive fist. "I speak the truth, and the truth speaks me."

As she spoke, the scales tilted slowly in Jack and Anna's favor, until they were standing high above Maat's head, almost level with Anubis himself. The whispering grew louder.

The angels bent to hold the scales while Maat stepped off of them. Jack and Anna were lowered slowly to the ground. Still clutching each other's hands, they stepped onto the stone floor and watched as first the scales and then Maat were carried away.

Finally, Anubis banged his gavel and the room fell silent. Jack and Anna drew closer together.

"Jack, Anna, your hearts have been weighed on the Scale of Justice. They are lighter than the Feather."

A roaring filled Anna's ears. The room and the spectators contracted around her, pressing against her in the sudden darkness. She felt her whole body being squeezed until she was certain she would be crushed, and then the pressure relaxed. The world exploded in a cacophony of light and color and sound.

Epilogue

Nathan parked his car on the side of the road next to the gate. As he got out, he stuffed two bags of gummy worms into his pocket. He shut the door firmly and looked around. There weren't any other cars, just a purple-and-white bicycle propped against the fence.

The sun warmed the back of his neck as he walked through the open wrought-iron gates into the small cemetery. He passed the graves of the veterans with their tiny flags, and the graves of the Cyr family who had been buried here for eight generations and filled at least a third of the plots.

Anna was in a cove created by a pair of overgrown shrubs. "Hey," he said. He didn't really believe she could hear him, but he always found himself talking to her anyway. "I brought you these."

He set a bag of gummy worms down between a geranium in a clay pot and a blue lantern his mother had left there the day they'd buried Anna. A tiny flame flickered inside it. He was glad it was there. Anna never had liked the dark.

He stood, looking at his sister's name on the gravestone. A bar of gold sunlight cast it in high relief. He dug the toe of one shoe into the grass. It was hard to believe that he was older now than Anna had been then. He turned away.

Jack's grave was farther on, surrounded by empty plots on either side. His family had probably bought up the spaces so they could be buried near him when the time came, but for now it was a lonely spot. Or would have been, if it hadn't been for the girl kneeling next to Jack's gravestone with her white-blond hair shielding her face.

Nathan didn't say anything, but let his feet make extra noise as he approached.

Ella looked up. "Hi," she said. Her eyes were red around the edges.

"Hey."

Ella stood up and brushed grass off of her knees. "I haven't seen you around much."

"I started college this year. Stanford."

"In California?"

"Yeah," Nathan said.

"Cool."

They fell silent. Nathan pulled the packet of gummy worms out of his pocket. "I didn't mean to bother you," he said. "I just came to leave these."

"I'd wondered where those came from," Ella said.

Nathan set them on the grave. "I bring some by every time I'm home. They were Anna's favorite." He straightened up.

"Eight years," Ella said.

"What?"

"That's how long it's been. Eight years, but it's still . . . You never get over it, do you?"

"No, not really, you just sort of get on with it, you know." He bit his lip. He wished he had something more comforting to say. Something that didn't sound so empty.

"I know," Ella said without looking at him. "I was only six, but I remember exactly how it felt when I found out. Sometimes I think it's my first real memory."

Nathan stared at the grass. He could still remember the way the light fell through the blinds of Anna's hospital room.

Ella said, "Back right after it happened, I had a . . . a dream that Jack talked to me. He told me to be good."

"That's such an older sibling thing to say."

"It is, isn't it?" Ella smiled. She shaded her eyes and looked up into the blue sky. "Do you think they're out there somewhere, watching over us?"

Nathan was silent for a moment. "No," he said finally.

Ella looked stricken. "No?"

Nathan hurried to explain. "They're out there somewhere, yes. But they're too busy having wild adventures to spend time watching our boring lives."

Ella looked away again, down at her brother's gravestone. "It's what they always wanted," she said. "Wild adventures, I mean."

"Yeah."

Nathan started to turn away, and then turned back. "It's kind of hot," he said. "Why don't you throw your bike in my car and I'll give you a ride home."

They walked out of the cemetery, past the veterans' graves and Cyr family plots, and through the open wrought-iron gates, their shadows running along before them.

ABOUT THE AUTHOR

Emma G Rose intended to become a kick-ass girl reporter like Nellie Bly. Until the Christmas Eve she stood on a riverbank waiting for rescue divers to pull a body from the water. She stopped waiting and wandered off to explore the world instead. People who keep track of this sort of thing call her writing speculative fiction. It's a fancy name for what you get when you mix up a dash of sci-fi, a dose of fantasy, and a sprinkling of humor, then add in one of the big life-shaping questions. You know the ones. They usually start with "why." As in: "Why are we here? What did this happen? And why should we keep hoping for the future?"

Follow Her Adventures
Facebook @lifeimperative
YouTube @lifeimperative
Instagram @nothingseverlost
www.emmagauthor.com

Look for Emma's next book:

Near-Life Experience

Coming July 2020

Aknowledgements

I swear this is the most difficult part of a book to write. Thanking everyone who made this book possible would mean thanking every person, animal, and probably plant that I've come in contact with over the last 30 years. Many of them have found a place in these pages. There are a few people, however, who contributed in tangible ways to the publication of this book.

Kelsie Witt who created cover art that wasn't what I had pictured but was exactly what I wanted. And Ashley Hinson Dhakal who turned that art into a book cover.

Lanette Pottle, my coach in both life and business, who encouraged me to stop waiting for the universe to align and make my dream happen to myself. I did it, Lanette. I don't think I would have done it without your support and encouragement.

Kim Smith, who looked at me as a "real author" long before I had anything published. Your faith and your example has encouraged me.

Jamie Clark, who created a magical place where women could come together to get better at business and better at life. For the record, it was Jamie who introduced me to both Lanette and Kim. So, Jamie, this is pretty much all your fault.

Zac and Lauren Platt, you know what you did.

Madeline Clark Frank, my constant supporter, friend, writing buddy, and adventuring companion. When you're done solving the global climate crisis and revolutionizing education, I hope you'll get around to publishing that series.

Matt Dean, Amanda Bruce and the rest of the writers group that used to monopolize the corner booth at various Panaras in and around West Ashley, South Carolina. You shaped this story with your thoughts, your criticism and your laughter. In a real way, this book belongs to you.

My Brother Noah, who somehow managed to serve as the model for both Nathan and Michael in this story. The conversation between Michael and Ella was for you.

My parents Ron and Sue Potvin. You encouraged my curiosity and my writing. I hope I've made you proud.

And if I can be indulged so far as to thank a man I've never met, Sir Terry Pratchett, whose books I've read over and over and whose fiction changed the way I look at reality.

Thank you. All of you.